Praise for Linda Ford

"A lovely story of love, forgiveness and accepting God's guidance in difficult times."
—*RT Book Reviews* on *The Cowboy Tutor*

"A tender love story with characters who are strong-willed and caring."
—*RT Book Reviews* on *Dakota Father*

"Ford's sweet, charming love story has well-written characters that demonstrate strong faith, even though they stumble along the way."
—*RT Book Reviews* on *The Cowboy's Baby*

Praise for Karen Kirst

"Second in the Smoky Mountain Matches series, this story creates a great sense of place, with a bit of suspense."
—*RT Book Reviews* on *The Bridal Swap*

"Kirst's debut knocks it out of the park. It's a gem of a story with a thrilling roma[illegible]"
—*RT Book Reviews* on [illegible]

LINDA FORD

shares her life with her rancher husband, a grown son, a live-in client she provides care for and a yappy parrot. She and her husband raised a family of fourteen children, ten adopted, providing her with plenty of opportunity to experience God's love and faithfulness. They've had their share of adventures, as well. Taking twelve kids in a motor home on a three-thousand-mile road trip would be high on the list. They live in Alberta, Canada, close enough to the Rockies to admire them every day. She enjoys writing stories that reveal God's wondrous love through the lives of her characters.

Linda enjoys hearing from readers. Contact her at linda@lindaford.org or check out her website, www.lindaford.org, where you can also catch her blog, which often carries glimpses of both her writing activities and family life.

KAREN KIRST

currently lives in coastal North Carolina with her marine husband, three boys and Andy the parrot. When she's not writing or dreaming up characters, she likes to read, visit tearooms, play piano, watch romantic comedies and chat over coffee with friends. She's incredibly blessed to be able to do what she loves, and gives God the glory.

LINDA FORD

KAREN KIRST

The Gift of Family

Love Inspired

Recycling programs for this product may not exist in your area.

ISBN-13: 978-0-373-82935-4

This edition published by arrangement with Love Inspired Books.

www.LoveInspiredBooks.com

Printed in U.S.A.

CONTENTS

MERRY CHRISTMAS, COWBOY

Linda Ford

To those seeking a home and acceptance.
May you find a place of welcome
especially in the Christmas season.

For there is no difference between the Jew
and the Greek: for the same Lord over all
is rich unto all that call upon him

—*Romans* 10:12

Chapter One

Edenvale, in what is now Alberta, Canada.
Winter 1880

He was about two minutes from freezing to death.

Colt Johnson grunted defiance, though the sound never left his icy lips. There'd be no freezing today. Not with two children burrowed against his chest and swathed beneath his heavy winter coat.

He reached the Eden Valley store, managed to dismount while still clutching the children and left his long-suffering horse at the rail so he could stagger to the door. His stiff hands struggled to turn the knob. The rattle of his efforts alerted the storekeeper, and through the frosty window Colt made out the shape of a person moving toward him.

The door opened. Colt blinked and tried to clear his vision as he stared into the face of the most beautiful white woman he'd ever seen—blond hair so curly that bits of it escaped her braids and hung around her face. Her eyes were as blue as a midsummer sky, and her smile rivaled the sunshine.

Simply looking at her made his insides start to warm.

This must be Macpherson's daughter. He'd never seen her before, having stopped only briefly at the store as he rode toward the hills and the cabin where he meant to spend the winter.

"Step in before we all freeze." Her voice was sweet as birdsong.

He didn't move, as much from not knowing how to react to her presence as because of the cold frosting his veins.

She grabbed his arm and pulled him forward, then shut the door behind him. "Brr. It's cold out there." She wrapped her arms across her chest and peered out the window.

Colt couldn't disagree, but he spared no more time considering the woman as he hurried toward the stove, sat on the first chair he reached and threw open his coat.

Marie's big eyes regarded him solemnly, full of trust.

"Are you okay?" Colt asked.

She held her little brother protectively to her chest and nodded. The little guy managed only a whimper.

It had been a long ride in cold that worsened with every mile.

The young woman sprang toward a stack of blankets and whipped off several. "You all need to get warm." She draped the blankets before the fire to warm, then held them toward Colt. "Give me one of the children."

But Marie pressed tight to Colt, and her eyes filled with fear.

"I'll take care of them." He took the offered blankets and wrapped them about the pair. With the fire's heat and the children on his lap, his front side soon began to warm, but his back remained as cold as the outdoors.

"You're shivering," the woman said. "Lean forward

and I'll slip this blanket over your shoulders." She stood behind him and waited.

He couldn't move. Couldn't think. Had she been so concerned about the weather she'd failed to take note of him…his black eyes, black hair and swarthy skin? A half-breed. White women did not have anything to do with the likes of him…at least not well-bred women. He could tell this woman fit that category by the way she moved—graceful as a deer at a brook—the way she spoke—her voice gentle and sweet—and even the way she dressed—her clothes sparkling clean.

Her hands touched his shoulders, spreading the blanket.

Without deciding if he should or not, Colt leaned forward, allowing her to tuck the warm material around him. His throat tightened with a combination of fear, surprise and longing at the way she patted his back as she adjusted the blanket. When had he felt the gentle touch of a woman's comfort? Anyone's comfort, for that matter? He pushed the question to the far reaches of his mind.

"You'll soon be warm." She moved around to face him.

At that moment, Macpherson entered the store from a back room. His presence brought stoic indifference back to Colt's thoughts. He didn't require comfort. He was full grown and on his own.

"I'll need to build more shelves to accommodate supplies." Macpherson rubbed his hands together.

Colt couldn't say if the man was cold or expressing pleasure at having to store more supplies.

The ruddy-faced man, with a shock of hair that was as red as it was brown, jerked to a halt. "We have visitors. Didn't hear you come in." He squinted at Colt.

"Say, didn't you stop here day before yesterday to get some supplies?"

"Yup."

"You're the young man who bought that book, *Flora and Fauna of Western Canada.* Your choice surprised me."

Colt gave the man a steady look, refusing to reveal any rancor at the comment. Did Macpherson think it strange a half-breed could read? "Like to know the names of things."

"Uh-huh." Macpherson's gaze darted to the children and back to Colt. "Don't remember you having any young 'uns when you stopped here earlier."

"They ain't mine."

The man's eyes narrowed. "Whose would they be?"

With long-suffering patience, Colt tamped down his irritation. Macpherson didn't need to get all suspicious.

"I didn't steal them, and if I had, I wouldn't likely show up at a white man's place of business, would I?" He kept his voice low and calm, but the way Macpherson blinked and straightened, he knew he'd managed to get his point across.

His daughter gasped. "Pa, surely you don't think such a thing. Why, he wrapped his coat about the children, braving the cold to protect them." She flashed Colt a bright smile that melted every remnant of frost in his body and all resentment in his brain. "It was very brave and noble of you."

Macpherson made a rumbling sound in his throat. Colt wondered if it was meant as warning to his daughter or to him.

"Didn't mean to suggest anything wrong." But Macpherson's expression showed no sign of relenting in his judgment. "Just wondering whose they are and why you have them."

"Zeke Gallant, a trapper west of here, married a Blackfoot girl. These are their children."

Macpherson nodded. "I met the pair a couple years ago. They had a baby with them." He smiled at Marie. "I guess that would be you."

Marie gave a shy smile then buried her face in Colt's shirtfront.

It amazed him these children trusted him so easily. After all, he hadn't seen Marie but once or twice, and Little Joe only once when he was a tiny mite.

Macpherson's smile flattened as he waited for Colt's explanation, but Colt was momentarily distracted as the fine young woman reached over and patted each little head. She was so close, he could see the light catching in her hair and smell the fresh, clean scent of her skin and clothing.

"Where are the Gallants?" the storekeeper prompted.

Colt jerked his attention from the woman and steeled himself to reveal nothing of his thoughts. He didn't immediately answer. He didn't like to mention the harsh reality he'd discovered. Not with little Marie watching him with big dark eyes, and listening to every word. Thankfully, her little brother had fallen asleep against Colt's chest…double reason to be grateful. He guessed when Little Joe woke up and saw he wasn't at home, he would let them all know his displeasure.

Colt's ears still rang from the racket the tiny boy made in protest to being taken from his home and parents.

"My ma and pa are dead." Marie dropped the announcement into their midst with a distinctive, husky voice. Not that it took her voice to give away her mixed race. Dark hair and black-as-coal eyes proved it. There would be no hiding the fact that this pair was part Indian.

Macpherson's eyes widened at the announcement, and his daughter again leaned closer and reached for Marie as if wanting to hug her. She settled instead for stroking Marie's head.

"I'm so sorry." Her words seemed filled with tears.

Against his better judgment, Colt looked into her face. Indeed, her eyes were watery, but she favored Colt with a trembling smile that shook him to the core. Was the light so poor she hadn't noticed what sort of man he was? Had she failed to notice the obvious heritage of these children?

He jerked his attention to Macpherson. Saw the curiosity and concern in his expression as he regarded the children. Colt explained what he'd found when he stopped at his friend's place. "Their mother was already gone. Buried under a tree. Zeke was barely alive when I got there. Figure his concern for his kids kept him going long past what his body wanted. I buried him next to his wife this morning." Some wouldn't dignify the union by calling the Indian woman anything other than a squaw, but Colt didn't feel that way.

"Pa said someone would come for us. He happy to see Colt. Said Colt will take care of us."

The young woman squatted to eye level with Marie.

Colt stiffened, drew back. He darted a glance at Macpherson, expecting the man to step forward and push Colt away from his daughter. But the man's gaze rested on Marie, his expression—near as Colt could decipher—full of sympathy.

Colt wasn't sure if he trusted the compassion he saw.

He'd witnessed very little of it in his lifetime. He waited for the expression to shift and grow hard.

He pulled the children closer. If necessary, he would move on. If they were fortunate, he'd find shelter in a barn. Otherwise, the river was nearby. The trees would offer some protection. He had the skills to build a shelter of branches. They'd survive.

Except the children deserved more than he could offer them in an outdoor camp. They at least needed food and more warmth than a fire struggling in the wind would provide. But, he reminded himself, this pair must learn to survive the opinion of white folks, the uncertain welcome of the natives. They would need to be tough.

The woman remained unaware of Colt's troubled thoughts and tense waiting.

"My name is Becca." She stroked Marie's head. "What's yours?"

Marie stared into the blue eyes, likely as mesmerized as Colt by the sweet voice and warm smile. "Marie," she answered.

"Marie. What a nice name. How old are you?"

"Four." Marie held up the correct number of fingers.

"A big girl now. With a little brother. What's his name?"

"Little Joe. He's two." Marie held up two fingers.

Little Joe, disturbed by his sister's movement, jerked awake. He sat up, looked about, wrinkled his face—

Colt balanced Marie on one knee as he pulled Little Joe to his shoulder, hoping to prevent what he knew would follow. But Little Joe turned as wriggly and uncooperative as a newborn calf and as loud as a pen of angry mountain cats. Colt's ears rang from the boy's cries. He had his hands full trying to make sure Little Joe didn't launch himself headfirst to the floor.

Miss Becca stood to her full height and stared at the boy, as amazed by the noise one small boy could make as Colt had been the first time he'd heard the racket.

Little Joe squirmed away and stood on the floor, his mouth open wide as he bellowed his displeasure.

"Shush." Colt patted the boy's back and tried to calm him. Being mixed race was already enough to see them turned out into the storm. This noise would make anyone with ears reconsider an offer of shelter.

"Little Joe, it's okay. Don't cry." But the kid merely sucked in air and released it in a louder scream.

"Ouch." Colt covered his ears. "That hurts."

Macpherson shuddered and backed away while his daughter stared.

Marie giggled. "Mama said he was loud enough to call down rain from the sky."

Colt could barely make out her words in the din.

"I'd have to agree," Becca said. "But we don't need rain, do we, Little Joe?"

Little Joe paid her no mind. The volume didn't diminish at all.

Marie went to her brother and patted his back. She murmured Indian words Colt recognized from his past as speech meant to comfort. They were always spoken for another, but he remembered a time he'd allowed himself to pretend they were for him. He shook his head, driving away the useless memory.

Little Joe stopped screaming and clutched Marie's hand.

Becca's sigh filled the air. "That's better. Thanks for calming him."

"He's my brother." Marie gave Colt, then Becca, a dark-eyed look of fierceness as she pulled Little Joe closer to her side.

Becca smiled, which filled her eyes with beams of sunshine. "He's a fortunate boy." She turned her blue gaze to Colt. "I don't know your name."

He gave it. Would she ask him to leave now?

But she only smiled and said, "Nice to meet you."

Colt kept his face expressionless and slid a look at Macpherson. Would *he* ask Colt to leave? The man's face showed a thousand things Colt could only guess at, but his gut informed him the man did not feel any welcome toward his guests.

"We'll be on our way as soon as the children are warm enough. I'll get more supplies before we leave." He hoped the promise of a sale would allow them to stay for a brief period. He'd never been one to pray. Didn't seem to be any point in praying to a white man's God. Truth was, he wasn't sure whose God he should pray to, but at the moment, he petitioned the only God he'd heard much about...the white man's.

Please stop the storm and guide me to a shelter for these kids.

"Nonsense," Becca said. "No one will be going out in this weather. There's plenty of room here, isn't that right, Pa?"

"I certainly wouldn't expect man nor beast to venture out in this storm." The words were spoken kindly enough, but Colt didn't miss the slight hesitation before they came, any more than he missed the protective look Macpherson fixed on his daughter.

Colt could assure the man he would not harm her in any way. He would only speak to her when necessary, and he'd stay a goodly distance away. He knew better than to ever look at a white woman in a way to invite the ire of a white man.

Marie pulled Colt's head down to whisper in his ear. "She's nice."

Colt nodded, but kept his attention on the child. Nice white women did not associate with half-breeds.

Becca watched the black-haired man with his head bent over Marie, listening to her murmured comment. She couldn't hear what the child said, but she ached for the gentle way he held her. Almost as much as she ached for the plight of the children. Orphaned, half-breed children didn't face a happy future, from what she'd observed. If it was in her power, she would do something, but what could she do? She'd promised Ma on her deathbed that when she turned eighteen, she would return east to family back there. She was set to keep that promise. Her trunk stood packed and ready near the door, waiting for the stage-coach due tomorrow. The first leg of the journey would take her to Fort Macleod. From there she would go south to Fort Benton. Eventually a train would carry her to her destination, though it pained her to think of leaving Pa alone.

Colt lifted his head, as if aware she watched him. His gaze collided with hers. A jolt raced through her veins at the intensity in his black, almost bottomless eyes. Except they weren't. Looking into them, she felt her heart hit something solid. Something deep inside, almost hidden. She knew somehow, that he was a person one could trust through thick and thin. A heart could find perfect rest in his care.

She shifted her attention to a display of hardware behind his shoulder and wondered when she had grown so silly.

Marie turned to Colt. They studied each other, then she grabbed his hands, opened his arms and indicated he should lift her and Little Joe to his lap. He arranged one on each knee and pulled a blanket around them. Marie glanced up at Colt and smiled, as if being in his arms made her feel safe.

Becca's eyes stung at how tender he was with the children.

Colt looked up and caught her watching. Again, she felt that unexpected jolt of surprise, and something more that she couldn't name. Meeting his gaze, however, made her aware of an unfolding inside her. How unusual for her to take so much note of a customer. Or even a visitor.

She must stop thinking about Colt and focus her attention on these orphaned children. Because of her promise to her mother, she could not offer them all the things she longed to—shelter, acceptance and love—but while the storm raged outside, she could give them a taste of what her heart longed to provide.

Pa cleared his throat. She realized she'd been staring at the trio far too long, and turned toward her father. He went to the window to look out.

"Good thing you got here when you did. The wind has picked up. Anyone out there now would be in danger of freezing."

"We was pretty cold," Marie said.

Colt grunted. "You mean to say you weren't cozy and warm under my coat?"

Marie quickly corrected herself. "Most of the time."

"It's okay, little one," Colt said. "I knew you were cold. But there wasn't anything I could do about it."

"I know. It's okay."

Becca chuckled at the way Marie tried to reassure him.

Pa wandered about the store, paused to adjust the

cans of tomatoes, and secured the lid on the barrel of crackers. "I hope this doesn't last too long."

"We're all safe, Pa."

He sat on a chair by the fire. "The stagecoach won't run if this keeps up. You won't make it to Toronto as we planned."

"I'll be safe here. I can go later." She didn't object to a delay in her travel plans—although Pa insisted that the sooner she went, the better. But she hated to leave before Christmas.

"I promised your mother you'd leave when you turned eighteen."

"I'll be eighteen for a whole year." She smiled encouragement at her father, then glanced at Colt to see his reaction to the conversation.

He watched them with guarded interest.

Deciding to change the topic, she asked him, "What are your plans for the children?"

He paused as if to measure his words. "I thought the children should go to Fort Macleod. I hear there's a teacher there who takes in orphan children without any regard for their race."

Suddenly, the first leg of her journey didn't seem so lonely and frightening. With Colt and the children along, she'd barely have time to think about all she was leaving behind.

Colt fixed his dark eyes on her, bringing her thoughts to a crashing halt.

"Miss Macpherson, seeing as you plan to take the stagecoach, I hope you'll agree to take them with you and turn them over to the teacher."

"Me?" She couldn't tear her gaze from his.

"Makes sense," Pa said.

Becca did not think it made any sense whatsoever.

She saw herself clutching two sad children, tears flowing silently from three pairs of eyes, as they huddled alone and cold in a stagecoach racing farther and farther away from everything familiar. Though perhaps the tears wouldn't be silent on Little Joe's behalf. She blinked, reminded herself of her promise to her mother, and managed a soft answer.

"Of course."

"So much depends on the weather." Pa again wandered about the store, poking at supplies.

Marie shifted to look into Colt's face. "You not take care of us?"

"I'll make sure you're safe."

His reply satisfied Marie, and she snuggled against his chest.

Colt had the most peculiar expression on his face. As if unsure how to handle the children, and yet he was so gentle and natural with them.

Becca couldn't stop watching him.

Pa cleared his throat, and guilty heat burned across her cheeks. Pa always guarded her closely, making sure she didn't spend too much time in the company of the men who visited the store. Not that he'd ever had to run interference before.

"It will soon be supper time," Pa said.

"Of course. I'll see to it." She hurried into the living quarters, grateful to escape the three visitors. She stared around the kitchen. What was she to prepare for them? Would they enjoy clustering around the table? When had she ever been so disturbed by unexpected guests? It wasn't as if they hadn't had occasional visitors over the few years they'd been here. But none that stirred her heart the way this man did.

The innocent children, too, of course. Only it wasn't

the idea of the children sitting at the table that had her thoughts all aflutter.

She grabbed her apron, tied it about her waist and put a pot on the stove.

Tomorrow she would depart on the stage. She glanced toward the window. If the storm let up. Otherwise—she sucked in air that seemed strangely empty—they would be stranded until such time as the weather improved. No doubt she should be somewhat dismayed at the idea of a delay. But she smiled as she browned bacon, peeled potatoes and cubed them into the pot for thick, nourishing potato soup. She turned to get a can of milk from the shelf. Out of habit, her glance slid to the picture of Ma on the small side table beside the burgundy armchair where she'd so often sat to read or knit.

"Ma," she whispered. "It's only a delay." And only if the storm lasted. "I haven't forgotten my promise."

Yet her insides felt as tangled as a sheet left too long on the line. Yes, she'd go to Toronto because she'd promised to do so. Her mother had wanted her to enjoy more opportunities than the frontier provided. More social life, more suitable acquaintances. But she wouldn't regret a delay in her travel plans. Surely Ma would understand that some things couldn't be helped—like the weather.

And if her heart welcomed the delay, who was to know and judge?

The soup was about ready and the table set when Becca heard a scream that caused her to drop a handful of spoons.

Clutching her skirts, she dashed for the doorway to the store. "What's wrong?"

The two children stood before the outer door. Marie

held the blanket out to her brother, but he tossed his arms about, refusing her efforts to comfort him.

Pa stood by his chair, looking as startled and confused as Becca.

She glanced about. "Where's Colt?" Had he walked out on these children? If so, he wasn't the man she'd judged him to be.

Her question made Little Joe scream louder. She closed her eyes and grimaced. "He's so loud."

Pa shook his head. "I can't hear you."

At least, that's what she guessed he said. She moved closer to him and shouted, "Where's Colt?"

"Said he had to take care of his horse. I told him to put the animal in our barn."

"He's coming back, isn't he?"

Pa nodded. "Don't think he has much choice. He wouldn't get far in this weather." He escaped into the living quarters where the din of Little Joe's crying would be softer.

There must be a way to calm the boy. Before she could think what to do, the door swung open and shut again. A cold wind blasted through the room, carrying a generous dose of snow.

They all turned to look at Colt as he brushed himself off.

Little Joe let out a wail and ran to him as fast as his little legs allowed. He didn't slow down when he reached the man, but crashed into his legs.

Colt swung the boy up in his arms. "Young man, you are going to have to learn to stop without using my legs as brakes."

Little Joe buried his face against Colt's chest and peeked out from the corners of his eyes.

No mistaking the gleam of victory.

Becca laughed. “You little scamp. You’re just pretending.”

Colt quirked a black eyebrow. “What’s he pretending?”

She fell into Colt’s gaze and had no idea how to answer him.

Colt shifted to consider Little Joe. “What have you been up to, young fella?”

At the grin on Little Joe’s face, Becca laughed and smoothed his hair. “You’re going to do just fine.” So long as he found somewhere he felt safe and loved.

Little Joe wriggled to be put down, and Colt released him. The boy darted from one thing to another in the store, touching gently but never pulling at anything.

Becca remained at Colt’s side, watching. “They seem like fine kids.”

“I think Zeke had been warning them to be good. If they misbehave, people will say it’s because they’re savages.” His voice deepened as he said the word.

“Well, those people would be wrong. They’re simply children learning how to operate in the world.”

Pa appeared in the doorway. “I moved the soup off the heat. Thought it might burn.”

“I forgot.” She dashed to the door, pausing to call over her shoulder, “Supper is ready. Come on in.”

Colt looked like she’d shot him rather than invited him to join them for the meal, but she didn’t have time to ask for an explanation if she meant to save the soup. And provide Colt and the children with a good meal. Plus something more from her heart—welcome and blessing.

Chapter Two

Colt stared after Becca. The idea of going into their private quarters sent a quake up his spine.

"Everything is ready," Macpherson said. "Who's hungry?"

"Me hungry." Little Joe headed after Becca.

Marie hesitated, watching Colt. When she saw he wasn't moving, she came to his side. "I'm not hungry."

He knew it couldn't be true. Except for some cold biscuits, they hadn't eaten since breakfast, and his stomach growled as if to remind him of how long ago that was. He was at a loss to explain why Marie felt she had to side with him, but seems she did. If he refused the invitation, she would, too.

"I'm kind of hungry," he said, and took a tentative step toward the door, and then another.

Marie followed hard on his heels.

Macpherson stepped back to usher them into their living quarters. Colt faltered. These were white people. He'd been taught in every way possible that he had no place with them. Sure, he could eat with the cowboys, or the servants, but not at the table with—

"Grab a chair." Macpherson indicated where they should sit.

Colt swallowed hard and made his stiff legs carry him to the table. He sat gingerly on a chair.

"If you all bow your heads, I'll say the blessing." Macpherson waited for them to obey, and even Little Joe did so.

Colt closed his eyes, more to contain a thousand surprised and uneasy feelings than out of any reverence. Though his conscience reminded him of the times he'd sat in the back of a church and listened hungrily to the words of love from the preacher. Words that he guessed did not apply to him.

"Amen."

Colt jerked up his head and looked directly into Becca's flash-of-sky eyes.

"I hope everyone likes potato soup."

He nodded, tried to force a word to his tongue, but couldn't. In desperation he grabbed the glass of water before him and downed it.

"I like soup." Marie's eyes never left the ladle as Becca filled her bowl.

"Me like, too." Little Joe reached for the bowl.

Becca grabbed his hands to keep him from sticking them into the hot soup as she filled his bowl. She ladled soup into Marie's bowl, then filled Colt's.

He murmured his thanks. "Smells good." And it did.

She filled her pa's bowl, and then her own before she sat down and checked the temperature of Little Joe's soup. "Still too hot. Here, start with a slice of bread."

"Okay." Little Joe didn't seem to have any problem with that and ate it heartily, then tackled the soup. He had a little trouble coordinating the spoon, but Becca didn't appear to notice.

Colt would have been content to eat in silence, but it seemed a practice the Macphersons didn't hold to.

Becca paused with her spoon halfway to her mouth. "I hope everyone is safe in this storm. I can't help thinking of Russell Thomas."

Macpherson spoke directly to Colt. "Old Russell lives out in the mountains all summer, but comes to town about this time of year to hole up in a rough cabin that has cracks so big between the logs, you could throw a cat through 'em. We haven't seen him in town yet but he knows the country better than most. He can take care of himself." He addressed the latter reassurance to his daughter.

Little Joe's eyes widened. "Frow cat?"

Becca laughed. "It's an expression. No one really throws a cat."

Both kids looked relieved.

Colt forced his eyes not to shift in Becca's direction. But he couldn't stop his thoughts from going that way. When had he ever heard a woman laugh so often, so readily? And when had he ever heard such a joyful sound? Maybe in the woods on a sunny day, when every bird within twenty miles seemed determined to sing the loudest and cheeriest.

"Won't keep out much of this wind and snow, but it's better than being without shelter." She sounded so worried, Colt half decided to go find the old man right then and there and bring him to town, never mind the storm.

Macpherson chuckled. "He knows how to survive better'n most men. He'll show up here in a day or two asking for more tobacco."

Little Joe finished his soup and looked longingly at the empty bowl. Becca obligingly gave him more.

Colt cleaned his bowl and ate two thick slices of

bread. He refused offers of more, even though his stomach craved it.

Becca gave a low-throated chuckle. “I wonder how Miss Oake likes her first taste of winter here.” She directed a sweet smile toward Colt. “Miss Oake came out to join her brother at the OK Ranch. She was a teacher back east but said she craved a little more excitement. I wonder if this is enough adventure for her.”

Her pa answered. A good thing because Colt could think of nothing but blue skies and cheerful birds.

“I expect she’s enjoying a cozy fire and a good read. She had a heavy case of books with her.”

Little Joe’s head rocked back and forth, and he tipped forward.

“Looks like it’s bedtime,” Colt observed.

“No.” Little Joe jerked up. “I not tired.”

But even Colt could see that he could no longer focus his eyes. “I’ll take them to the barn.”

Becca leapt to her feet. “You’ll do no such thing. Pa?”

Macpherson pushed his chair back. “You and the children can bunk here.” He sounded as if none of them had a choice.

Here? In their living quarters? Surely he didn’t mean that. “Thanks. I’ll throw down my bedroll in the storeroom.”

“Nonsense.” Becca sounded determined. “There’s no heat there. We’ve had people spend the night before. They don’t seem to mind sleeping on the floor.” She waved her hand to indicate the space in the living quarters between the kitchen table and the easy chairs, and gave him a challenging look as if to ask if it didn’t suit him.

“That will be fine,” he mumbled, his tongue thick

and uncooperative. His skin would itch with nerves all night at sharing white people's quarters.

"I'll put Little Joe down right away." She chuckled as the little guy's head bobbed from side to side. But when she lifted him from the chair, he turned into a squirming, screaming ball of fury.

Colt sighed. "Sure does have a powerful set of lungs." He grabbed the boy as he wriggled from Becca's grasp.

Marie looked about ready to fall asleep in her chair as well, but with a deep sigh, she climbed down and went to Little Joe's side. Again, she murmured Indian words to calm her brother, then led him to one of the chairs, climbed up and pulled Little Joe after her. The pair cuddled together.

"He'll be okay. I will take care of him," Marie said.

"That's so sweet," Becca murmured.

"Yup." Colt hoped his voice revealed none of his churning feelings. Little Joe would likely never know how his sister buffeted the harshness of life for him. But understanding what lay ahead for both, he wished he could find a home where they would be admired as much as Becca admired them. Just listening to her laugh as she dealt with them caused cracks in the walls he'd built around his heart.

A shattering cry jerked Becca awake. It took two seconds to remember the source of such a piercing sound. Little Joe. She blinked away sleep and tried to guess the time of day…or was it night? Stumbling from her bed, she danced about on the cold floor.

The stove top rattled. Pa was up. She'd slept the night through.

She hopped to the window, scraped away the frost and peered into the gray light. Snow piled against the glass. The wind battered the side of the building. The snowstorm continued.

Shouldn't she be disappointed?

But she wasn't. Instead, she hurried into her clothes and fixed her hair, pausing to study her reflection in the misted mirror. The cold made it impossible to stand still long enough to assess her likeness. Not that she needed a mirror to tell her what she knew already. Skin that stayed porcelain white—a fact that had pleased her mother, but mattered not at all to Becca. Hair that refused to behave itself. She braided it tightly, then dashed from the room and huddled near the stove, stretching out her hands toward the growing heat.

Little Joe's cries had settled into sobbing misery.

Becca glanced toward Colt and the children. The three of them were bleary eyed.

"You look like you never slept."

"I tried." Colt sounded resigned. "But have you ever tried sleeping with two kids kicking you in the ribs all night?"

"Can't say as I have." She grinned at him, enjoying the mental picture of him spending the night with the children. It wasn't the kicking she imagined, but the way Marie leaned against him, as trusting as a kitten with its mother.

"I expect they're hungry." She pulled out griddles and sliced bacon to fry. She mixed up batter for griddle cakes, and to complete the meal, she opened a jar of applesauce she'd preserved a few weeks ago.

As Becca pulled out dishes to set the table, Marie jumped from the easy chair she shared with Colt and Little Joe. Her brother scrambled after her. "You stay with Colt," she told him.

Little Joe hesitated, as if deciding whether or not he

wanted to comply, then nodded. "Okay." He gave Colt an expectant look and Colt stared at him.

"What do you want?"

"Up."

Colt's face registered surprise, then he lifted the boy and settled him on his knee.

Becca studied them a moment. He met her gaze, his eyes full of dark depths. She got the feeling Colt found every welcoming, accepting gesture unexpected and wasn't quite sure how to handle it. She wondered about his parents and what sort of things he'd encountered to make him so wary. Though she'd seen enough of how people acted toward those who weren't like them to guess at the way he'd been treated. It brought a stab of pain to her heart. She turned away to hide her reaction.

Marie stood at her side. "I will help you."

She realized Marie meant she would like to set the table.

"How nice. Thank you." Becca bent over to give the child a quick hug, then handed her the plates. The least she could do was prove to these children that not everyone would treat them poorly.

"Breakfast is ready." The words were barely out of her mouth before Little Joe flung himself from Colt's lap and grabbed his hand, tugging at him to hurry.

"Eat. Me hungry."

Colt laughed. "So I see."

Becca's eyes widened. She'd never heard the man laugh before, though he had a shy smile and quiet chuckle that seemed to escape often, and likely without his permission. But his laugh did funny things to her insides—making them smile in secret. She jerked her fanciful thoughts back into order as Pa settled at one end of the table and waited for her to sit so he could say the blessing. Guilt stung her cheeks at the way Pa studied her. She sat and bowed her head.

As Pa asked God to bless the food, she asked Him to guard her thoughts. She knew what she must do—honor her promise to her mother. There was no room for wishing for something else.

The food was well received. After several helpings, Little Joe finally slowed down with a sigh.

"All done."

Becca shook her head. "I can't believe you ate all that."

He nodded, flashed a wide grin and patted his tummy. "Full now."

Colt snorted. "Better plug your ears." He addressed Little Joe.

"Why?" Marie asked.

"I know there isn't room for all that food in a little-boy stomach. It has to go somewhere, so I figure it will start coming out his ears."

Little Joe clamped his hands over his ears and scrunched his face in deep concentration.

Becca laughed. "He's joshing you." She sent Colt a scolding look and almost choked as he laughed—his mouth open, his eyes flashing.

He reached over and tapped Little Joe on the shoulder, gaining his attention. "It won't really come out your ears."

Little Joe slowly removed his hands, checked his palms. "No food."

Colt chuckled. "It's all in your tummy."

Little Joe looked relieved.

Pa cleared his throat and reached for the Bible he kept on a shelf near the table.

"If everyone is done, we always read a chapter every

morning. As my father often said, it's a good way to start the day."

Becca settled back to listen. She would miss Pa's morning reading when she left. Yes, she read her own copy of the Bible, but hearing Pa's slow, strong voice was part and parcel of her faith.

He read a chapter from Matthew, then closed the Bible. "We always pray for the day ahead of us."

As Becca bowed her head, she allowed herself a glance at Colt. He watched Pa with an expression combining surprise and what she could only guess was admiration.

"God in heaven, bless us this day. Protect any travelers in the storm. Please see fit to bring an end to this storm so Becca can begin her journey. Take Colt and the children on whatever journey You have for them. Amen."

Pa drained his cup of coffee and suddenly tipped his head to one side. "Listen to that. The wind has stopped blowing. I do believe the storm has ended."

For the first time in her life, Becca resented the sun that broke through the clouds and turned the frost on the window to a thousand sparkling diamonds.

Pa rubbed his hands together and looked pleased as he went to the store, hoping for customers.

Colt pushed away from the table to follow her pa from the room. Little Joe scrambled from his chair and raced after him. "Me go, too. Me go with you."

Marie followed her brother, her eyes echoing his words.

Colt turned slowly to contemplate the children, then faced Becca. "I have to go."

"Go? As in leave?"

He shifted his weight from foot to foot, as if anxious to be on his way.

"Don't go," Marie begged, clinging to his hand.

Little Joe puckered up, ready to set his ear-splitting cry on them again.

Colt swept the boy into his arms. "Don't cry. Please."

"You not go?"

The poor man looked torn between a desire to flee and the demands of two little children.

"They've lost so much already," she murmured. "You could at least stay until the stage comes."

His expression could have been set in stone for all he revealed. Then he nodded. "Very well. I'll see them safely on their way first."

"You stay?" Little Joe demanded.

Colt nodded, and Little Joe patted his cheeks lovingly. "You good boy."

Laughter filled her throat at the child's innocent approval, and she knew her eyes brimmed with amusement.

Colt looked her way, saw her barely contained laughter and grinned crookedly.

"Must be nice to be appreciated," she managed, though her words seemed a little garbled by the welling laughter.

"Guess there's a first time for everything." Suddenly he turned away and strode into the store, Little Joe clutched in his arms.

"Anything I can do to help?" she heard him ask Pa before the door closed between them.

If she didn't miss her guess, he sounded desperate.

"I'll help with dishes," Marie offered, pulling Becca's attention from the activity in the store.

But it did not stop her from trying to guess what sent Colt skittering away so fast.

First time for everything.

As if he felt neglected because only a two-year-old child saw fit to show appreciation. A self-pitying statement if he'd ever heard one. Dare he hope she'd think he was only joshing? But he feared he'd seen a flicker of something in her eyes before he ducked from the room. Whether it was pity or something else, he would not consider.

The storm was over. He should be on his way, but the kids would soon be off to the fort with Becca where they'd be treated kindly…as kindly as mixed-race children could expect, and he knew from experience it was hit or miss—mostly hit of the physical sort, as it turned out.

The outer door blew open and a weathered, bewhiskered man entered the store.

"Seems we survived the first big blow of the season."

"How do, Petey. You planning to head out soon?" Macpherson glanced out the window. "Don't see the stagecoach."

Colt watched the pair. So this was the driver. Seemed his promise to stay until the kids were on their way would be short-lived.

Petey strode to the stove and held his hands toward the heat. "Came to tell you I ain't going 'til after Christmas."

Macpherson straightened and stared at the man. "You don't say." He didn't sound pleased by the announcement.

"Rufus invited me to stay with him."

"At the livery station?"

"Rufus and me go back a long ways. 'Bout the closest thing we have to family. Figure we should spend Christmas together."

"Of course." Macpherson strode to the window and peered out.

Colt didn't move. Tried to become invisible, but Little Joe squirmed and chattered, drawing Macpherson's attention and a glower.

Petey glanced at the little boy then at Colt. "You taking that kid out in this weather?"

Macpherson answered. "They're going to the fort on the stage."

"Then it looks like you'll have visitors for Christmas."

Macpherson did not look pleased at the prospect, but moved to tend to Petey's order.

A few minutes later the man left with a bundle of goods that Colt figured would be used to celebrate the season.

Colt and Macpherson stared at each other, then Macpherson headed to the living quarters. Colt hung back, Little Joe playing in his arms. Christmas was a family time. Even Petey knew that. Colt wasn't family. He'd buy a few supplies and be on his way.

Macpherson paused in the doorway. "You better come along."

Colt knew what to expect. He'd be leaving within the hour.

"Don't suppose you heard Old Petey out there." Macpherson sounded weary as he spoke to Becca.

Becca had been supervising Marie washing the table. Her smile faded. "He's here already? I thought—"

"He's spending Christmas with Rufus at the livery barn. I can't imagine why he'd choose to stay cooped up in the tiny room at the back of the barn when he could enjoy Christmas at the fort."

Becca clapped her hands. "That's the best news I've heard in a long time."

Colt stared in disbelief and confusion.

Macpherson grunted. "Why is that?"

"I can spend Christmas here with you." She spoke directly to her pa, then shifted her gaze to the two children who had gone to the corner to play. "And I can give them the best Christmas ever."

Her words hit Colt like a blow to the stomach. It meant he'd have to say goodbye to them right away, but he acknowledged it would be best for them. Only it would be lonely for him.

He was being plumb ridiculous. He'd been alone most of his life, even when he found shelter with a family.

"You are most generous," he murmured, letting his gaze rest momentarily on her face, taking in her sunny smile and sky-colored eyes. He would never forget her. Recalling her features would warm many cold, lonely nights. He jerked away to confront Macpherson.

"I'll get those supplies now and be on my way." He headed for the door, expecting Macpherson to follow.

But before her pa could take a step, Becca sprang forward and grabbed Colt's arm.

"You can't mean you intend to leave." She kept her words low so the children wouldn't hear, but nevertheless, they rang with accusation. "They'll be so upset, they won't be able to enjoy Christmas. You must stay and help me make it special for them." She pleaded silently, her eyes soft, then her face filled with determination. "Didn't you promise them—and me—you would stay until they were on the stage?" When he didn't answer, she turned to her pa. "Tell him to stay. Tell him we need him to make this work. Tell him—" She ran out of steam.

Macpherson studied his daughter for some time, then shrugged and turned to Colt. "Really doesn't make sense to ride out on your own unless you're in a hurry to get someplace."

Was he? Part of him said he should leave now before he was driven away. Leave with his pride intact. His heart untouched.

"Please stay," Becca murmured.

Her voice made him forget all the sound reasons for going.

"For Christmas?" Was it really what she meant?

"We'll make it the best Christmas ever."

Did she realize she hadn't added "for the children"? Was it worth risking all the solid walls he'd built around his soul to find out?

"I'll stay."

A large portion of his brain told him he would be less thankful before this sojourn ended, but he could only hope he'd be able to say it had been worth whatever pain it brought.

Chapter Three

Colt meant to see that no one regretted having him spend Christmas here, so when Macpherson returned to the store, Colt followed hard on his heels, scooping Little Joe into his arms again before the boy could start his ear-splitting cries. Marie seemed content to keep Becca company.

"Can I do something to help?" he asked the older man.

"Thanks. I could use a hand." Macpherson prepared to move a barrel to the other end of the counter.

Colt put Little Joe down. "Stay here."

"If I take the bolts of fabric off this table, I can shift it closer to the corner and give me room for a better display of tools."

"I'll do that." Colt lifted the bolts to the counter. Little Joe stuck to his heels like a tick on a warm dog. He wanted to warn the boy not to get used to Colt being there.

Even at the fort they could expect to be shunned by both races because of the blood of the other flowing through their veins. Colt learned a person fit nowhere but in his own skin. He'd found his place by doing what he liked best, what he was good at—caring for horses and riding the high pastures.

The table was empty, and Macpherson indicated Colt should help shove it into the place he'd chosen. That done, he handed Colt a rag. Little Joe tagged along after Colt's every step.

"Might as well clean it while it's empty." The older man grabbed a broom and swept the floor.

"Nice prayer this morning," Colt said. The man's words stuck in his brain. Did he really mean them, or had he simply uttered them out of habit?

"My pa, God rest his soul, believed a man could only order his days aright if he put God first."

"You really think God cares about a man's daily activities?"

"I do believe so."

Colt wondered if that only applied to a select few. "I suppose it's only for white men."

"Nope. For everyone. Seems to me if God makes all men, then He must like different skin colors." Macpherson scooped up the pile of dirt and dumped it in the ash bucket.

"Hmm." No doubt the sound contained more of Colt's doubts than he meant it to. But he'd seen the caution and warning in Macpherson's expression as he watched Colt when his daughter was around.

Macpherson leaned into the counter and considered his words. "Maybe it's like a farmer with his animals. Think about it. Sheep, goats, chickens, pigs, horses, cows…each is so different, yet of great importance to the farmer." He shrugged. "Here, give me a hand putting the fabric back."

Colt welcomed the task providing, as it did, an opportunity to consider Macpherson's words without having to comment on them. He'd seen no evidence that God cared for a man of mixed heritage.

Or—he jerked up and stared at the display of harnesses and yokes—was he mistaking man's actions for an indication of what God thought? Interesting concept. He'd have to give it some study.

They finished rearranging things to Macpherson's liking. The man circled the room, as if hoping to find something else to do. Little Joe trotted after him. Finally Macpherson went to the counter and sighed. "I have accounts to deal with. You might as well take the little guy into the living quarters. Maybe Becca can find something to amuse him." Every time either one of them turned around, they practically tripped over Little Joe.

Colt's thoughts reined to a skidding halt. He could not get his brain or his feet to function.

"We go." Little Joe grabbed his hand and led him toward the door.

Colt followed like one of those mindless sheep Macpherson had mentioned. He stepped into the living quarters and stared at Becca bent over the table with Marie.

She glanced up. "You're just in time. I'm showing Marie one of the books I read as a child."

Little Joe trotted over to his sister, pushed a chair close and climbed up beside her, chattering away about the pictures.

Becca's expression indicated she waited for a comment from Colt.

"That's nice." Certainly not very profound, but it was the best he could do. Thankfully, she seemed satisfied.

"This is one of my favorites. It's a Bible story book. Maybe you're familiar with it." She waved him over to examine it.

He managed to make his feet move to the table and bent over the children, aware Becca did the same thing next to him.

She turned a page. "Look how worn the edges are. That's because it was my favorite. The story of Jesus born in a manger."

"Will you read it to us?" Marie asked.

"I'd love to." Becca straightened and looked at Colt as she told the story. Once she turned a page, but she never referred to the book.

Colt suspected she had the words memorized perfectly, but he didn't turn from her gaze to look at the page, so he couldn't say for certain. He was trapped by her voice and blue eyes…and something more that he couldn't name. A sense of being drawn forward by a woman who would remain forever out of his reach. At the same time, a memory pulled him to the past.

"I spent Christmas one year with a family at the fort." The words came slowly and without forethought. He simply spoke the memory as it formed in his mind.

"The mother read this same story." Her three children had gathered round her knees. Colt had been allowed to listen from a distance. But the words enticed him then, even as they did now.

"I like the story," Marie said, pulling Colt back to the present.

He stepped back until the big armchair stood between himself and Becca.

Marie continued. "Papa told us this story just before Mama died. He said Mama went to live with Jesus." A sob escaped her lips before she clamped them together. Silent tears tracked down her cheeks.

Becca gave Colt a despairing look, as if hoping he could somehow fix Marie's pain. He couldn't. Tears made him itch with discomfort as he recalled being cuffed across the head for shedding a few of his own when he wasn't much bigger than Marie.

But Becca seemed to know what to do. She lifted Marie from the chair and sat down, cradling the little girl in her lap. She rocked back and forth, making comforting sounds.

Little Joe scrambled from his chair and edged close to his sister to pat her leg. "Not cry. Not cry."

"It's okay little guy," Becca soothed. "She's not hurt."

Marie struggled to contain her tears, but seemed powerless to stop their flow.

Little Joe wrinkled up his face. An ear-piercing wail rent the air.

"Don't cry," Colt ordered, which only made him cry harder.

Becca tried to pat both children but couldn't quite manage. She shot him a look so full of appeal he couldn't resist. He sat on the chair next to her, pulled Little Joe to his lap. Imitating Becca, he patted the boy's back. Little Joe's cries softened to shudders as he clutched Colt's shirtfront. Colt tried to decide if this felt right or if it threatened his careful self-containment.

Marie sat up. "I'm better. Thank you." She stood before the table and paged through the storybook.

"You done, too?" Colt asked Little Joe, then tried to put him down, but he burrowed his fingers into Colt's shirt and hung on.

Becca chuckled at the sight. "Guess he needs to be held a little longer."

Colt settled back. "Guess so."

Becca gave him a look brimming with warmth and—he swallowed hard—approval? She chuckled again.

"He seems very content."

"Huh?" Oh, Little Joe. Of course. "Probably worn out from kicking me all night."

Becca laughed, and Colt allowed himself a grin.

But Little Joe wasn't prepared to sit quietly for long. He wriggled down and began to trot about the room. He stopped in front of a small table near one of the chairs and reached for a picture. Glass. If he broke it—

Colt leapt to his feet and crossed the room in three strides, capturing the picture before Little Joe got it.

"This isn't for little boys," he explained to the startled child.

Little Joe giggled. "You run fast."

"Guess so." He looked at the picture. A beautiful woman in a fancy outfit.

Becca crossed the room to his side. "My mother."

"I see the resemblance."

"She's the reason I'm going east. Here, I'll put it out of his reach." She took the framed photograph from Colt and set it on top of a cupboard.

Colt tried to sort out his scrambled thoughts, but they were so tangled he needed a rake to arrange them. With a mother like that, Becca didn't belong in the untamed West. No wonder she planned to leave. Yet she seemed the sort of woman the West needed. She seemed unfazed by the storm, as well as the challenge of frontier life. She was gentle, accepting of half-breed kids…

He allowed one thought to surface. She'd been kind to him as well, as if oblivious to his mixed race.

Little Joe ducked behind the chair and poked his head around. "Peek."

Becca nudged Colt. "Someone wants to play with you."

"Me?" He sucked in air. She thought he should play with the boy? The idea both thrilled and frightened him.

Little Joe poked his head around the chair on the other side. “Peek.”

Colt laughed.

Becca grinned. “He’s adorable. They both are.”

Colt sobered. “Too bad everyone won’t see that.”

“What do you mean?”

He shook his head. He wouldn’t voice his reasons in front of the kids, knowing how much it hurt to hear the words people would use to describe them. Instead, he hunkered down and crab-walked forward until he was at the front of the chair. He waited for Little Joe to poke his head around the corner.

“Boo.”

The boy jumped and then giggled. “You scared me.” Mischief flashed through the child’s eyes seconds before he rushed forward to tackle Colt, catching him off balance. The pair tumbled to the floor, and Little Joe bounced happily on his chest.

Marie sidled up to them, searching Colt’s face as if to make sure he wasn’t upset.

“Come here, you.” He grabbed the girl, pulled her down beside him and tickled her.

Becca sank down in the chair, so close her skirts brushed his arm. She chuckled, her eyes brimming with amusement and—he would not make the mistake of thinking she smiled approval on him. But when had he ever felt so…so…

As if he’d arrived where he belonged?

The children’s laughter washed through him. Becca’s smile melted the edges of his heart.

He shifted the kids to the floor, pushed to his feet and brushed himself off—more because he needed to collect and arrange his thoughts than because he’d found any dirt on the floor. He strode to the window. Every nerve in his body screamed to leave right now.

While every beat of his heart longed for each minute to last forever.

Thankfully, Macpherson chose that moment to step into the room. "The temperature is dropping." He glanced around the room, and Colt wondered if he resented having his space invaded by three visitors. But Macpherson smiled.

"I think some games for the children would be a good idea." The man might not approve of Colt, but at least he didn't seem to look at the children with the same narrow-eyed concern.

"Games?" Marie's eyes widened with hope.

Becca clapped her hands. "Oh, yes. Pa, do finger puppets for them."

"Very well." He pulled pen and ink from the cupboard.

"I'll show you on my own finger." Macpherson dipped the pen into the ink and drew a simple face on one finger.

"This is a little boy. He can hide." He curled his fist and the puppet boy disappeared.

"He can dance." Macpherson sang a little ditty, and the finger danced.

"He can talk." He held the finger to his ear and listened intently, nodding as if he understood a whispered secret.

"Who wants to go first?"

Marie edged forward and held out her hand.

"I can make one or a whole family. Which would you like?"

"A family. A mama, a papa, a little girl and a littler boy."

Colt realized the importance of Marie's choice—her own family. He couldn't look at Becca, but heard her suck in air. It drew his attention. He glanced her way to see if she was okay. Her blue eyes glistened with tears, and she pressed her lips together. She looked at him and gave a watery smile.

He returned her smile, wondering if his lips trembled just slightly.

"There you go," Macpherson said, and Colt jerked his attention back to Marie, who thanked the man and stared at her fingers. A slow, dazzling smile filled her face, and she pressed her hand to her chest.

This time Colt dared not look at Becca. Instead he forced his attention to Little Joe, who stood before Macpherson with a fist held out.

Macpherson took the tiny hand and drew a face on the index finger. Little Joe backed away, staring at his finger. He circled the room holding the finger up, turning it toward objects then back toward him.

Macpherson chuckled. "It doesn't take a lot to amuse children."

"Or make them happy." Becca's voice rounded with emotion.

Marie sat cross-legged on the floor, murmuring softly to her finger people.

"I wish they could be protected from the harshness of life." Becca spoke softly, so only the adults would hear her comments.

Her pa went to her side and wrapped an arm about her shoulders. "Life is generally what we make of it. If what I've seen of this pair is any indication, their parents have prepared them to face things with calm assurance. That's bound to go a long way."

Colt shifted to block Becca and her pa from his view,

and wished he could likewise block their words from his mind. Sometimes a child didn't have any opportunity to make good or bad of his life. Other people did that for him.

He concentrated on slow, deep breaths. He was no longer a child. Now he could make what he wanted of his life. A few days ago he had no doubts about what that was—an isolated cabin and a pen of horses to work with over the winter.

Now long-buried, long-denied wishes seemed determined to reestablish their useless presence. All because of two children who needed a home and acceptance. Their requirements so clearly mirrored what he'd wanted, but never had, as a child.

I am no longer a child. I no longer need or want those things.

He didn't succeed in putting his thought to rest.

Chapter Four

Becca ached to pull the children to her lap and hold them close. If only she could protect them from the cruelties she knew they'd face.

The children weren't the only ones she wished she could help. She'd seen the hurt in Colt's face before he turned away. It pained her to think of the sort of memories that brought such a reaction. A shudder started in her chest, and she stepped away from Pa. With his arm across her shoulder, he might feel it and ask the cause. She began lunch preparation, determined the children and Colt would leave this place with memories of kindness and good food. She stared at the stove a moment, trying to think how she could make the meal special. Smiling, she pulled out pots.

Her mother had always made tomato soup for special occasions. She would do the same, though she'd never managed to make it as good as Ma did.

A little later the soup was gone, as was the bread she'd served with chokecherry jam.

Little Joe had purple jam smeared on his face, along with a look of satisfaction.

Marie managed to eat more neatly, and smiled at Becca. "Thank you."

"You're welcome, sweetheart."

Colt's head jerked up, and his dark eyes bored into her. What had she said to make him look at her that way?

He shifted his attention to Little Joe. "I think a little boy is ready for a nap." He swung from his chair and lifted the child.

"Put him on my bed." She rushed ahead and opened the door.

Colt hesitated.

"He'll get a good rest here." Still, the man did not move. "Is something wrong?"

Colt's gaze found hers, and she saw confusion.

"Oh, give him to me and I'll put him down." But Little Joe fussed and clung to Colt.

Marie marched ahead and climbed on the bed. "I'll take him."

Little Joe went eagerly to his sister, and the pair cuddled together. Becca covered them with a quilt, then turned to speak to Colt but he'd disappeared.

"Pa, where did he go?"

Pa yawned and stretched. "Said it was a good time to check on the horses. He'll be back when he's done." He went to his room and closed the door. He'd sleep maybe an hour before returning to the store. If a customer came, Becca would wake him.

Suddenly she was alone. Would Colt take all afternoon to complete his chores? She wanted to ask him some questions.

After she finished cleaning the kitchen and doing some chores of her own, he stomped into the store. A few seconds later he stood in the doorway.

"Come on in."

His gaze darted about the room. "Where's your pa?"

"Resting." She tilted her head toward the closed door.

Colt began to back away.

"Don't go. Sit and visit awhile."

He swallowed loudly.

She thought he would turn tail and run, but he slowly crossed the threshold.

She sat in one of the big chairs and waved him toward the other, but he slowly circled the room and came to a stop in front of Ma's picture. "Is your ma back east?"

"No. She died two years ago."

"I'm sorry. I didn't know, or I wouldn't have mentioned it."

"There's no way you could know without asking."

He nodded. "You ever been east?"

"Once. When I was fifteen. Ma had been sick quite some time, and Pa sent her to Toronto to see a doctor."

"Did you like it there?"

She thought of the strangeness of the city…the dirt, the noise and the way people rushed about. "Not really."

"So why are you going back?"

"My mother asked for my promise as she lay dying. The least I could do was agree."

He turned toward her, his eyes watchful. "The least? Why do you say that?"

"Because it was my fault she didn't get better." The words she'd never confessed to another soul fell from her lips.

The way he raised his eyebrows requested an explanation.

"I was unhappy in Toronto. I missed Pa. I missed the open prairies and the sight of the mountains. I asked

Ma to let me go home. She agreed and we returned, but she wasn't better. She never got better."

"I see."

The way he said it made her curious. How could he possibly know what it was like? "What do you see?"

"You blame yourself for her dying, though it seems to me if you believe what the Bible says, you have to believe it's God's doing."

The words jolted through her with the power of a flash flood, upending roots of guilt and regret. "If I hadn't been such a crybaby, she would have stayed and gotten better."

"You know that for a fact?"

"Certainly." She faltered. "I always thought so."

"Maybe you thought wrong."

She stared at him, not really seeing him. Rather, seeing the accusations she'd flung at herself. Had they been unfounded? No one had ever said Ma should stay and get more treatment. No one had ever suggested she might get better if she stayed in Toronto. Had she blamed herself needlessly? How could Colt have seen it so quickly? Yet she wasn't sure she believed it. If only she hadn't cried to return home.

Time to change the subject before she was forced to examine her opinions more closely.

"Tell me about your parents."

He jolted as if shot and turned away, staring at Ma's picture. "Ain't nothing to tell."

"How can that be?" Had they been so cold and uncaring he didn't allow himself to mention them?

"I don't know who they are. Never met them."

"Never?" Shock rattled her thoughts. "Colt, how dreadful."

He shrugged and turned away. "It's neither here nor there."

"But—" Of course it was. No wonder he carried a wounded look.

"How long do you think the kids will sleep?"

She understood what he didn't say. As far as he was concerned, the subject was closed. But she ached for him and wished she could say something to comfort him, although words could not adequately convey her sympathy any more than they could erase the pain of not knowing who his parents were. She wanted to ask who had raised him. Had he known happiness as a child? But she sensed he wouldn't welcome any probing.

"I really can't say." If the kids slept an hour or better, it would give her a chance to question Colt further. Perhaps he guessed at her curiosity, for he crossed the room.

"I'll check the stove in the store." The door closed behind him.

She sighed, suspecting an equally solid door had closed in his mind. He clearly did not want to talk about his parents. She sensed the depth of his pain and wished she could help him.

A little while later, Marie stood in the door, Little Joe at her side.

"We're awake." She glanced around the room. "Where's Colt?"

Little Joe, seeing his friend missing, opened his mouth and let out a wail that threatened to lift the roof from the building.

"He's in the store." Becca pointed, knowing they likely couldn't hear her.

Marie headed that direction, a yowling Little Joe in her grasp.

The door swung open and Colt stepped in. He swept Little Joe into his arms and let the boy burrow his head against his shoulder. The crying ended in a couple of relieved sobs.

How on earth did he expect her to pry these children from him and take them to the fort when they wouldn't let him out of their sight for a moment?

But she had a few days over Christmas and intended to use it to give these kids a chance to adjust to the truth: their parents were dead, but there were still people who would care for them and love them.

Pa stepped from his room, stretching and yawning. He shook the kettle. "Anyone care for tea?"

"Me, me," Little Joe crowed.

Becca would put her few days to the best use possible. She pulled cookies out of the pantry and made tea, weakening the children's with canned milk.

Pa downed his before it had a chance to cool, and grabbed a couple of cookies. "Might have customers show up." He headed for the store.

When Colt shoved his chair back, the sound reverberated through Becca like thunder.

"I'll go see if your pa needs help. I heard him say something about shelves." He headed for the door.

Little Joe scrambled after him.

Colt stopped and squatted to the boy's level. "You stay here with Marie. I'll be right there." He pointed toward the door.

Marie joined them and took Little Joe's hand. "I'll look after him." Her voice trembled.

Becca guessed Marie hated to let Colt out of her sight as much as her brother did, but intended to be brave for Little Joe's sake.

Colt straightened slowly, his gaze finding a place on

the floor to study. Then he lifted his eyes to Becca, and she saw regret and resignation. He clearly understood the children's fear. And no doubt knew better than most what their future held.

He squatted before them and pulled them both to his chest. "I won't ever leave without telling you first, so if I say I'm going to help Mr. Macpherson, you can count on me coming back. Okay?"

"Okay." Marie straightened and pulled Little Joe to her side. "You go help. We'll help Becca."

Colt chuckled. "There you go. We all have something to do."

Becca's throat tightened with emotion. If only she had the power to change what the future held for these children.

Colt had no trouble getting Macpherson to let him tackle making shelves in the storeroom. He concentrated on sawing lumber to the right length and affixing sturdy shelving to hold a dizzying array of goods.

"The country is opening up," Macpherson said as he moved crates and adjusted boxes. "The Gardiners have a lease and are establishing a large ranching operation. I expect I will get the most of their business." He held the end of a board while Colt nailed it to the supports. When it was in place, Macpherson shook it hard.

"Needs to be good and solid." He nodded with satisfaction when the shelf didn't budge. "The OK Ranch was here first, but they've had some problems with managers. The Gardiner place won't be having any such problems. Not with Eddie Gardiner himself running it. Calls the place Eden Valley Ranch."

Colt measured and cut another board, but curiosity

overtook his normal silence. "Why is Eddie Gardiner so important?"

"He's the son of some rich lord, or something fancy like that, back in England. I hear they're rolling in money."

A fine rich man. The sort who would look down his nose at half-breeds, and likely kick them in passing.

Macpherson continued talking. "I rode out that way during the summer. Impressive place, indeed. Those buildings will stand for a hundred years or more." He looked about the storeroom. "They have a supply shed as big as this room. The whole place is laid out like a little town. Very impressive. You ought to go have a look."

Colt gave a noncommittal grunt.

"Say." Macpherson studied Colt as if seeing him for the first time. "You any good with horses?"

Colt grinned. "Some think so."

Macpherson chuckled. "I expect that's your way of saying you got a reputation to uphold."

"Could be." He measured for the next shelf.

"If you're as good as you say, you might consider signing on with the Eden Valley Ranch."

Colt gave a snort of laughter. "Don't recall saying I was good."

"That's what made me figure you were." Macpherson grinned at Colt.

Colt kept his attention on his work. Seems Macpherson liked him a whole lot better when he wasn't around his daughter. Nothing surprising about that. Colt didn't suppose it would ever change. Yet the way Becca smiled at him, the way she spoke to him, her look and words so inviting…

He realized he grinned foolishly at a length of board and stilled his silly thoughts. But it took more than the normal habit of pushing aside his feelings to quiet his heart.

A customer came into the store, and Macpherson left to wait on him.

Colt continued working steadily throughout the afternoon. But his disobedient thoughts kept harking back to Becca—the way she spoke so gently and kindly to the children, the way she smiled at him.

He paused, a hammer dangling from his hand. His experience warned him that the children's future would be unlike this visit here. How happy would they be? At least the teacher would give them a home. He could only hope—and perhaps, pray—they would find much more in her care.

Marie stepped into the room and smiled up at him. "Miss Becca says to come for supper."

Colt hesitated. Was he only making things worse for her and Little Joe by accepting Becca and her pa's kind invitation? But what could he do? He'd given his word.

His choices were either stay and guard his heart, or leave and break his word—and likely two tiny hearts. Really no choice at all. He followed Marie into the store.

Becca stood in the doorway, favoring them all with a shining smile. "It's ready and waiting. Marie helped with the potatoes."

"Well, then." Macpherson rubbed his hands together. "We'd best see if she did a good job or not." He nodded at Colt. "Come along."

Colt's feet felt like lead and his heart clenched with a well-developed caution, but how could he refuse with Marie looking pleased with herself and Becca smiling a welcome? It wasn't as if her father seemed reluctant. Maybe he should accept this blessing for now. Then he would go back to being Colt Johnson, a loner half-breed.

"Let's taste those potatoes."

He scooped Little Joe into his arms and followed after Marie and Macpherson. The warmth of the room, full of savory smells, welcomed him as no other meal had. Only he knew it wasn't the room or the scents. It was Becca's smile.

Simply the politeness of a well-bred woman, he reasoned. No need for him to think it meant anything else.

They sat down and waited as Macpherson said grace, then Becca saw to passing the food around. A richly flavored pot roast, boiled potatoes in odd clunky shapes, gravy and turnips.

Marie watched him carefully as he took a scoop of the potatoes and poured on gravy.

"Yum. These are the best potatoes I've ever had." And they were. He understood it had nothing to do with the flavor of the food, but everything to do with two pairs of eyes—Becca's blue ones and Marie's black—observing him. As if his opinion mattered a great deal.

He tried in vain to bring his thoughts into rational order, but they tripped along their merry path, undeterred by his silent warnings.

He pushed aside the mental warfare to address the eager-eyed child. "You did a fine job, Marie."

She wriggled with pleasure and turned to Macpherson for his opinion.

"I do believe Colt is right. Best potatoes ever."

Marie practically glowed, and Becca looked as pleased as if she had received the praise herself.

A most generous woman. A very unusual woman. He couldn't see her fitting in back east, though his only way of judging that was through the people he'd met from that direction. Mostly stiff, judgmental individuals who saw Colt and those like him as oddities, or much worse.

His skin tightened as he recalled the name a pair near the fort not so many days ago had applied to him. Dirty savage.

The meal over, he sprang to his feet to walk to the window. Marie scampered from her chair and insisted on helping with the dishes.

He listened to Becca instructing her, sweetly and patiently. Kindly.

"It's dark already." He hoped forcing his thoughts to the outdoors would eliminate any possibility of thinking of things he shouldn't be.

Becca hung the towel and came to his side to look out into the night.

"Look at all the stars. They're so beautiful. I wonder if it was like this the first Christmas night."

He forced his gaze to remain on the scene through the window. It took supreme effort not to look at Becca. But even without seeing her, he pictured her starry eyes and beaming smile.

How was he going to get through the next few days without letting her sweetness shatter the protection he'd built around his heart?

Chapter Five

Becca barely contained her desire to dance across the floor. Christmas at home with her pa, Colt and the children. If she never got another Christmas present in her life, she would die content with this one.

She couldn't stop grinning as her mind twirled with plans. But her joy stuttered as she watched Colt retreat to the far corner and hunker down beside the kids. She guessed it wasn't a desire to play with them that took him there, but why did he act as if staying would be an ordeal?

Well, she'd prove to him it wasn't. She'd make this the best Christmas ever for him, too.

She waited until the children curled up on their mats and fell asleep to signal Pa and Colt to the table. "Let's make plans."

Colt leaned back as if he wanted no part of this. "I wouldn't know what to do."

"What would you normally do?" She hoped he'd share a special memory.

He blinked hard then grinned. "Normally I would ride out to the prettiest place I could find and enjoy nature."

"Alone?" She sounded as shocked as she felt.

"Nature is the best company I know of."

She tilted her chin upward. "I intend to prove you wrong. We're pretty fine company, aren't we, Pa?"

"Your ma seemed to think so."

Becca's smile slipped at the mention of her mother, then she dismissed any sadness and regret. She'd been offered a reprieve. Even if it was only temporary, she intended to make the most of it.

"You must have done something fun and special during Christmas. After all, you're—how old are you?"

"Near as I can figure, I'm about twenty-one."

Near as he could figure? Didn't he know anything for certain about his past? "There you go. In twenty-one years you must recall something special."

His jaw tightened and he looked stubborn. She wondered if he meant to deny any such knowledge, then he gave a little chuckle.

"I was once given a wild, rank horse. I expect it was more of a joke than any kindness, but by spring I had a mount that many a man envied."

She sighed in a way meant to be long-suffering. "Not exactly the kind of thing I think would be useful in planning Christmas for the children. I have a few ideas, though."

She turned to Pa. "With your permission—"

"Child, do whatever you'd like. I'm sure we'll all be pleased."

She nodded. "I do believe you will." Her head buzzed with ideas.

Pa yawned. "Time for bed."

Becca sprang to her feet. "Good night to you both." She paused at her room. "I can hardly wait until morning to put my ideas into effect."

* * *

The next morning, Becca hurried from bed, her head full of plans. Colt had not looked nearly as enthusiastic as she would wish, but she'd soon change that.

As soon as breakfast was over, she asked the others, "Have any of you made taffy?"

The children shook their heads, and when she shifted her gaze to Colt he blinked.

"Me?"

"Have you?"

"No." He sounded far more cautious than curious, which made her even more determined to make this the most fun he'd ever had.

"My ma taught me how to make pulled taffy. She made it every year for Christmas. I didn't realize how good she was at it until we went to Toronto and her family begged her for a taffy pull." She spoke to Pa as he headed for the store and the hope of customers. "Did you know she was the best candy maker?"

"It's why I married her. Didn't you know?" His eyes twinkled and she laughed.

"But didn't you say it was because she made the best rice pudding? Oh, wait, wasn't it because she baked the best biscuits, or was it because she had such a nice reading voice?"

"Yup. And lots more."

Becca held his gaze a moment as they both silently acknowledged how much they missed her. Then Pa stepped into the store.

"Pa, don't you want to take part in the candy making?"

He paused and sucked in air. No doubt the activity carried bittersweet memories for him. But Becca wanted so much for him to remember the good times they'd had and cherish them. A wish she had for everyone in the room.

"Call me when it's time to pull it, and I'll come back if I'm not busy with customers." He turned to smile at Becca. "It will remind me of all the times I helped your mother."

"She'd want to know you remembered all she taught you."

She and Pa smiled shared love of her mother, then he closed the door behind him.

Becca glanced at Colt. He jerked his attention to a spot behind her, but not before she caught a glimpse of hunger, as if he liked hearing her talk about her mother...maybe he enjoyed hearing about a regular family. She made herself another promise—she'd show Colt what it was like to be in a family.

She pulled out the kettle Ma had always used. "The first time I remember Ma making taffy, I was about Marie's age. We had just moved west. Ma had a job as a teacher in Fort Benton. She made taffy for the children on the last day of school before Christmas. I remember feeling so proud because all the children seemed to think she'd done something special." She poured the sugar, water and vinegar into the kettle as Marie watched her every move. Colt stood back, Little Joe in his arms.

"Bring him closer so he can watch." She saw eagerness in both expressions but Colt did not move, even though Little Joe wriggled, trying to force him to do so. She held Colt's gaze, feeling his caution and reluctance. Her determination to give him good memories intensified. "Better pay attention in case you ever want to make this."

At that he relaxed and chuckled. "Horses seem to

think carrots are candy." But he sidled closer to observe the ingredients in the kettle, close enough that she could feel him alongside her, even though they didn't touch.

"It's beginning to boil. Now we don't stir it or jar it until it's reached hard-ball stage. In the meantime, we get ready." She pulled out the large pan her mother had always used. "It needs to be buttered. Marie, why don't you and Little Joe do that?"

Colt put Little Joe at the table beside his sister, and Becca showed them how to dip their fingers in the butter and spread it on the pan.

"Can'y ready?" Little Joe asked.

"No, now we wait."

When the boy moved toward the stove, Colt lifted him into his arms and held him where he could see but not grab the kettle.

"It takes time to cook," Becca warned the anxious trio. She dropped a bit of the candy mixture into a cup of cold water. It dissolved as she pressed it with the spoon. "Not ready yet."

"Why do you do that?" Colt asked.

She explained that it indicated how hot the syrup was. "When it stays in a little ball, then it's ready to take off the stove." She noticed with warmth that he forgot to be reserved with her. "It takes a bit of practice to recognize the right degree, but Ma taught me well. I'll try and do the same for you just in case you decide to treat the horses." *Or maybe decide to get some people friends.* But she kept that thought to herself rather than drive him back into his shell.

She'd gladly—willingly—be his friend. But she couldn't even offer that. She'd made a promise to her mother and was obligated to keep it. She checked the syrup again. "See how the little ball stays in shape?"

She tipped the cup of water toward Colt for him to study. "When I take it out and press it, it holds its shape." She held out her hand. "See for yourself."

Colt extended a finger, and she slipped the candy onto it.

Flesh on flesh sent a jolt through her. She wanted to prolong the touch, examine her reaction, analyze the accompanying emotions—excitement, aliveness—but Colt, oblivious to her reaction, pulled away and felt the candy.

"That's amazing."

Yes, it was, though she understood he meant how the texture had changed. But what amazed and pleased her was the way he'd forgotten to be nervous and distant around her.

Little Joe leaned forward, his mouth open, his tongue out, begging to taste the sample.

"Can he eat it?" Colt asked.

"Certainly," Becca answered.

Colt let the boy lick up the candy, and Little Joe smacked his lips. "Good." He angled toward the kettle. "More."

"It's not ready yet. But it's almost time for the fun part." She poured the mixture into the prepared pan. "We all have to wash our hands while it cools."

They washed and then waited, rather impatiently, for the candy to cool.

Pa came in and sat at the table, anticipating the time for pulling.

Becca turned the candy from the edges several times so it would cool equally. She tested it. How hot could the children handle? "It's still a little warm. Pa, what do you think?"

"I'll partner with Marie and show her what to do. You can show Colt and Little Joe how to pull it."

That wasn't exactly her question, but she readily agreed. Pa took half and showed Marie how to stretch and double it. Becca did the same with Colt as he held Little Joe in his lap. They held the candy mixture gingerly. She folded her end toward his, and their hands brushed. She was again so aware of him that her insides felt liquid. "We are working in air to make it light. Sometimes, if there's any left overnight, it turns all creamy. Yum." Think of candy. Think of how everyone will enjoy this. Think of anything but this silly reaction to a simple task.

Somehow she managed to explain every step until the candy was too stiff to work further, and they put it on the pan and cut it. "We could wait for it to cool and harden more. Or—" She let her voice trail off and laughed as three faces looked at her with wide-eyed begging. It felt so good to see all of them relaxed and enjoying themselves. Step one in making this the best Christmas ever for them.

"Or we could have some right now." She grabbed the big knife and sliced off a piece. She handed a small piece to Little Joe. He plopped it into his mouth and his eyes grew big.

"Good." Drool dribbled from his lips.

She grabbed a wet cloth and patted it away. "Anyone else want some?"

Marie nodded and received a piece.

"I do believe I'll have some," Pa said.

She cut a piece for him, then faced Colt. His eyes brimmed with eagerness, but his mouth remained flat. As clearly as if the words were written on his forehead, she understood he wanted to enjoy himself but feared to venture too close, perhaps cross a line that had always brought repercussions.

"It's very tasty," she teased, cutting off a piece and waving it before him.

"I wouldn't know. Never had the stuff before, but I'm game to try it." He'd asked for it without really asking.

Laughing, she let him take it from her fingers. She waited as he sucked the treat. Her heart felt light with success when his eyes widened with pleasure and he made appreciative noises.

They ate several more pieces until she suggested they should save some for the next day. "Wouldn't want anyone to get a tummy ache." She washed the children's hands and faces.

"Pa, didn't you put a box of my old trinkets in the back closet? Maybe Marie and Little Joe would like to play with the things we saved."

"I suspect they would. I'll fetch it." He went to the closet past the two bedrooms and returned with an old satchel. He brought it to the table, where he opened it and began to pull out items.

Becca grabbed a little rag doll. "Ma made me this for Christmas one year. It was the first year we were in Fort Benton." Her heart full of sweet memories, she smiled at Pa. "Just before she met you. Before you married her and became my new Pa." She handed the doll to Marie. "Would you like to play with it?"

Marie took it gently. "I'll be very careful."

Becca let her gaze find Colt. But instead of the pleasure she expected, she saw a harsh expression.

"What's wrong?"

"What if she damages it?"

"I don't expect she will, but if she does it's only a toy."

"A special toy," Pa said.

Becca shot him a questioning look.

"I think Colt is asking, will the child be punished if something happens?"

Becca's insides twisted. "Do you think I would be angry with her?"

Colt's eyes narrowed, and she sensed a heap of pain.

Her annoyance died as quickly as it came. "It's what you've experienced, isn't it?"

"Anger can make people very cruel."

He didn't need to explain further. She didn't want him to. Her imagination filled in the details and they weren't pleasant, but she knew Colt had experienced the cruelty of anger. Knowing the forms that could take brought the sting of tears to her eyes. She blinked them away, but not before Colt noticed.

The hardness in his face fled. "A person learns to be tough."

"Sometimes a person can learn to be too tough."

Pa paid them scant attention as he explored the contents of the bag and pulled out a wooden horse with moveable legs. "Do you remember this?"

"Uncle Martin sent it to me from Toronto one Christmas. I played with it for hours at a time. Look, Little Joe." She showed him how she could make the horse walk across the table, then handed him the toy.

He scrambled from Colt's lap, and the two children sat on the floor nearby playing.

Pa took the satchel back to the bedroom and set it on his bed. He stayed there, his back to them as he looked through the contents.

The bedrooms opened off the kitchen so Becca was able to watch him. She wondered why he chose to look at her toys in his room. Then she saw his shoulders rise and fall in a huge sigh, and a tiny suspicion grew in her thoughts. She knew he missed Ma. But perhaps he was also remembering the first time he saw her. Recalling all the fun they'd had together. Maybe even regretting their promise for her to leave. She didn't want him to be sad when she left, though they'd both find the separation difficult.

If only they hadn't promised Ma. If only Becca hadn't insisted they return home.

Was she in any way responsible for Ma's death because she'd begged to come back? She'd never asked, never considered it a possibility. And now it was too late. Responsible or not, she had given a promise and she meant to keep it.

But glancing at Colt, she wished she could stay. Yes, Colt made it very plain he meant to move on, but surely he'd come back. For supplies, if nothing else.

Perhaps if she stayed, another reason for him to return might develop.

If ifs and ands were pots and pans, there'd be no work for tinkers' hands.

Ma had said it often when Becca got caught up in wishing for things to be different. It was a good reminder for her again now. There were things she could not change.

She could not change her promise nor, likely, Colt's desire to be alone.

But she could make this a Christmas they'd never forget.

Chapter Six

When had he felt so immune to anger? Colt watched Becca studying her pa. Pain and regret filled her expression. She loved her pa and didn't want to leave him, but because of her guilt and a promise, she would.

Too bad the stagecoach wouldn't stay parked for the winter. It would mean he could stay, too.

What was he thinking? He knew better. He'd already extended his stay longer than was wise. Not that he had much choice. He'd given his promise to help the kids have a good Christmas. He wasn't sure it was a promise wisely made. Would having such a memory make the reality of the future better or worse?

Becca sighed and turned toward the children, a smile erasing her worries as she watched them play.

An unfamiliar warmth flooded Colt's chest. She truly seemed fond of these little half-breeds. How was it possible? She was a white woman—a fine white woman with proper upbringing.

Yet she shared her quarters, her table and even her toys with him and the kids. And she went out of her way to amuse them. She made plans to brighten their days, going so far as to make candy.

When had he ever partaken of such pleasure? Only his thoughts weren't of the candy, but of Becca's sweet smile. Guilt cooled his insides. A man could be shot for looking too long at a woman like Becca. Good thing a man couldn't be shot for his thoughts. He pulled his lips in to hide a grin. But there were men who would shoot him simply for being so bold as to sit at the same table. If he had a lick of sense, he would immediately head toward that mountain cabin.

Instead, he watched Little Joe playing with the toy horse. After all, if he tried to leave Becca would fuss, and it didn't seem fair to cause her concern after she'd been so kind.

Little Joe turned and held the horse out to him. "Make horsee run."

Grateful for the diversion, Colt sat cross-legged on the floor beside Little Joe and played with him. Marie moved to the table and talked to Becca about the doll.

An unfamiliar peace settled about Colt's shoulders. It was temporary, but maybe for a few minutes he'd let himself experience what it felt like to be part of a family, and maybe even, foolish as it was, he'd pretend he belonged.

Little Joe trotted the horse up Colt's leg and arm, across his neck and down again, making funny little horse sounds. The feel of the little boy's hands and legs as he climbed over him did strange things to Colt's guarded thoughts. Peeled away layers. He discovered he liked being touched. Didn't realize it was something he'd missed until this very moment.

Little Joe trotted the horse up again. This time he went over Colt's head. The horse tangled in Colt's hair. Little Joe tugged.

Colt squinted against the pain of having his hair pulled.

"I'll get it." He tugged and twisted, but the toy would not come free.

"My horsee." Little Joe whined and screwed up his face in preparation for a yowl.

"Don't cry," Colt begged. He'd never be able to get the toy out of his hair if he had to cover his ears.

"Do you need help?" Becca asked.

He couldn't look at her. "I can get it." He yanked, bit back a groan, yanked again. The toy did not come free.

"You're only making it worse." She stood behind him. "Let me."

He felt her with every nerve in his back. He itched to put more distance between them. She touched his head. His scalp tingled, and he knew an unusual sense of comfort. He held his breath, expecting her to jerk the toy free without consideration for his tender scalp, but her fingers gently separated strands of hair from the toy. Each touch was like a kiss. A blessing. A calming massage. He closed his eyes against the pleasure. He should never have allowed her to do this.

A smile caught at the corner of his mouth. She hadn't exactly waited for permission.

"Got it." She handed the toy to a tearful Little Joe and stepped back.

Marie stood before him. "He didn't mean to hurt you."

"I know. He was only playing."

"You aren't angry?"

"No." He couldn't even manage to be angry at himself. Whatever line he had crossed was worth it for the pleasure of her touch. He'd gladly face whatever repercussions came.

Marie edged closer and patted his cheek. "Are you okay?"

He smiled, letting all his happy emotions surface for a moment. Being touched in loving, gentle ways felt so right and good, he wondered how he had survived up until now. And facing the future knowing he would not experience it again filled him with bleak despair.

Nothing had changed. Nor did he expect it to. These few moments would make his future less lonely. Or would they make it worse, having learned the beauty of the human touch?

Becca went to the stove to start preparations for the noon meal. Marie hurried to her side to help.

Colt watched. Every step of Becca's work was slowed by letting the little girl assist, but she didn't seem to mind as she gently explained things, always smiling as she did.

If only Marie and Little Joe could find such a home.

If only frogs could fly.

He'd seen the children in the teacher's care. She insisted on a certain standard of behavior, as well she should. Orphaned children—especially if mixed race—faced unreasonable criticism. The kindest thing the teacher could do was teach them to act in such a way as to avoid repercussions. But from what little he'd observed, the teacher offered minimal affection. She appeared to consider the task of caring for the children her duty. And she did it well. No one could fault her for the fact that she seemed to find little joy in it.

After the meal, the children again fell asleep on Becca's bed.

Colt headed for the store. He would spend time with the horses in the barn and help Macpherson with whatever chores that needed to be done.

"Wait." Becca's word stopped him in his tracks, his hand suspended at the door. "We need to talk."

Talk? Talk meant bad news. Had she changed her mind? Would she ask him to leave? His heart hit bottom as he realized how much he wanted to stay.

"Come. Sit down. Have another cup of coffee."

She waved her hand to indicate the chair opposite her. As he considered his options, she poured coffee.

He sat, cradled the cup and waited.

"I'd like your help in planning gifts for the children."

He stared in disbelief. "You just gave them toys to play with. That's enough."

She shook her head. "I want them to have something they can take with them and keep. I want them to look at the gifts and remember their Christmas with us." Her words slowed and her voice softened. "I plan for them…you…us to have the best Christmas ever."

His mind swirled worse than the wind during the recent snow-storm. Best Christmas. Welcome memories.

"What's the matter?"

He realized he shook his head back and forth. "I don't know if that's a good idea."

She frowned, and he almost retracted his words so she'd smile again. But he couldn't.

"What's wrong with it?"

"They'll be going to the fort. Likely whatever they own will be shared with anyone else the teacher is sheltering. You're just setting them up for hurt."

She sat up straighter. "Won't they be allowed to have their own things?"

Wishing he'd never started this conversation, he shrugged. "Can't say for sure one way or the other."

"But I take it your experience makes you think they can't."

"They're orphaned half-breeds." He wanted her to be clear how that affected the way the kids would be treated.

"It shouldn't make a difference."

He stared at her. Her blue eyes blazed like a bright summer sky. Her chin jutted out. And she looked ready to fight anyone who argued with her. Did she really think it shouldn't matter? Did she mean in a general sense? Did it matter to her? Sure seems it didn't.

"But it does." The words were as much a reminder to himself of the facts as they were for her. "But they're strong. They'll survive. And they have each other."

Her gaze probed his thoughts. He felt her questions, although she didn't voice them. And he turned away because he didn't want to delve into his past. He faced the future as a man of mixed race, making the best of his life, but not dreaming of enjoying a family such as he glimpsed here. Yes, someday he might find someone like himself, an outcast, who might be willing to share his life. But every time he considered the idea he balked at it. Didn't seem right to bring more children like himself into the world, knowing they would never be accepted by more than a handful of people. Best he restrict his friendships to horses.

"It is unacceptable that they aren't allowed their own possessions."

He shrugged again. Her opinion didn't change the facts.

"Marie and Little Joe are going to get presents to take with them and remember happy days here, and if anyone says otherwise—"

He could have told her there would be plenty of people who would say otherwise, but heeding his well-developed sense of caution, he decided he wouldn't be the first.

Taking his silence for agreement, she gave a decisive nod. "Good. Now what can we make for them?"

"We?"

"You do want a part in making this a time they'll remember with joy, don't you?"

Well, shoot. If he said no, he would sound cruel and he'd be lying. But if he said yes…he had no idea where it would lead him.

"I thought you would. Now this is what I have in mind." She rattled on about things her pa had in the store that he'd be willing to give them. "But we should do something extra special."

"Uh-huh."

"I think I can make a doll for Marie. She certainly seems to enjoy the one I lent her."

"Uh-huh." He had nothing to add to this discussion.

"What do you think a little boy would want?"

He swallowed hard.

"What did you like as a boy?"

A thousand long-buried memories burst, forbidden, into his mind. A long eagle feather he'd found. A shiny rock he'd hidden in the far corner of a barn. A broken wooden wheel off some other child's toy. None of them had followed him in his many moves.

He realized Becca watched him, and he steeled his expression to indifference. "Nothing special." Aware of the sympathy in her face and hoping to keep her from probing deeper, he rushed on. "Little Joe enjoys the horse you gave him to play with. If your father wouldn't mind letting me use some scraps of lumber, I could make one like that."

"Wonderful. It's going to be so special. Thank

you for helping." She reached across the table as if to squeeze his hand.

He bolted to his feet before she could make contact. "I'll go speak to your pa right away." He made it through the doorway before he took in a breath.

Macpherson readily agreed to Colt's request for wood pieces, and Colt welcomed the excuse to spend the afternoon in the storeroom working on the toy.

He refused the invitation to join them for tea when the children wakened, using the excuse that he wanted to keep at the task, but he couldn't refuse the call to supper without being rude.

Besides, he half suspected Becca would come looking for him and demand an explanation if he didn't show up, and he had no reason except this whole setup was pushing him far beyond his safe borders. Sooner or later he would pay the price for agreeing to go along with her.

It was as certain as the dawn.

The only thing he didn't know was whether or not he'd consider it worth it in the end.

Somehow he made it through supper without saying or doing anything to make anyone suspect the restlessness of his mind. He'd vowed to keep his attention off Becca. But despite his best intentions, he was often startled out of his determination by her quick laugh or something she said. Each time he glanced her way, he felt a flash of sunshine. He found it hard to keep his mind closed to such pleasures.

He'd never been so glad to see bedtime, and gladly settled the two kids in their bedrolls. Little Joe fussed every time Colt moved away, so he edged down between the pair and opened his book to study the illustrations. Becca and her pa remained at the table talking softly.

"Pa, the children are so sweet. They need to be loved and cherished. Like you and Ma cherished me."

"I bless the day God brought you and your mother into my life."

Colt knew Macpherson was her stepfather, though he would never have judged it by the affection between the two.

"Me, too." Colt heard the smile in her voice.

"These children deserve as much." Becca's voice rang with feeling.

Macpherson sighed heavily. "Becca, remember your promise to your ma. A promise we both gave without reservation."

"I haven't forgotten." No mistaking the resolve in her voice. And he thought he picked up on a thread of sorrow or perhaps regret, too. Of course, she would feel both at the thought of leaving her pa.

"Don't get so involved with the kids that you regret your promise."

"Pa, I'll keep my promise. I have to." Her voice rang with determination.

"Just be sure you don't get sidetracked by other things."

Colt closed his book and squirmed into his bedroll. *Don't get involved with a half-breed cowboy.* Macpherson hadn't said the words but they hung, unspoken, in the air…a reminder to Colt.

Becca would leave after Christmas. She'd take the children to the fort, and Colt would resume his journey to the isolated cabin where he'd spend his time caring for horses. That would take an hour or two of his day. And then what? His book. His own company. It had been enough most of his life.

But now it seemed empty, lonely, barren.

I'll get used to it again, he vowed. He repeated the words over and over. He had almost fallen asleep when he was jarred alert by one child screaming and kicking. The other patted his cheek.

"Colt, Little Joe is scared." Marie sounded frightened, too.

He scooted up and pulled Little Joe to his lap. "Hush, little guy. You're safe and sound."

"I want Mama."

That he couldn't provide. Nor could he convince Little Joe he was okay. The boy continued with his earsplitting cries. And Marie sobbed quietly, pressing her face into his side.

He closed his eyes and sucked in air. He knew how to calm a horse, but was powerless to comfort this pair.

"Colt," Becca's voice came as a whisper from her bedroom. "Are you okay?"

No doubt she meant the kids. "They're missing their folks, and I can't seem to calm them."

"Can I help?" She didn't wait for him to answer. "Are you decent?"

He'd only taken his boots off to go to bed. He knew that's what she meant, but he thought of far more. Was he decent enough to be around people like her? He wished the answer could be yes.

"I'm fully clothed."

"I'm decent, too, so I'm going to help with the children." She set a lit lamp on the table, and a golden glow touched the furniture. Then she appeared in his view. Her hair hung down her back in waves of gold.

He swallowed hard. "You shouldn't be here."

"Nonsense. No one would expect me to ignore the cries of a child." She moved closer and bent over them.

He pressed himself into the wall, but escape was impossible. Distance could not be gained.

"Come here, Little Joe. I'll hold you."

The boy held out his arms and cried, "Mama."

"I'm not Mama, but maybe I'll do." She sank down beside Colt and hummed as she rocked the little guy.

Marie scrambled into Colt's lap, buried her face against his shirt and cried quietly, in direct contrast to Little Joe.

He couldn't deny them this bit of comfort. But if Macpherson—or anyone else—discovered him sitting with Becca after dark…

Becca cuddled Little Joe close and hummed a lullaby she remembered from her childhood. Little Joe cradled into her arms like he'd found home. He clutched a corner of the blanket. Within a few minutes he'd fallen asleep. Marie's sobs quieted and she, too, seemed to return to the forgetfulness of sleep.

"Ma used to hum that tune," she whispered to Colt. "It always soothed me, though now I can't say for sure if it was the tune or simply the fact that Ma always patted or rubbed my back when she hummed it." She told him how she lay in bed with the gripe at twelve, feeling like she wanted to die, and Ma had sat on the edge of the bed rubbing her back and humming.

"When Ma lay dying—" Her throat closed off temporarily. "I did the same for her." Ma had seemed comforted by Becca's efforts. Becca had found it soothing, as well.

"It sounds nice."

"I miss her a lot." She tried to imagine what it would be like not to have memories of a mother's love. Or a father's, either. Who had raised him? Where did he belong?

"'Spect you do." He shifted. "You think they'll stay asleep now if we put them back on their beds?"

"We can try and see."

They shifted about and each lowered a child to their respective bedrolls. Little Joe protested in his sleep, and Becca again rubbed his back and hummed the lullaby until she was certain he was settled.

Colt stood by, watching.

Becca straightened to stand by his side and study the sleeping children.

"I hate to think of them going to the fort." A pain twisted through her at the thought.

"They'll survive."

"I take it you talk from experience."

"That and observation." He backed away, went to the stove to lift a lid and add a hunk of wood.

She followed him and put a kettle of water on, as much to delay ending this evening as for any other reason.

"Colt, don't you know anything about your parents?"

He shrugged, but she couldn't believe it didn't matter to him. "I suspect my father was a soldier who took advantage of an Indian woman. My earliest memory is of living with a native woman, but I knew I didn't belong. I wondered if she was my mother. I know her husband didn't much care for me."

"What happened?"

"One day when the woman was out picking berries, he took me to the fort and dropped me off at the gate." He said the words with cold indifference, but she couldn't believe he didn't hurt.

"Did someone take you in?"

"Yes." His one word said so little, and yet so much.

"But what?"

"They figured I was good enough to sleep in the barn and help with the horses."

She touched his elbow, felt him tense. "I'm sorry."

"Nothing to do with you."

"Maybe not directly, but don't we all share responsibility, and maybe blame, as to how others are treated?" Her thoughts shifted back to the two innocent, sweet children asleep only a few feet away. What was her responsibility? To take them to the fort. After that, their care was out of her hands. She ached clear through as she acknowledged the fact.

"I was fed and I liked the animals."

Another bald statement that said so much more than the few words. "Didn't anyone offer you a proper home?" The kettle steamed and she set it off the heat, wondering why she'd thought she should fill it.

He sighed. "Why are you asking so many questions about me?"

She tried to come up with a reasonable answer but couldn't find one. "Because—" I care? Or was she simply curious? Or she could pretend it was about the children, which, in part, it was. "I'd like to have some idea of what will happen to Marie and Little Joe."

He stared at the stove as if it hid a hundred secrets. "Why do you care so much what happens to two half-breed kids?"

She fell back a step at the harshness of his tone. "What difference does it make if they are Indian or white? People are people."

"Easy for you to say when you're white. Your family is white. You're accepted in a white world."

"I would hope—" she spoke slowly, enunciating each

word carefully "—I would never be so narrow as to judge a person by the color of his skin. I think all people are created equal."

"That kind of talk could land you in a lot of trouble."

"It's what I believe." She realized he'd managed to sidetrack her from her original question.

"Colt." She touched his arm again, felt again how he stiffened at contact that was barely there. "Did you spend your childhood in a barn taking care of horses? Who took care of you?"

"I mostly took care of myself." He ground out the words as if each one hurt. "I learned to mind my own business. I learned to make myself useful while being invisible."

Her heart near broke in two at the pain each word revealed. "No one loved you?"

He made a dismissive noise. "A kid who belonged to no one? To no race? I was glad to escape the anger most people expressed."

She didn't quite manage to muffle her cry, and he turned as if to see if the noise came from her.

"Colt, I'm so sorry. No one, child or adult, should be treated unkindly."

"Noble philosophy, but someday you'll learn that not everyone is created for love."

She knew he tried to sound mocking...dismissive... but he failed. She heard the ache in his voice as clearly as if he had cracked open his chest and shown her his bruised and battered heart. Acting instinctively, she leaned close. Standing on tiptoe, she planted a kiss on his jaw. "Someday you'll learn that everyone is."

He jerked back and stared at her as if she had fallen through the roof and landed at his feet. "Are you crazy?"

"No one has ever suggested it."

"Do you know what would happen if someone caught me kissing you?"

"You didn't. I kissed you."

"No one would believe that."

She tipped her head and studied him. "What would happen?"

"I'd likely be lynched, or if people were charitable, I'd be run out of town."

"Not if I had anything to say about it." She was pleased with herself. She'd liked the feel of his rough whiskers on her lips as she kissed him. Even more, she liked breaking through his self-contained composure and seeing how deep his feelings flowed.

"Miss Macpherson, I think you should go to bed."

She felt mischievous. "And if I don't?"

"Then I shall leave." He tried to edge around her in the direction of the door, but she didn't budge and he was trapped unless he physically moved her aside. She could tell by the way he shuffled and twitched that he wouldn't do that. He hesitated to even touch her.

"It's dark. You can't go out."

"Might be safer than in here."

She laughed. "I'm not going to hurt you."

"Not thinking of you so much as your father, or anyone else who thinks I've been a little too bold."

"Fine. I'll go to bed and leave you in peace. Besides, you can't go because the children would be upset. Little Joe would deafen us with his cries of protest. And didn't you promise to stay for Christmas?"

"A promise I regret."

"How can you think of abandoning the children?" He flinched, and she realized her remark had cut deeper than she intended. "I'm sorry. I didn't mean to suggest that you would do that."

"However, it's the truth."

She held her tongue, though she might have pressed the matter.

He stared at her with dark, shuttered eyes. "Aren't you going to your room?"

She nodded. "One more thing I must say. God loves you and wants you to be part of His family."

He didn't give any indication he heard, though she knew he had.

She grabbed the lamp and headed for her room. "Good night."

Just as the door closed, she heard him whisper, "Good night."

God loves you and wants you to be part of His family.

How could she be so certain? She almost convinced him.

Colt lay on his back staring up at the dark ceiling. He smiled crookedly. He'd told her more about himself in those few minutes than likely anyone else knew. His smile flattened, and he scrubbed his jaw where she had kissed him.

What if her father had seen it? Or anyone?

She simply had no idea how harsh people could be. If he hadn't promised he'd stay until after Christmas, he would leave before she earned herself an undeserved reputation as an Indian lover, or worse.

Little Joe squirmed about and delivered a sharp kick to Colt's ribs. Colt welcomed the pain. It was nothing compared to what adults would inflict if they thought he had eyes for a white woman. And he did. He smiled. Becca was a noble and idealistic young woman. Too bad she was white. If she were mixed blood, he might allow himself to think about her in friendlier terms.

Finally he slept. He was up and had the fire burning and the coffee boiling by the time Macpherson rose.

"You're up early."

"Hard to sleep with two kids tossing and turning." Only he'd been the one unable to settle, his thoughts alternately accusing and rejoicing. A beautiful, decent woman seemed to like him. He knew well enough how foolish it was to let his thoughts follow that trail, so he pushed them away.

"Besides, I need to work on that toy." Christmas was only two days away. And then this special time would be over. Becca and the children would take the stage-coach. He'd continue west to a lonely cabin.

Little Joe jerked to a sitting position. Saw Colt was not beside him and crunched up his face for a good cry.

Flinching at the thought, Colt crossed the floor and scooped up the little guy. "I'm right here."

Little Joe wrapped his arms about Colt's neck and hung on like his life depended on it. Colt closed his eyes against the pain of knowing he must say goodbye to these kids. If only he could offer them a home. But he was a homeless cowboy. He couldn't provide the supervision and care they needed.

Though he could sure enough give them the acceptance they might not find anywhere else.

Becca stepped from her room, her hair braided in a long plait that hung down her back, her blue eyes dancing with what he expected was joy, and a smile as wide as all his tomorrows.

"Good morning, Pa. Morning, children. Morning, Colt. Isn't it a marvelous day?"

Colt could find no sound in his head but a grunt, and knowing it would make him sound dull and stupid, he kept silent.

Macpherson chuckled. "You're a little ray of sunshine this morning. Any particular reason?"

"Thousands of them. I just love life. Always have. You know that. Besides, I have another day to enjoy being with you." She kissed her pa on the cheek.

Her gaze captured Colt's, and her eyes twinkled.

He couldn't breathe. Surely she didn't mean to start over with her inquisition. Or worse. What had she said?

Everyone was made for love. Did she intend to pursue the idea? His heart beat a frantic tattoo against his ribs, and for the life of him he couldn't say whether it was fear or anticipation that made it hammer so hard.

Marie sat up and rubbed her eyes. "Is it morning?"

"Yes, dear. It is. Why don't you help me make breakfast?"

Marie gave her brother a cautious look as she slipped from the blankets. "He sure cried loud last night."

"That's a fact," Colt agreed.

Macpherson shifted his gaze from Marie to Colt. "The little fella cried? I never even heard him." He directed his attention to Becca. "Did you?"

She bent over and helped Marie pull on her sweater, then grabbed a brush to fix Marie's hair, but Macpherson waited for her answer.

"Yes, Pa. I heard them."

Macpherson studied her. Did he suspect there'd been more to it? If he knew his daughter had kissed Colt, even if only on the chin—

Colt stiffened. He'd likely be leaving in the next minute.

"I wasn't in bed yet, so I came and helped settle Little Joe. He seemed to find Ma's lullaby a comfort just like I always did. You remember how I hummed it for her at the end?"

Her pa nodded. "I remember." Then he shifted his attention back to Colt. Did the man suspect his daughter had been too bold?

Colt resisted an urge to rub his chin, lest it make him appear guilty.

Becca clapped her hands in joy. "It's only two more days until Christmas, and we are going to have a spectacular celebration."

"What's a celebration?" Marie asked.

Becca bent down to smile into the child's face. "It's when we have lots of fun to remember forever. But this celebration is for Christmas. Did you do special things for Christmas?"

Marie studied Becca's face, reached out and touched her cheek. Then she slowly nodded. "My mama and papa would take us out to the woods, and we'd spread grain and stuff for the birds and animals. Papa said God made everything and—" She crinkled up her face. "I can't remember the rest." Her voice quivered.

Becca pulled Marie into her arms and patted her back. "It's okay. You'll remember when you need to. In the meantime, maybe you could help me with some of the things we like to do."

Marie nodded. "What things?"

"Would you like to help me make sugar cookies?"

Marie smiled agreement.

"I help, too," Little Joe yelled.

"Everyone can help." Becca's gaze invited Colt.

He didn't indicate he understood her silent invitation, and gratefully took the cup of coffee Macpherson handed him.

Becca turned her attention to breakfast preparations, and they soon sat around the table.

Colt knew the routine now. Macpherson said grace.

They ate. Then Macpherson read from the Bible and prayed. Colt found it reassuring. Maybe if he ever had a home of his own, he would do the same thing.

As soon as Macpherson finished, Colt pushed to his feet. "Got things to do," he announced and hurried out the door.

He planned to finish Little Joe's toy, but he had a lot more in mind, as well.

First, he went to the barn and took care of the chores out there. When he'd stated his intentions, Macpherson had thanked him for sparing him a trip out in the cold.

He spent longer in the barn than the chores required, finding peace in the company of the animals. Only his usual peace was fractured with long-buried, long-denied yearnings. If only he wasn't who he was—a half-breed with no family—he might allow himself to think of the future. He could imagine Little Joe running to greet him every day, growing into a fine man. And Marie becoming sweeter and more gentle as she matured. He thought of how Becca held her and comforted her.

He bolted to his feet and rushed outside, hoping the cold would snap his thoughts back to someplace sensible.

His dreams could never come true.

He headed for the woodshed and chopped until his arms ached. Even then, he only stopped because Macpherson came to get him.

"Becca says to come. Soup is ready."

Colt put the ax away and loaded his arms with wood before heading for the house. Macpherson carried in wood, as well.

The kids rushed forward as he entered, reminding

him of the things he'd been struggling all morning to forget.

"We dec'rate cookies," Little Joe said. "See." He pointed to the cookies laid out on the cupboard. Each had a hole with a bit of yarn through it. Looked like Becca planned to hang them. No doubt part of her celebration plans.

Marie grabbed his other hand and led him to the display. "Becca says we can hang them to fancy up the place."

Both children beamed with pleasure.

Pale green icing smeared on star-and-tree-shaped cookies. "They look nice."

The children looked even happier than they had a moment ago.

"They did a very good job," Becca said, and against his will, Colt's gaze sought hers.

Every dream, every wish he'd ever had burst fully formed into his heart.

"Let's eat." Macpherson's words jerked Colt back to reality.

Colt spun about, put Little Joe in his chair and took the one he customarily used. For two more days, then this time away from time would end.

Somehow he made it through the meal without paying undue attention to Becca, though he felt her every move, breathed her sweet scent with every inhalation and clung to every word.

"As soon as the children have their naps, we are going to make decorations," Becca announced. "Colt, maybe you'd like to help."

He shook his head.

"Please." Marie's voice seemed to indicate it was important to her.

"You help." Little Joe had made up his mind, and the way he stuck his chin out, Colt expected he would cry if he refused.

He thought of the unfinished toy. He thought of escaping to the safety of the barn. His brain warned him he should put as much distance between himself and Becca as possible. But his mouth said, "I don't know anything about making decorations."

"Becca's going to show us." Seemed it was settled in Marie's mind.

Colt didn't have the heart to say no. Besides, he rather liked having an excuse to agree. "Guess I can help."

While the children napped, he ducked out to the storeroom. Every thought warned him of the dangers of this situation. Except for a disobedient one in the attic of his brain that had become loud and impossible to dismiss. It shouted, *This is what you've always wanted. Enjoy it.*

He might as well listen to the loudest, most demanding voice and enjoy himself.

Even knowing he'd pay later did not quench his smile.

He worked on Little Joe's toy, taking his time and great pleasure at cutting each tiny piece and smoothing it to perfection. He hoped Little Joe would get hours of pleasure from the simple object—and perhaps think of Colt with fondness in the passing months.

The door to the living quarters opened, and Marie said hello to Macpherson.

Colt quickly hid the toy behind a stack of goods and turned as she entered the room.

"We're awake now."

He smiled at the sleep lines on her cheeks. "You're sure?"

A smile drove the lines away. "Little Joe is in a hurry to make things." She reached for his hand.

As they stepped into the living quarters, Becca looked up and smiled.

Colt almost stumbled. Did she mean to be so welcoming? Or was it only good manners? Her fine upbringing? He informed himself he should look away. But he couldn't. Seeing the warmth and welcome in her eyes made it impossible to think, to move.

"We ready," Little Joe said.

Marie tugged on Colt's hand. Slowly his world righted. He sucked in air and tried to clear his brain, with little success. He sat at the table and looked at the plain brown paper before them. Store paper. Nothing special about it.

"This is decoration?"

Becca chuckled. "Don't sound so dubious. You'll be amazed what we can create. First, we cut the paper into strips like this." She cut several lengths an inch wide. "Then we weave them together." She pasted two ends at right angles, then folded them back and forth. "Here, Marie, you do this one. Colt can help you if you need it."

"I'm all thumbs."

"Thumbs?" Little Joe bent over to study his hand.

Startled by how literal the child was, Colt shifted his attention to Becca, saw the amusement in her eyes, and they both laughed. When had he ever shared such simple, profound pleasures with anyone?

Never.

His joy cooled. When he left here, would he ever again experience this feeling of unity and acceptance?

His arms stiffened with the knowledge of what he'd miss when he had to go. He was unable to help Marie fold her paper. Thankfully, she managed on her own.

They continued to fold paper chains. As they finished sections, Becca glued them together.

"It's like a paper snake," Marie said, which brought a shriek of laughter from Little Joe. He grabbed the chain draping over the edge of the table and shook it.

"Snake." He made gruff noises.

"A growling snake. How unusual." Colt could barely contain his amusement.

Becca laughed. The infectious sound released Colt's laughter.

Marie understood the joke and giggled.

Little Joe simply enjoyed the attention, and continued to shake the paper snake and make sounds more appropriate to a dog or bear.

Becca wiped tears from her eyes and leaned over to plant a kiss on top of Little Joe's head. "You are so much fun." Her eyes, round with pleasure, captured Colt's gaze, inviting him, it seemed, to acknowledge shared joy in this little boy and his sister.

He smiled and nodded. No way he could pretend they weren't a great pair of kids. But his enjoyment was bittersweet. Not many hours from now, he would say goodbye and turn them over to others. He wasn't much for prayer, but every day he would ask God to bless and protect these children.

He had no one but himself to blame for the agony he knew he'd have to accept. He'd known from the start he should guard his heart against caring for the kids. And Becca. He'd tried. And failed.

Somehow he would endure the pain of saying goodbye—or die trying.

Chapter Seven

"Snake broke," Little Joe said, about to cry.

Becca rescued the torn snake. "I'll fix it." She glued the battered pieces together. It didn't matter that the chain was less than perfect. The children had enjoyed making it, and then playing snake with it.

She and Colt had shared laughter.

And something more. A deeper, heart-touching look. Sorrow intermingled her joy.

They'd enjoy Christmas, then they would part ways. She would take the children to the fort and leave them with a teacher who would give them shelter and hopefully much more. She'd go on to Toronto. Despite family and the crowds of people in the city, she knew she'd be lonely. Yet for her mother's sake, she must do this.

She set aside the paper chain. "We'll hang it over the windows and doors after the glue dries." She pulled out pretty paper she'd saved from cards and gifts of the past year. "We can make little hangings from these." She showed the patterns her mother had used over the years—balls, stars and bells. Sadness tugged at her throat. Christmas had been empty without her last year, but this year there was reason to celebrate, reason to do something special. There were two children and a lonesome man to give Christmas to.

A smile filled her heart and eased the sadness.

She showed them how to draw around the shapes on the colored paper. "Then we cut them out, and we can hang them up."

"Where will we hang them?" Marie wanted to know.

"From the paper chain—"

"Snake," Little Joe said, setting both children giggling.

Becca and Colt smiled at each other.

"Or we can hang them in the window."

The door rattled. "Pa has customers." There had been a few during the day.

Booted footsteps sounded on the floor. The muted sound of voices reached them. Then Pa opened the door. "Becca, we've got company."

She looked up. "Eddie. Roper. Ward. Welcome."

The three cowboys followed Pa into the room. He turned to Colt. "These men are from the Eden Valley Ranch I told you about. Eddie Gardiner owns the spread, and Roper Jones and Ward Walker are two of his ranch hands. Boys, meet Colt Johnson. He landed here with these two kids in the middle of the storm. They'll be spending Christmas with us."

Colt got to his feet and shook hands with the trio. He didn't return to his seat, but backed away from the table.

She watched him as he studied the cowboys with narrowed eyes. What did he see? Eddie was pretty ordinary-looking—brown hair, brown eyes, a steadiness about him as if aware of his responsibilities and determined to fulfill them. Roper was more solidly built, with hazel eyes and also brown hair that was lighter than Eddie's. Ward had black hair and blue eyes.

They and others from the ranch came to the store often enough that she considered them friends.

Eddie stepped forward. “Cookie sent you this turkey and said to tell you Merry Christmas.”

“How generous.” She took the bird and put it in a pan. “Another way to make this Christmas special.”

“These are Zeke Gallant’s kids.” Pa introduced them. “He and his wife are gone.”

Roper jerked like he’d been jabbed. “They’re gone? But what will happen to the kids?”

“Becca is escorting them to the fort when she goes.”

She didn’t want this constant reminder that she would soon be leaving. “The stage isn’t running until after Christmas, so we are going to give these kids the best Christmas ever.”

Roper twisted his hat round and round, his eyes dark with emotion. “I grew up in an orphanage. Sort of know how Christmas is often overlooked in places like that. Boss, if you’ve a mind to let me, I’d like to help make the day special for these two.”

“Good idea,” Eddie said. “We’ll all help.” He glanced about. “I see you could use a Christmas tree. We’ll get you one. Anything else?”

Becca hadn’t considered a tree. It had never been part of their celebrations.

Roper gave a snort that was half laughter, half mockery. “See, boss, that’s the difference between people like me and people like you. I was thinking maybe an orange, though I don’t know where I’d get one. Or maybe a new pair of socks. You’re thinking trees and likely other gewgaws and trinkets.”

He and Ward jostled each other in amusement.

Eddie shrugged, unaffected by Roper’s observation.

"A tree is part of our tradition. We'll get one and bring it tomorrow."

Pa clapped Eddie on the back. "Most generous of you."

"You're welcome to stay overnight tomorrow and enjoy Christmas day with us," Becca offered, knowing Pa would approve.

Roper brightened. "What do you say, boss?"

"If Cookie agrees. We don't want to be in her black books." He headed for the door. "But for certain we'll be back tomorrow. Good day."

Pa followed them out and closed the door behind them.

"I should leave," Colt said.

"No go." Little Joe let out a wail of distress, and Marie looked ready to cry, as well.

Becca bolted to her feet, and went close enough to Colt for him to hear her above Little Joe's cries.

"You can't go before Christmas. You gave your word. How can it be a good Christmas if you leave?" With a start, she realized she didn't mean for the kids, but for herself. "Besides, why would you go?"

"Those men—"

"What do you think they're going to do?"

He looked everywhere but at her. Little Joe threw himself against Colt's legs. Colt picked him up and pressed him to his shoulder. The boy's cries subsided.

"How can you even think of leaving them?" she murmured.

His fiery gaze lit on her. "What choice do I have?" He stepped past without giving her a chance to answer, and put Little Joe down to play with the toy horse. "You two stay with Becca. I have something to attend to in the store."

Little Joe wrinkled up his face, set to cry again.

"I'll be right next door. I'm not going anyplace else."

"You sure?" Little Joe asked.

"I'm sure."

"Okay."

Becca stared after him. He certainly got all nervous when there were others around, but at least he seemed committed to staying. Just as she was committed to giving him a Christmas to remember, and…

Her thoughts stalled and slowly, almost reluctantly, she finished the idea.

She'd prove to him that others were prepared to accept him.

God, help me. He needs to know You love him, and others will, too, if he gives them a chance.

Before Colt could escape, Pa opened the door, forcing Colt to step aside.

"Becca, have you got coffee and some of those biscuits from breakfast? Russell showed up. He's cold. Come on in and get warm." He waved to the man behind him.

Colt shifted back to where the children played.

Russell entered, a whiskered man, short and stocky. His nose was red from the cold. Frost clung to his whiskers, melting and dropping to the front of his buffalo-hide coat. He nodded a greeting at Becca, but his eyes never left the table as she set out a plate of biscuits along with butter and jam. He didn't even glance around the room.

"Much appreciated, Miss Becca. Just got back to town. I've been out of 'baccy for two days." He settled himself and waited only until Macpherson sat down across from him to take two biscuits, which disappeared in four bites.

“You sure do make the best biscuits.” He drank a long gulp of coffee, set the cup down and sighed.

“How did you folks weather the storm?” Russell glanced about for the first time, saw Colt and the children and jerked back. “What are they doing here?”

The way he screwed up his face and puckered his lips, Becca half expected him to spit a brown stream of tobacco on her floor. He swallowed hard, and his eyes narrowed to slits.

Pa answered the man’s questions. “Our guests. This is Colt Johnson. The children are Marie and Little Joe. You might remember Zeke Gallant? These are his kids. Zeke and his wife have passed on. Colt found the children and brought them here.”

Both children drew back, and Marie clung hard to Little Joe.

Russell snorted. “Should have left them to starve. Would have done us all a favor.”

Becca drew back. “Mr. Thomas, hold your tongue.” Only her good manners prevented her from telling the man to leave immediately. She didn’t bother looking to see what Russell thought of her order as she watched Colt and the children.

Marie and Little Joe looked frightened.

Colt’s face had hardened to expressionless. Only his eyes revealed his anger and disgust.

“Half-breeds. Mongrels. Best you get rid of them immediately.”

Pa rose to his feet. “Russell Thomas, these people are guests in my house, even as you are. I will thank you to treat them civilly.”

“So that’s the way it is.” Russell jerked to his feet, sending the chair skidding away. “Didn’t take you to be an Indian lover.” He headed for the door. “Well, I ain't no Indian lover. I'll be finding some other place to conduct my business." He stomped from the room.

No one moved as they listened to him thumping across the store and slamming the door as he departed.

"Oh, Pa, that was awful," Becca whispered. Her stomach churned at the insulting way the man had spoken.

"He's an ignorant man who doesn't deserve our attention." Pa suddenly chuckled. "Wonder where he plans to take his business. The closest store other than ours is the fort." He left the room, still laughing softly.

Becca turned to the others.

Marie's eyes were wide with dismay, but Little Joe had returned to his play, blissfully unaware of the hatred behind the man's words.

Slowly Colt brought his gaze to Becca's. "Just knowing me brands you with ugly names." He rushed from the room.

Colt looked neither right nor left as he crossed to the storeroom. At least the Eden Valley cowboys were gone. He wondered if they would have sided with the whiskered old man or with Macpherson. And did Macpherson mean anything by his defense of Colt and the children? Or was he only defending helpless children?

He'd wondered how to explain to Becca how others had always treated him. This incident informed him in every way possible that he didn't belong with people like her. She'd never known anything but acceptance and wouldn't understand. But now she'd seen it for herself.

He knew how most everyone would view her associating with him. An Indian lover. She'd be judged harshly, and he'd be judged even worse. For her sake he should leave now.

Yet he could not go before Christmas. He didn't want to. But he must be cautious and not overstep unseen boundaries.

For the rest of the afternoon he remained in the storeroom. He sorted and stacked goods for Macpherson. The man went so far as to say, "You're turning out to be mighty handy. Makes me think I could use a man like you once it gets busier again in the spring."

Had he so soon forgotten Russell's comments? And Russell wouldn't be the only one. "Lots of men looking to come west," Colt answered.

"Yup. The country is opening up. I expect we'll see more and more people coming every year."

"Uh-huh." The man seemed inclined to talk. Colt wasn't opposed to letting him, hoping it would drown out the ugly words and despairing thoughts drumming inside his head.

"I don't think I told you how I met Becca's mother."

"Nope." He opened a crate of ready-made wear—mostly trousers made of wool or denim. "Might buy myself a pair of these."

"I had in mind to find a place to open a store in the Territories. Knew it was about to open up. Stopped at Fort Benton for the winter. Elizabeth was teaching school. She was prettier and sweeter than an English rose. A widow, but that hadn't made her bitter. She was determined to take care of herself and Becca." Macpherson chuckled. "At first, she wouldn't give me the time of day, but I took my time about winning her. Figured I had all winter. I think it was little Becca who made Elizabeth take a second look at me. That little girl and I fell head over heels in love from the first. My, but she was a sweetheart." He had been staring into the distance, and now brought his gaze back to the present with a hard look at Colt.

"She's still something special. I want to see her get the best." He stomped away, leaving Colt to finish filling the shelves on his own.

Macpherson had made himself plenty clear...Becca deserved better than the likes of Colt Johnson.

He kept to himself in the storeroom until Marie came to fetch him for supper. He would have said he wasn't hungry, but the little girl's eyes shone with excitement. "Come and see what we made."

He vowed to guard every thought and feeling as he followed Marie back to the living quarters.

Becca stirred something on the stove and glanced over her shoulder at his entrance, favoring him with a smile that slipped past his defenses and landed soft and sweet in the middle of his heart.

Aware of Macpherson watching from the end of the table, Colt lowered his gaze and allowed Marie to lead him toward the little table by the armchair.

"See all the bells and stars we made. Becca says we can hang them on the tree."

"Mine." Little Joe patted a small stack that could best be described as odd-shaped stars.

Colt chuckled. "I can hardly wait to see them hanging on the tree." Behind him, Becca laughed softly. Her chuckle danced inside him. He could only wish it would stay there permanently.

Forcing his face into a mask of indifference, he went to the table and sat, keeping his attention on his plate. Even after Macpherson said grace and Becca passed the food, he managed to concentrate on the meal and not on her.

He'd give her pa no reason to pull him aside and suggest it was time Colt moved on.

Relief came when the meal ended. He planned to use the excuse of checking on the horses to leave the room, but the children were excited by all the Christmas plans. Little Joe ran around in circles, making a noise like the howling wind.

"He needs some playtime to wear him out," Becca said.

She didn't say Colt should provide the play, but he guessed that's what she meant so he caught Little Joe and sat down, giving the boy a horse ride on his foot.

"Do more," Little Joe begged every time Colt stopped, until finally Colt's muscles complained.

"Where's the little horse Becca lent you?"

Little Joe scampered off to find it behind the bedrolls. He climbed the toy up and down Colt's arms and legs, crawled over Colt's shoulders and finally perched there, his face next to Colt's. He patted Colt's cheek. "I like you."

Colt grunted and held still as his insides teetered back and forth. It was the first time in his life anyone had said such words. It mattered not if they came from a child. The words held the power of a thousand storms, and innumerable clear nights. They blew away dirt and debris of many unkind words.

He'd never known the value of hearing such things. Little Joe had given him this gift, and he would return it. He pulled the boy off his neck and sat him on his knee. "I like you, too."

Little Joe nodded, cuddled up to Colt's chest and promptly fell asleep.

Glad of a reason to avoid looking at anyone else in the room, he gently settled the boy in his blankets.

"Marie, come to bed," he called, and the little girl obeyed.

She paused at his side. "I like you, too." She kissed his cheek and crawled into her bed.

Colt tried to smile. Didn't quite manage.

"You're a good kid." He brushed strands of hair off her cheek. Not wanting to face Becca and her father, he spread out his bedroll, lounged back and opened the pages of his book.

Becca pulled out a sewing basket and took out the doll she was making for Marie.

Holding his book so it looked like his attention was on the pages, he watched her. She smiled as she worked, and after a few minutes held up the doll to examine it. Hair of black yarn, and black eyes. Nodding as if satisfied, she embroidered on lips and lashes.

"I'll make a dress and coat for it tomorrow, then it's ready." She glanced toward Colt, caught him watching her. "Is Little Joe's gift ready?"

"Just have to paint it tomorrow." Macpherson had seen the toy and offered some enamel.

Her father closed the book he'd been reading. "Daughter, it's time for bed."

"Yes, Pa." She set the basket in the cupboard, out of sight.

Macpherson waited for her to go, then took the lamp and went to his room.

Colt stared into the darkness. Tomorrow was Christmas Eve day. The next day, Christmas. He couldn't help but be a little excited, even though he knew it would all come to a crashing halt the day after that.

Becca hurried to get breakfast ready. She had a lot to do this day. Meal preparations for the big dinner tomorrow topped the list. For the first time in years, they would have many to share it with. She paused long enough to glance at Ma's picture. Still nothing would quite make up for her absence.

What would Ma do in Becca's place?

Vaguely, she recalled the winter they had spent at Fort Benton. The man who had been her Pa for almost fourteen years had been there. Truth be told, she barely remembered the presence of others, but now that she thought about it…seems there had been another young woman with two children older than Becca and….

She concentrated. Wasn't there a boy of about fifteen or sixteen with black hair and buckskin clothes? An Indian—a half-breed like Colt? She hated the word half-breed, and vowed she would use the gentler form used widely in Canada—Métis.

The children clamored to the table, and she hurriedly served breakfast.

"We make something today?" Little Joe asked.

"I have an idea," Colt said.

Becca blinked in surprise. Up to this point, the man had been reluctant to take part in anything.

"I wonder about what Marie said. You know, about her papa taking food to the birds."

"And animals," Marie added.

"It looks to be a pleasant day. We could— I could—"

"Excellent idea." Becca beamed her pleasure around the table. "Would you like to come, Pa?"

"I don't want to close the store in case people need last-minute things, but you go ahead."

Becca thought of meal preparations and the Eden Valley cowboys returning later in the day. But not for anything would she forgo the pleasure of an outing with

Colt and the children. "Give me an hour or so to do a few things, then let's go."

Marie wriggled with happiness. "I'll help you."

Colt ducked out of the room with a murmured excuse. She guessed he wanted to complete work on Little Joe's toy, though he likely welcomed a reason to be alone. Seemed he preferred his own company to that of others. She hoped he was learning there was a pleasant alternative to loneliness.

She turned her attention back to Marie. Truth was, Becca could do the work in half the time, but she would not deny the little girl the chance to help—and herself the pleasure of working side by side with the child.

They prepared stuffing for the bird and vegetables for the following day. They'd likely be late in returning, so she put a pot of soup to simmer, then paused. What would she serve for the evening meal with three more to feed? Something easy so she wouldn't waste a minute of the day at the stove. She tossed vegetables, meat and a bit of broth into a pot and stuck it in the oven.

"There." She grinned at Marie. "We're done. You're turning into a great little cook."

Marie beamed her pleasure.

Becca hugged her and kissed her forehead. "Now, let's find Colt."

She and Marie put on their warm clothes. Marie needed new moccasins. Hers were getting small for her. If they had more time, Becca could have arranged for a native woman to make some, along with fur-lined mittens. She found a pair of woolen mittens that were only a little too large and dressed Little Joe, and they headed to the barn.

A few minutes later they were on their way. They

marched through fresh snow along the river until Marie pointed to a tree. "There. It's perfect."

Becca wondered why this tree, and none of the many they had passed.

Marie looked at it with wide eyes. "Papa says the tree has to be big and wide to shelter many birds and animals."

"Then this tree is perfect." Tiny birds fluttered from the branches as they neared it.

Colt put the feed sack down, opened it and let the kids scoop out grain.

Becca watched him, noting his tender way with the children. Not once had she seen him mock them or ignore them or even become annoyed.

He turned her direction, and she read as clearly as any mirror the same regret she felt. They both cared about these children. They ached at the thought of what the future held.

If only things were different. If only she hadn't promised Ma. If only—

Marie waited. "You, too."

Becca and Colt sprang forward as if caught in a guilty act, and filled their hands.

The four of them marched around the tree, sprinkling the grain until the bag flattened.

Marie stood before the tree and held out her hands. "We held hands and Papa prayed for God to give us a good winter, enough to eat and a warm home." She glanced at the others.

Colt reached for Marie's hand. Becca reached for Little Joe's and then stopped. Her hand was inches from Colt's free one.

"We need to hold hands," Marie said.

Becca reached toward Colt, sensed his hesitation, but

then he gripped her hand. Warmth and a million sensations raced up her arm and crowded her heart. Joy and longing, dreams and belonging. In that instant, she knew their hearts beat as one.

Even as she knew it could never be acknowledged.

She had a promise to fulfill. Out of guilt or honor? She couldn't answer.

"Colt, you pray like Papa would." At Marie's words, Colt stiffened so quickly his hand tightened on her.

"I don't know if I can."

"Why not?"

"I don't know if God listens to me."

Becca knew he wouldn't say because he was a half-breed. It would ruin Marie's faith.

"My papa says the only thing God doesn't hear is a prayer we don't pray."

"Huh?" Colt considered the statement. "Okay then. I'll pray. 'God in heaven. Seems you hear if we pray, so I'm praying the same prayer Marie's papa would. Please give us a good winter with enough food and a warm home. Amen.'"

None of them let go of each others' hands for a moment.

Becca added her own prayer. *God in heaven, send a miracle for these children and fill Colt's heart with love. Give us all the best Christmas ever.*

Chapter Eight

Colt pulled his hands away from Becca and Marie, and grabbed the feed sack. He scooped up Little Joe and led them back to Edenvale. Was Marie right? Had her papa been correct? Did God hear every time someone prayed? Was it that easy, or did it only seem so because Marie was a child?

He tried to dismiss the questions, but they refused to leave him. He acknowledged an ache deep inside that longed to believe as plainly as Marie did…to know as surely as her papa had that God heard the prayers of a man like Colt.

They returned to the frontier town and passed the livery barn.

A deep voice called out, "Good day, Miss Becca."

"It's a beautiful day," Becca called back. "A Merry Christmas to you, Rufus."

"And to you."

They continued on to the store and stepped inside. The smell of food cooking, the warmth of the room and the smile Macpherson gave them tangled with Colt's troubled thoughts. For a brief second he envisioned himself in a real home full of warmth and welcome.

Then he shuttered these useless thoughts behind a thick door and set Little Joe on his feet.

"We can eat right away," Becca said, and they all sat around the table.

Little Joe nodded before he finished, and Marie readily went to Becca's room to nap with him.

The outer door opened, and Macpherson hurried away to care for a customer.

Colt pushed from the table, glanced about.

"Don't rush away," Becca said.

"I don't think—"

"You can help with dishes. The Eden Valley cowboys will show up any time, and I want to be ready."

His thoughts stalled, restarted with a jolt. She wanted him to help her? Wouldn't that mean standing elbow to elbow at the little cupboard?

She handed him a towel. "You can dry."

His mouth felt parched. But what choice did he have? And he honestly didn't mind the predicament. It provided an excuse to stand close enough to smell the fragrance of her hair—wild flowers and honey.

Trouble was, she wanted to talk. He didn't. His tongue seemed thick and numb.

"Marie is so sweet and smart. I love it when she quotes her father."

Colt wasn't sure he liked it so much. The words had the tendency to stir up things in his heart he would rather remain quiet.

"He must have been a wise man."

"Does that surprise you?"

She jerked about to face him. "No. Why should it?"

He shrugged. "He married an Indian woman."

Her gaze bored into his, demanding, unrelenting. "Are you saying only a stupid person would marry an

Indian?" Her words were low, but he did not miss the angry tone.

"I'd guess that's what most people think."

"And you think people view you in the same light, I suppose?"

Yes. No. He grabbed a bowl and scrubbed it dry. "I know who I am. What I am. I'm happy enough with the knowledge." Only he wasn't. And it was all her fault. All his hard work at building walls about his feelings, pursuing his own interests while staying away from trouble…it was all coming undone, thanks to her insistent kindness. He did not feel any gratitude for how his foundations had been cracked and were now about to crumble.

She stopped working to study him.

He tried to concentrate on the dish in his hand, tried to remember he meant to dry it. Did his best not to look at her. But he failed to control his eyes, and when he met her gaze, he forgot every argument, every lesson he'd learned.

"Colt, you are a good man. I appreciate who you are. But I think I see you differently than you see yourself. Even more, I think my view is right and you know it."

He couldn't speak, couldn't argue, though he knew he needed to. Instead he was trapped by her blue-sky eyes and her sunshine smile.

She touched his arm with her damp hand, sending a spray of warmth up his limb and into his heart with the welcome of spring. "Colt Johnson, you are a good, decent, kind, thoughtful, loving man."

He tried to swallow the lump in his throat. She saw all that? Oh, how he wanted to believe it. How he wanted to respond to it. If he could speak, he would say yes, that is me. That is the me I've buried deep.

She increased the pressure on his arm, filled his heart to overflowing with her smile. “I’m right, aren’t I? That’s who you are behind your pretense of not caring.”

“Becca, I wish I could be who you see.” Without conscious thought, he touched the back of her hand where it lay on his arm. His strong walls shattered. But it couldn’t be. He mentally gathered the pieces and reconstructed the wall. A little less secure than it had been, but it was there. He stepped away, forcing her to drop her hand to her side and leaving him adrift in a sea of regret. He realized he still held a bowl, and set it aside.

“Looks like we’re done. I’ve got to finish Little Joe’s toy.”

He hurried to the storeroom and stared at the shelf loaded with goods. He had come perilously close to crossing a forbidden barrier. For a heartbeat, he’d considered pulling her into his arms and letting the pain of his past disappear in holding her and believing her. Good thing he came to his senses in time. Saved himself being run out of town. Or worse.

He touched the spot where her hand had rested on his arm, and for a moment let the rush of emotions have free rein in his heart. If only… If only he could tell her how he felt. How her concern had given him a glimpse of hope. How it had stirred a longing he’d learned to deny. But he knew he must push such wayward ideas back behind solid walls. Even though those walls trembled with an emotion he could not confess. If he knew what love was, he might think that was what he felt.

He examined the little horse. Earlier in the day, he’d painted on black eyes, a black mane and black hooves. The paint would be dry by morning, and Little Joe would have a toy of his own.

Would the teacher allow him to keep it? Or would

it simply get "lost" as so many of Colt's things had in the past?

He puttered about in the storeroom for the afternoon. A few times Macpherson came in to get something or to pace the room. Colt's nerves twitched. Why was the man so restless all of a sudden? Was he trying to come up with a way to ask Colt to move along?

He didn't need to. Colt would be leaving tomorrow, as soon as Christmas was over. Or early the next day, at the latest.

He steeled himself against the pain shafting up his spine and into the base of his skull. Thankfully, someone entered the store at that moment and Macpherson rushed out.

He recognized the voices of Eddie, Roper and Ward, and listened to the discussion about bringing in a tree. Then the men went into the living quarters, and the closed door muffled the conversation.

Colt sat down on a crate. With all his heart he longed to join them in the Christmas celebration, but the thought sent every warning bell in his head ringing with vigor.

"Colt."

He jerked up at Marie's voice. "Didn't hear you come in."

"Becca says come so we can decorate the tree."

"You go ahead without me." He didn't belong. Never would. Never could. But he wanted to with a ferocity he hadn't admitted since he was Marie's age.

Marie shook her head. "Becca said to bring you back."

He sighed, guessing Becca knew he wouldn't be able to refuse Marie. He rose and let Marie take his hand, then they returned to the others.

The three cowboys greeted him pleasantly enough. Macpherson was busy making a pot of coffee. Becca smiled.

"Now we can start." Her gaze lingered on Colt.

He forced himself to look away first. The cowboys struggled to right the tree, and he rushed over to help.

The tree was soon secure, and the children hung their decorations. Becca assisted Little Joe. Colt lifted Marie so she could hang the colorful balls and stars on the upper branches.

The cowboys stood back and watched, nursing mugs of coffee provided by Macpherson.

Colt forgot the others as he and Becca helped the children. He would let himself enjoy the moment. Accept the sense that this was right and good. Believe that he fit into the picture.

Tomorrow was soon enough for facing reality.

Having given himself permission to enjoy the present, the rest of the day passed pleasantly. Seemed everyone was prepared to set aside any differences and focus on making the season special for Marie and Little Joe.

They played games in the afternoon. In the evening, they enjoyed popcorn and hot chocolate. Later, when the children had fallen asleep, Colt prepared to retreat to his mat.

Becca saw his intention. "Why don't we sit around the table and enjoy Christmas Eve?"

The Eden Valley cowboys eagerly joined her. Colt could not refuse without appearing churlish. But he wondered what she had in mind.

"Why doesn't everyone tell us where they were and what they were doing last Christmas?"

Colt shrugged. His answer would be simple enough.

Becca began. "Last year was hard for me. It was

our first Christmas without my mother. I don't think either of us knew how to celebrate without her." She touched her pa's hand. "But you tried so hard to make it special for me. Thank you." She turned to the others. "What I remember most clearly is that Pa and I went for a walk after dark on Christmas Day. The sky was so clear. The stars so numerous. It made me think of what it must have been like that first Christmas. I felt blessed and loved."

Macpherson cleared his throat. "I remember last year as both sad and happy. I was sad Elizabeth was gone, but so happy to have Becca with me. And it pleased me to see so many new ones coming into the area." He nodded toward Eddie. "You were one of those I welcomed."

It was Eddie's turn. "Last year was my first year at the Eden Valley Ranch. I had nothing but a little log cabin, but our cook house was finished and Cookie made sure we celebrated Christmas proper—as she described it. We had turkey and pudding. And she gave all of us mittens she'd knitted." He nodded. "I missed my family. Still do. But I love this new country and am happy to be part of it." He turned to the man beside him. "Roper?"

"Last year I spent the holiday with strangers at a stopping house in Idaho." He sucked in a deep breath. "Like I said the other day, I know what it's like to have little in the way of Christmas celebration. Not that I was unhappy. But it's not like having Christmas with family and friends."

Indicating he was done, he turned to Ward.

Ward grinned widely, as if pleased with his memories.

Colt studied the openness in the man's face. What must it be like to feel so free before others?

Ward continued. "I've got my own little ranch. Going to live there someday."

Roper chortled. "Yeah, when he finds some woman silly enough to agree to marry him."

Ward only laughed. "Shouldn't be a problem."

Roper rolled his eyes. "I expect they're just lined up waiting for you to give them the 'come here' signal."

Ward shrugged. He seemed completely unconcerned with the teasing and ignored Roper. "I already have a little cabin built. That's where I spent Christmas." He looked past all of them as if seeing his ranch.

Or his dreams.

Colt tried to imagine what it would be like to have such solid dreams. To make such firm plans. He thought of his money in a bank back in Fort Benton. Almost all of his wages were in that bank. Someday, he might get a ranch, too. Would he have someone to share his life with? He kept his eyes fixed on the table.

Ward nudged Colt. "How about you, partner?"

Colt had known this moment was coming. He was prepared. All he had to do was pull back his wandering thoughts.

"I had a good Christmas last year. I was in a cabin in the mountains, and the day was so sunny and bright it felt like spring. I had a horse I'd been training, and he was ready for a good workout so we rode for hours. Saw some beautiful scenery. Stopped to make dinner at a little stream just about frozen over, so it had interesting shapes of ice. A big whitetail buck came down to drink and stood watching me." He sighed. "It was a great day."

"Sounds like it," Roper said.

None of the others commented, and Colt guessed

they thought it sounded lonely. It had been, though he hadn't realized just how lonely until now.

"Where was the cabin?" Roper asked.

"West of Great Falls."

"Say. I wasn't that far away." The conversation drifted to comparing places they'd been until Macpherson yawned.

"Tomorrow's a big day. We better get some sleep," the older man said.

As Becca went to her room, Colt hustled to his bedroll. The cowboys tossed theirs nearby. Then Macpherson took the lamp and the room grew dark.

Colt compared this Christmas with the one previous. He'd enjoyed last year at the time, but nothing he'd ever experienced held a candle to this year. Friends and children, attention from a beautiful woman, a special meal…

He fell asleep with visions of turkey and children's laughter dancing in his head.

Becca listened to the sounds from the other room. Pa had risen a few minutes earlier, and she heard the men moving about. Little Joe cried once and Colt calmed him. She pictured him holding the little boy to his shoulder. There was an obvious affection between the pair.

Tomorrow—

She shook her head. She would not waste a speck of today's joy worrying about tomorrow. Deeming it safe to leave her room, she hurried out. "Merry Christmas, everyone."

Marie raced out to her. "Is it Christmas now?"

"That's right." She could hardly wait to see the children with their gifts.

But first she served them breakfast, and then Pa read

the Christmas story as he'd done every year since he and Ma married.

While she and Marie washed dishes, the men ducked out of the room, returning in a few minutes with strange-looking parcels wrapped in Pa's store paper.

They put the packages under the tree and sat back, smiling in anticipation.

"Are those presents?" Marie whispered.

"I believe they are."

"Who are they for?"

"Why don't we see?"

Pa handed out the gifts. There were mittens for the children.

"Bought them off the natives near the ranch," Eddie said.

Pa had supplied a little storybook for each child.

Marie opened the package containing the doll. "Oh. Is this mine to keep?"

Becca hugged the child. "It's yours."

"Thank you."

Then Little Joe opened the horse. "Horsee."

"It's yours. Colt made it for you."

Little Joe threw his arms around Colt's neck and hugged him. "Fank you."

There were still a few remaining parcels. Pa handed them around. Becca had made each of them framed pictures of pretty scenes she'd saved from old calendars. Pa gave each adult a book.

There remained one more gift.

Pa read the label. "To Mr. Macpherson and his daughter, from Colt." He held it toward Becca. "You open it."

"What is it?" It was bulky and oddly shaped. She glanced at Colt, hoping for a clue. He watched without expression, though she detected a flicker of something in his eyes—whether caution or hope, she couldn't say.

"Open it and see," Pa said.

She untied the strings and folded back the paper. A deer carved from pale wood stared up at her. "It's beautiful." She turned it and saw a tiny fawn clinging to the side of the mother animal. So delicate. So tender. Did he have any idea what this carving revealed of his feelings toward mothers and family? "Did you do this?"

"Had a lot of time on my hands last winter."

"Look how nice it is." She handed it to Pa, who agreed that it was indeed a nice piece of work.

The cowboys took turns looking at it.

"I saw carvings like this back in Quebec," Eddie said. "The French Canadian Métis do a lot of this sort of work." He handed it back to Becca. "You do excellent work, Colt."

"Thank you."

Becca wondered if Pa would want to keep it, or if she would be allowed to take it with her when she left tomorrow.

She would not think of what the day held. But if Pa approved, she would love to take this carving and the memories it represented.

It was the last of the gifts.

The children played happily, and the adults sat back to read their books while Becca completed meal preparations. Soon they gathered around the table and ate until they were full.

"The pudding was excellent," Pa said. "As good as your ma made."

"She taught me well." If only she could erase the sorrow from Pa's face.

Eddie, Roper and Ward prepared to leave soon after.

"Cookie ordered us to be back in time to spend the evening with the Eden Valley crew," Eddie explained. "Thank you for a special Christmas." He turned to the children. "Wherever you go, remember this day and how much fun we had."

Marie nodded. "We will."

Some hours later, after the children had fallen asleep with their new possessions tucked under the covers with them, Pa put on his coat and new mittens.

"I think I'll go for a walk."

"Do you want me to come?"

"No, daughter, I need to be by myself for a little while."

She nodded. "I understand."

"I won't be long."

She'd hoped for such an opportunity to talk to Colt, and poured him tea now. "This is our last evening together," Becca murmured, not caring that she sounded as regretful as she felt.

"Knew it was coming."

"Of course we did. Doesn't mean I have to like it or welcome it."

She waited, hoping for some sign that he welcomed her friendship, her caring. When he offered nothing, she pressed him further. "What will you do? Where will you go?"

"Look after horses like I always planned." His voice carried a shrug.

She wanted to shake him from his stoic acceptance. "You could do something else. Give people a chance to know you." *Give yourself a chance to see that people can care. I care.*

His eyes filled with longing so deep, it ached at her

heart. She'd tried to make him see himself as worthy of love. He seemed so close to believing.

He studied the cup, turning it round and round. "Can't change what is."

"Exactly what *is?* Unfairness? Mean words from people like Mr. Thomas? I intend to do all I can to change that."

He lifted his eyes to her then, and she caught a glimpse of hope and despair intermingling. "Don't know how you can."

Suddenly she knew exactly what she could do. She had only to convince Colt. "We can change things."

"We?" He snorted.

The sound broke the last of her restraint. "Yes, we. You and I love these children."

He quirked an eyebrow.

"Don't bother to deny it."

His mouth fell open, and he stared. Closed his mouth and blurted out, "Love? I don't even know what love is."

"And yet you do. You love these kids. And I think you know God loves you. But you won't let yourself believe it. Or maybe you are afraid to trust it, even though you likely want it more than anything in the world. Colt, let yourself believe in love. Start by believing in God's love."

"You mean the white man's God?"

She ignored the bitterness in his voice and chuckled softly. "Have you read Genesis? Seems to me God created everything and everyone. So where does that leave your white man's God argument?"

"That was in the beginning, when the world was perfect."

"True. But man's sin doesn't negate God's love. Just

like in the beginning, we are all free to choose whether or not to believe."

"What does this have to do with the kids?"

"Maybe more than you know. You said you didn't know how to love. And I'm simply pointing out that love is available if you're willing to believe it."

"If you say so."

"It isn't that I say it. God says it. You feel up to arguing with Him?"

"If God is loving, then why don't these kids still have their parents?"

"It's easy to blame God, then refuse to help when it's in our power." She leaned forward and impaled him with her direct gaze. "You can give these children love. A home."

His face darkened with anger. "Becca, I cannot give them a home because I don't have one."

"Then get one."

He threw his hands into the air. "And do what? Leave them alone while I go hunting or breaking horses?"

"They deserve a home where they know they are loved. You and I can give them that."

As soon as she said it, she knew it was what she wanted more than anything. She loved the children. She loved Colt—whether or not he would accept it.

"It's the perfect solution."

He shoved back, but remained seated. He opened and closed his mouth twice, swallowed hard and shook his head. "What are you suggesting?"

"We can get married and give these kids a home."

"Miss Macpherson, that can never be."

When had she gone from being Becca to Miss Macpherson? "It can be if we decide it can."

"I will never marry a white woman."

His rejection stung. "Why not? There's no law against it."

"Perhaps not a written one." He clamped his mouth shut.

"Mr. Johnson, you know what your problem is? You're afraid to let anyone love you. You shove them away so they can't shove you away first. But I'm begging you to stay, and yet you're still running away. Colt, you're going to run out of people to push away and places to run and end up a lonely, bitter hermit. Is that what you want?"

He rose slowly to his feet, all expression erased from his face.

"I need to check on my horse. I'll be leaving first thing in the morning." He strode toward the door, not wasting time, his posture saying he didn't care what anyone thought.

"Colt, there are some things harder than not having a past. Such as not having a future."

"Haven't you forgotten something?" He paused, but she couldn't think what he meant. "Your promise to your ma to go back east." He left without a backward look.

She hadn't forgotten. But she wanted to stay.

What was she going to do?

Chapter Nine

Colt stumbled from the room. If only it was possible. Becca obviously loved the children. Her pa was kind enough to them. If she would keep them, it would be wonderful.

But to expect him to marry her!

The woman was blind if she thought others didn't see his mixed heritage.

Hope forced itself forward. She didn't seem to care about it. If only—

But how could Becca be so naive? Who would allow a man like Colt to make the kind of plans she suggested? He hurried to the barn and the safety of the horses. He couldn't go back to the house and the forbidden offers of love, acceptance and family, so he grabbed a couple of saddle blankets and hunkered down in the barn for the night.

The neighing of a horse wakened him, and he stretched and yawned. A glance out the door revealed the promise of a warm day. He looked at the sky. Not a cloud anywhere. That was good, he assured himself. It meant the stagecoach would travel. Becca and the children would be on their way. He would leave as soon as he saw them depart.

His useless wishes of the night before vanished in the reality of daylight. Becca didn't mean what she said about them making a home for the children. It had been only idle conversation. She was leaving for Toronto, and a life more suited to a beautiful white woman.

Macpherson poked his head around the corner. "So this is where you spent the night. Is Marie with you?"

"No. She was asleep with Little Joe when I left."

Macpherson jerked back. "Then where is she?"

"She's inside. You must have missed her." The men hurried to the living quarters to reassure themselves she was there.

Becca waited just inside the door, her hands twisting in her apron. She glanced behind Colt as he stepped in. When she didn't see the little girl, she met his look, her eyes wide with concern.

"She wasn't here when I got up. Little Joe doesn't know where she is."

"Marie gone," Little Joe said, as if to confirm this information.

Alarm skittered up Colt's spine, and he hunkered down in front of the boy. "Where is she? Do you know?"

He shook his head, and his eyes welled with tears.

"Don't cry. We'll find her. She's likely found something in the store to amuse her."

He joined Becca and her father at the doorway.

"I already checked the store," Becca whispered. "And every inch of this place. I can't find her. I hoped she was with you."

"Let's have another look." Macpherson headed into the store. "Maybe she's playing a little game."

Colt scooped Little Joe into his arms. "You can help

us find her." They called her name. They searched every corner. They looked in the new storeroom. Then he and Macpherson left Little Joe with Becca and searched the barn and woodshed out back. No sign of her.

"She can't have disappeared," Macpherson said, as the three adults sat around the table to plan their next move. Thankfully, Little Joe had allowed them to reassure him and was contentedly playing with the toy horse.

Becca gave Colt a look that was both beseeching and accusing. "Where would you go if you were four years old and afraid of being sent somewhere you didn't want to go?"

He knew what she meant. He'd been in Marie's situation. What had he done? "I suppose she might have headed back to their home. Or—is there an Indian camp nearby?"

Macpherson answered his question. "There are some up in the hills, but how would she know that, and besides, how could she hope to get there?"

Colt shrugged. "She's a strong-minded young girl. She might plan to walk. But I honestly have no idea where she'd go. Before we consider the Indian camp, we need to talk to folks living nearby and ask if anyone's seen her."

Macpherson was already on his feet. "Becca, you stay here with Little Joe. Colt, you go south. I'll go north."

Half an hour later they both returned without Marie. Colt's stomach bucked like an angry horse. Macpherson and Becca looked as concerned as he felt. Becca held Little Joe tight, perhaps as much for her own comfort as for his. Colt ached to pull them both into his arms and promise them everything would be okay. But he couldn't give such assurances, and he didn't mean only in locating Marie. He couldn't offer them what they needed, even though Becca had suggested he could. "I'll ride out and see if I can track her."

He returned the direction he had come several days ago. Why had Marie run off? It wasn't like she had any place to go. As he rode, he searched the trail for signs of her. Half an hour later he leaned over the saddle. "Horse, do you see that? A little girl's footprint." She'd been this way. "Likely she'll go back to the cabin that's been her only home." He rode on, catching more footprints to indicate she'd come this way. And then he saw her, seated on a log beside the trail, her knees drawn up to her chest and her head buried in her hands.

"Marie," he called.

She looked up, her face streaked with tears.

He dropped from his horse and ran toward her.

With a glad cry, she raced for his arms.

He swept her into a big hug. "Are you okay? I was so worried."

"I kept thinking if I walked and walked, I would get back home and everything would be like it was before."

He sat on the log she'd vacated and rocked her. "You know it can't be. You have to look forward, not back."

The words sounded so much like what Becca had told him.

It's harder to not have a future than to not have a past.

Marie pushed back to stare into his face. "Why don't you like us?"

"I like you fine."

"If you liked us, you wouldn't leave us."

The words said everything he'd been denying, everything Becca had been telling him. Likely she thought the same as Marie—if he left, he would be abandoning them and his only chance to fill the emptiness in his heart that called for love and family.

He faced a choice. Likely the hardest one he'd ever had to deal with. He could ride away and continue to live in self-imposed loneliness because of rejection he'd faced over his mixed heritage. Or he could trust God's opinion. Believe He saw not the color of a man's skin, but the condition of his heart.

On that knowledge he could accept the future Becca offered. She had made it plain as water she didn't care about his heritage. Was he willing to believe it? Was he brave enough to confess his love?

But even if he was, it wasn't possible. Becca intended to go east. He knew he and the children couldn't be part of her plans.

But he could not let her go without admitting what he'd been fighting since her first smile. He loved her. Her love had mended the tears in his heart and made him believe in the future. A future shared with her.

How long did she plan to be gone? He would wait for her to return.

In the meantime, he'd find a way to keep the children. Smiling, he said, "We better get you back to town. Becca was awfully worried about you. Her pa, too."

"I wish I could stay with them."

"I know you do."

Yet surely Becca had remembered her vow, and was already regretting suggesting they make a home for the children.

Becca watched out the window.

"There's nothing to do but wait for Colt to return," Pa said.

Becca glanced over her shoulder at Little Joe playing happily. She wished she could hold him, but he'd grown tired of her tight grasp. She did not want to let go of either of the children. She didn't want to see Colt ride away. She didn't want to go to Toronto.

"Pa, these children belong here."

Pa hurried to her side. "What are you saying?"

"I love them. I think you do, too. At the fort they might not be treated well."

"I can't take care of them. I run a store."

"Pa, why did Ma want me to go east?"

He looked out the window, though she suspected he didn't see the view outdoors. "She was afraid you'd never find a suitable mate out here. She wanted you to find a man who had more to offer you than an uncertain future in the West."

"But isn't love worth facing such things?"

He smiled. "I've always thought so." He sighed heavily. "Your ma only wanted you to be happy."

"This is where I am happy," Becca said. "This is where I belong."

Knowingly, her pa asked, "Even if Colt won't stay?"

Her heart gave a strange little jolt. She smiled shakily. "I hope he'll see he belongs here, too. But even if he doesn't, I know I do, and so do the children. You and I could raise them if Colt refuses."

Please help him to find Marie safe and sound. Please, God, don't let him ride away.

Her pa shook his head. "We promised your ma."

"But I think she would want me to follow my heart. Do what I know is best for me and for you, the children—even Colt."

His brow furrowed. "I would never force you to do something you didn't want to."

"I know, but your approval is more important to me than your permission." She waited as he fought an inner struggle.

"I've watched you since Colt and the children showed up. I saw this happening and tried to prevent it."

"Perhaps this is what my whole life has prepared me for."

"That sounds like something your mother would say." He nodded slowly. "I have a feeling she would approve of your decision."

"Oh, thank you, Pa." She flung herself into his arms and hugged him, then she returned to her post at the window, hoping…praying…to see Colt returning with Marie.

"Pa." Excitement made her voice high. "A rider. It's Colt—and he's got Marie! Praise God." Tears clogged her throat so she couldn't continue.

She rushed outdoors. As soon as Colt got close enough, she reached up for Marie. "My sweet child. I am so glad to see you." She kissed the top of Marie's head a dozen times.

Colt swung down from his horse.

Only then did she allow herself to meet his eyes, and her heart missed a beat at the look in them.

"Saw the stagecoach coming."

She nodded without moving.

"Shouldn't you be getting ready to leave?"

"I'm not leaving." She set Marie on the ground. "Honey, run in and see my pa. He's been worried about you."

Colt waited until Marie closed the door behind her to speak. "I thought I heard you say you weren't leaving."

"I did. I have what I need and want right here."

"What about your promise to your ma?" His guarded gaze searched her.

"It was given out of guilt and asked out of misunderstanding. Ma thought I needed to meet people like those who live back east. But they aren't my kind of people."

"Who is your kind?"

"Strong individuals who face all sorts of challenges and remain noble and true."

"Like your pa?"

"He's not the only one."

Colt swallowed hard. "Oh?"

"You're one of those men."

His eyes spoke volumes—hope and doubt combined. "What about Russell Thomas and people like them?"

"We might not be able to change Russell's opinion, but we can prove to others that this is the new West, and there are new rules of acceptance."

He continued to study her without responding.

"I'm staying with or without you. Those children deserve a home with people who love them. But I hope I don't have to raise them alone." She'd never be alone. Pa would help her, but that wasn't what she needed. She needed a man of her own to love and cherish her as she meant to love and cherish him.

"Did you mean it when you said we should raise the children together?"

"Indeed, I did."

"I believe a marriage should be based on love."

"So do I."

"Are you saying...?"

She nodded. "I love you, Colt Johnson." Her heart beat faster at the look of bewilderment on his face. It was replaced by disbelief, then finally, joy.

He pulled her into his arms with a shout of joy. "I have found here everything I've always wanted."

"Children?" she teased, all the while aching to hear the words.

"More than that. A woman who loves me, though not near as much as I love her."

She leaned back. "Say the words."

He smiled, his dark eyes full of emotion. "Becca, I love you now and forever."

And then, at long last, he lowered his head and captured her mouth in a kiss full of promise and love and everything her heart had ever dreamed of. She wanted the kiss to go on forever, but Marie's giggle at the doorway made them stop.

Colt grinned down at her. "We'll continue this later."

She nodded, her eyes brimming with happiness. "Let's go tell them the good news."

Epilogue

Spring

Colt stood in the street in front of the store. Becca and the children were in the wagon. His horse was tied behind.

Macpherson, who insisted on being called Grandpa now, went to the wagon, another parcel in his hands.

"This order came in on the stagecoach yesterday. New books for the kids." He handed it to Becca, who leaned down to kiss her pa.

"Thank you, Pa."

Colt heard the tears in her voice. He'd spend some time later comforting his wife. More than once, he'd offered to stay in Edenvale, but Becca was insistent they needed to start their own life.

When Eddie Gardiner heard that Colt wanted to settle down and start a ranch, he'd pointed out the availability of land not far from the Eden Valley Ranch.

"Our own land. Our own home." She'd hugged him.

"Guess the wages I've never spent were meant for this." Colt had hugged Becca as they agreed to buy the land.

Now they were loaded and ready to start their new life. A dozen people gathered in front of the store.

Becca smiled down at him. "Looks like our friends have come to wish us goodbye."

It was more than Colt thought possible. Not everyone was willing to be friends. Old Russell Thomas hadn't relented in his opinion, but he had to have his tobacco so he kept his thoughts to himself.

Six cowboys from the Eden Valley Ranch rode down the trail toward them.

"We've come to help you move," Eddie said.

Colt shook hands with Macpherson. "I'll take good care of her and the kids."

"I know you will. Don't be a stranger."

"We'll visit often, and I hope you do the same."

He climbed to the wagon seat and took the reins.

"Goodbye," everyone called as they drove away.

The cowboys rode behind the wagon.

Becca leaned close and pressed her cheek to his shoulder. "I am so excited."

Colt kissed the top of her head. "I have what I always wanted and never dreamed would be possible."

She turned her face toward him. "Tell me."

"A woman to love. A home and a family." He turned to pull the children up beside them. "We are so blessed."

With his arms about his family, they headed west to their new home.

* * * * *

Dear Reader,

I'm wondering what it says about me that I often write stories like Colt and Becca's—stories about injustices and strong characters who confront and conquer these issues. I hope at the very least it says I'd like to right wrongs, that I'd stand up to injustice and fight for the underdog.

And what better time than Christmas to let Becca and Colt face one of society's ills and find their own solution?

It was fun writing this story and trying to think of creative ways to celebrate Christmas with two children. I hope you enjoyed reading the story as much as I enjoyed writing it.

May each of you find God's love and human connections at Christmas.

I love to hear from readers. Contact me through email at linda@lindaford.org. Feel free to check on updates and bits about my research at my website, www.lindaford.org.

God bless,

Linda Ford

Questions for Discussion

1. What factors have influenced Colt's view of life? Which ones do you think had the most impact? Is his opinion valid?

2. How does Becca's upbringing differ from others, and how has that shaped her view of the world?

3. How does the arrival of two orphaned children affect change in both Colt and Becca?

4. Is the portrayal of prejudice realistic for the era? Can Colt and Becca hope to change things? How?

5. Is Becca's father prejudiced? Why do you think he acts the way he does?

6. What character do you most closely identify with? Why, and what does that say about you and the changes you can make in your world?

7. What challenges do you foresee in the future for this family?

SMOKY MOUNTAIN CHRISTMAS

Karen Kirst

In memory of my dad, Richard Kirst,
who passed away during the writing of this story.
I love you and miss you. Until we meet again.

The Lord does not look at the things people look at.
People look at the outward appearance,
but the Lord looks at the heart.
—*1 Samuel* 16:7b

Chapter One

Gatlinburg, Tennessee
December 1880

This Christmas would be different, Rachel Prescott vowed. No more wallowing in self-pity. No more regrets. Her life may not have turned out as she'd hoped, but she had plenty of reasons to be thankful. It was wrong to want more. *Help me, Lord, to be content with the blessings in my life.*

Chilled air seeped through the window seams and fanned across her already cold hands. She shifted to bring her face closer to the frost-edged glass. From where the church sat at the end of Main Street, she had a clear view of the storefronts draped with evergreen garlands and vivid red ribbons in anticipation of the holiday. Two youths exited Clawson's mercantile, dark heads bent over a shared bag of steaming chestnuts. A covered wagon turned onto the hard-packed dirt lane, and the horses' harness bells jingled a merry tune, temporarily masking the children's cheerful banter behind her.

Three more weeks. Surely she could survive twenty-one more days of fruitcakes and gingerbread men, hot cocoa and mistletoe and endless holiday cheer. With the annual Christmas Eve presentation to prepare for, the days between now and then would be blessedly hectic. There were props yet to build and paint, costumes to make, weekly practices and, of course, a church to be decorated. That left little time to dwell on the past, on her hasty Christmas wedding that neither she nor her groom had wanted.

Movement near the post office snagged her attention. A man she hadn't noticed leaning against the building straightened to his full height and seemed to stare directly at her. Rachel's breath caught. He was too far away for her to make out his features, but his lazy, defiant stance and the way he looped his thumbs in his waistband struck a warning knell in the recesses of her mind.

What if it was him? Alarm surged upward but she stemmed the tide. It *wasn't* him. Couldn't be. There was nothing for him here. The stranger tugged his fawn hat down and, pivoting on his heel, loped off in the opposite direction.

"The troops are getting restless, Rachel."

With a start of surprise, she whirled to find her friend Megan O'Malley regarding her with a puzzled expression. The rush of her pulse sounded loud in her ears. "I'm sorry, what did you say?"

The younger woman gestured to the group of twenty children now seated side by side on the wooden pews near the stage. "They're eager to be measured for their costumes." Megan hesitated. "Are you well? Your face has lost all color."

Rachel touched her cheek with ice-cold fingertips. "Have I? I didn't realize..." *Pull yourself together. Do you think he's the only man to stand just that way?* Sucking in a fortifying breath, she started down the aisle. "Well then, we mustn't keep them waiting."

The next hour passed in a blur. In their excitement, the children didn't seem to notice her uncharacteristic silence. She sensed Megan's concerned glances but didn't linger to chat after the last child had left. What would she have said, anyway? *I think I saw my estranged husband standing on Main Street?*

Impatient to reach the safety and solitude of her cozy cabin, her stop at her parents' home was a brief one. She declined their invitation to supper. Her mother would surely sense her unease, and she wasn't up to an inquisition. Besides, dusk had fallen, and she didn't like traveling the mile-long stretch between the two cabins in the dark.

Bundled in her roomy, fur-lined cape dyed the same deep green as the towering pines on either side of the path, she walked as quickly as her burden would allow. Her footsteps quickened when the clearing came into view and, beyond that, the cabin. Her home. The one her husband built for her, not out of a desire to please her, of course, but because it had been his responsibility. His duty.

Not so long ago, she'd actually believed in true love and soul mates and happily ever after. Those dreams died the night she and Cole Prescott were locked inside the storage room at Clawson's. Of course, they'd had to marry. It was either that or be shunned, subjected to whispers and cold stares. Cole was used to that treatment, but not her. Not the town sweetheart.

Forget the past. What's done is done. Bemoaning her lot in life wouldn't change a thing. Besides, she'd made a promise to herself that this year her smile would be real, her enjoyment genuine and not just an act to appease her parents.

Rachel stepped up on the porch. Soon she'd have the fire going and the leftover stew warmed up. Perhaps she'd fix a cup of that peppermint tea she'd splurged on last week and hadn't had time to sample. Then she would—

"Hello, Rachel."

Her heart jolted in recognition. The blood drained from her face. Unsteady, she turned to stare at the shadowy figure on her porch. Stars danced in the twilight.

Sixteen long months had passed since she'd last set eyes on him. Handsome in a rebellious sort of way, he looked the same and yet she detected differences. His light brown hair was cut in a more conservative style than before, his firm jaw clean-shaven and his skin tanned a nut brown.

"You're looking well." His hazel eyes, at all times guarded as if expecting the worst, studied her with lazy interest.

"Wh-what are you doing here?"

Hands shoved deep in his coat pockets, he stepped closer. "We have unfinished business, you and I." He cocked his head in the direction of the door. "It's cold. What do you say we continue this conversation inside?"

"I—" Rachel struggled to form words, her mind racing with the implications of his sudden reappearance.

"You don't have to look so worried, sweet pea, I don't plan on stickin' around. If you'll let me say my piece, I promise to leave you alone. For good, this time."

What business was he referring to?

The bundle beneath her coat squirmed, and the gravity of her situation robbed her of breath. Did he already know?

The stars in her field of vision multiplied.

So. Her instincts had been dead-on.

Cole Prescott was back in town.

Cole surged forward to catch Rachel before she hit the floorboards. Her body sagged against his chest, the faint scent of honeysuckle taunting him, awakening sensations he'd long thought dead and buried. Hooking one arm beneath her knees, he hauled her into his arms and grunted at the unexpected weight. Either he'd gone soft, or his wife had gotten heavier since he'd last seen her.

The hood of her cloak fell back, and he allowed himself the luxury of a long, thorough examination. She was lovelier than he remembered. The bold, arched eyebrows framed her expressive blue eyes now closed in unconsciousness, spiky black lashes resting against creamy skin. The small, straight nose and soft, petal-like mouth that could slip into laughter at a moment's notice. Her lustrous sable hair was tucked into a neat chignon. His gaze traced her hairline, snagging on the widow's peak she'd despised but he'd secretly found attractive.

Nearly a year and a half had passed since he'd held her close. He hadn't intended on consummating their forced marriage, hadn't wanted the emotional entanglement, but he was only a man, after all. He'd held out for seven of the eight months they lived together as husband and wife. Then, in a moment of weakness, everything had changed. Those final weeks were pleasure and pain all rolled into one, and when he'd realized his wife was slowly yet steadily penetrating the walls around his heart, he bolted.

Nudging the door open with the toe of his boot, he carried her inside the dim, cool interior and laid her on the quilt-covered bed. Moving away from her, he tossed kindling into the fireplace and lit it, watching as the flare of light illuminated the one-room cabin. He didn't stop to check the place for changes. Instead, he returned to his wife's side.

Despite long, grueling work hours and a mind-numbing whirl of card games, he hadn't been able to get her out of his head. The nights were the worst. Memories of his sweet wife struck when he was most vulnerable, asleep and unable to escape, dreams of her haunting him. He hoped that by officially ending the marriage, he'd gain closure and be free of her once and for all.

Her lids fluttered open, flaring wide with apprehension when her gaze focused on him. Anger he'd expected, but fear? What cause had she to fear him?

"The baby—" She scrambled back on the bed and placed a protective hand over her chest. "Who told you?"

Every muscle in Cole's body tensed. "What baby? Are you pregnant?"

His mind reeled. He'd remained faithful to their vows and had expected no less from her. The news hit hard.

"Where's the father? Is he someone I know?" He forced himself to remain calm. He was here to dissolve their marriage, so what did it matter if she chose to have another man's child?

"Get out."

"Excuse me?"

"You heard me." Eyes shimmering with unshed tears, she jammed a finger in the direction of the door. "I don't know what brought you here, Cole Prescott, and I don't care. You can turn around and walk right back out that door. How dare you insinuate—"

At that moment a baby's lustful cry burst forth

from beneath her green cloak. Ignoring him, Rachel unhooked the clasps and shrugged out of the sleeves. There, tucked snuggly against her chest in a homemade wrap, was a baby girl. At least, he thought it was a girl. Her brown corduroy gown was trimmed in pink and yellow roses. Whispering softly to soothe the infant's whimpers of protest, she loosened the material and, freeing her, hugged her close. Seeing his wife like that did odd things to his insides.

A horrible notion struck him. "How old is she, Rachel?"

"Six months."

He started counting backward. Was it possible?

Lifting her head, she speared him with a glance. "Her name is Abigail Rose, Abby for short, and she is your daughter, Cole. If you don't believe me, ask my parents. Or Doc Owens."

He'd never known Rachel to lie. The truth was there in her face along with a dozen conflicting emotions. His knees refused to support his weight. Sinking into the rocking chair beside the bed, he tried to process the news. He had a daughter?

The realization of all he'd missed made his chest seize up. His hands fisted. "You had my address. Why didn't you contact me? You know I wouldn't have stayed away."

Rachel closed her eyes against the anguish radiating from him. He didn't deserve her compassion. He *chose* to leave. To abandon her and, in doing so, thrust her in the midst of an even greater scandal than their hasty wedding had spawned.

"I don't have your address. Never have."

"As soon as I got settled, I sent you a letter with my

information in case you needed me. You're saying you never received it?"

In case you needed me... The words chafed. What good was her husband when he was miles away? Perhaps even states away? She had no idea where he'd been, and she wasn't planning on asking.

"That's right."

Shoving to his feet, his rigid stance radiated his displeasure. His nostrils flared. "Didn't you think this kind of news warranted some action on your part? A man has a right to know he's fathered a child. You could've hired a private eye."

Abby squirmed against her, and Rachel patted her back in an effort to soothe the both of them. Resentment and hurt warred in her chest. "And you could've stuck around."

His jaw hardened to carved marble. "Rachel, I—"

"Don't bother with excuses, Cole. Just tell me why you're here."

"I came to apologize and…to grant you your freedom."

The cabin walls seemed to close in on her. Cole wanted a divorce? It was one thing for him to walk away. Quite another for him to seek her out for the sole purpose of severing their union. She felt inexplicably ill. Shouldn't she feel elated? He'd be out of her life for good. Problems solved.

"Of course, that's no longer an option." His level gaze dared her to refute him. "Now that I know about the baby, I'm not going anywhere. It appears you're stuck with me."

Chapter Two

Rachel's throat constricted as her hard-won peace slipped through her fingertips like riverbed silt. Cole's presence would change *everything.* Her quiet, ordinary life would be reduced to a fond memory. Once again, she'd be the center of gossip, a specimen under a magnifying glass whose every move would be dissected and examined. He'd subjected her to this nightmare twice before. Not again.

Hugging Abby close, she edged off the bed and backed away. "No. You can't stay." She struggled to keep the panic from showing. "Haven't you put me through enough? First you marry me because of a cruel prank, and then you disappear. No explanation, no apology. Do you realize the humiliation I've suffered because of you?"

Emotion flickered deep in his eyes. "I'm sorry. Truly, I am. If I could go back to that night at Clawson's and change things, I would. I should've sensed something was off, but my attention was all on you...." He trailed off, his lips compressing as if to stop the flow of words.

She recalled that Christmas Eve, the flare of excitement his arrival at the mercantile had spurred within her. Cole had been darkly handsome, lanky yet strong, the dancing light in his eyes a heady invitation for a girl who'd always followed the rules. The owner's nephew, Gregory Moore, and another boy had lured them there separately with the promise to show them a shipment of goods from the Orient. It had been a ruse of course. A trick to get them there together. When the boys had slipped out, shut and locked the door, their raucous laughter fading as they left, it hadn't immediately registered what lay ahead. Reality soon set in. The mercantile was closed. No one would hear their yells for help. They were stuck. Overnight. Alone together. There had been no other option but to marry.

The uncertainty, sorrow and regret of those early days rushed back to choke her. Cole had accepted his responsibility with dignified resignation. He'd expressed no complaints, no pleas for leniency. And yet, he must've found life with her intolerable. What was it, she often wondered while alone in her bed at night, that made her company so undesirable?

"The minute people discover you're back in town, the gossip will start. Then the snide comments and fake concern for my welfare, when what they really want is to glean every detail of my life so they can hash it out behind my back." A private person, Rachel loathed feeling as if she were under constant scrutiny. "Surely you don't want to face it all again. If you thought people in this town disliked you before, imagine how they feel now that you've walked out on your wife."

He looped his thumbs in his waistband and shrugged. "I can handle it."

"You're prepared for the comparisons to your father?"

He exhaled sharply. "That's exactly why I have to

stay," he ground out. "When my pa skipped town, I promised myself that I'd never inflict that same pain on any child of mine."

And what of my feelings? Hadn't it occurred to him that his leaving would hurt her? While she hadn't been foolish enough to believe herself in love with her husband, she'd begun to care for him. How could she not, considering the intimacies they had shared? They had created a child together.

Abby was growing restless in her arms, her fingers grasping at Rachel's bodice. She would want to nurse soon. Smoothing the infant's dark curls, she swayed slowly back and forth.

"You're forgetting my parents."

Lawrence and Lydia Gooding had been against the marriage from the start, arguing that their daughter shouldn't be made to marry Cole Prescott, the no-account son of accused criminal-at-large, Gerald Prescott. Their protests hadn't changed the outcome, of course. And after the wedding, they made no attempt to ease the situation, verbally attacking Cole and making it clear he'd ruined all their lives. Rachel had been placed squarely in the middle of the war, if a one-sided offense could be labeled that. Amazingly, Cole had kept his cool. Not once had he defended himself or asked her to intervene. She remembered clearly the turmoil of those days and had no wish to repeat them.

"I deserve their animosity. And yours." His guard slipped, allowing her a glimpse of sincere contrition. "Leaving you the way I did was wrong. The act of a coward. I'm sorry, Rachel."

He regretted leaving? So what?

"I don't want your empty words. What I want—no, what I *need*—is for you to walk out that door and never come back. Leave town before anyone discovers you're here."

Out of patience at last, Abby howled her displeasure at having been kept waiting.

Cole's eyes cut to the infant, his resigned expression at odds with the determined set of his chin. "I'm not in the habit of making others happy. Thought you would've figured that out by now." His movements even and efficient, he strolled to the door and grasping the top of his hat with lean, tanned fingers, settled it onto his head and glanced over his shoulder at her.

"I'll see you in the morning."

Riding through the dark, deserted mountain town, Cole was wound tight enough to snap, memories and regrets clawing at him. Rachel was right about one thing—his reappearance was gonna stir up a hornet's nest of trouble. He hadn't counted on staying, hadn't figured on seeing anyone but his wife. One night, possibly two, would've been more than enough to complete his business. Now it seemed he was here to stay.

In his heart a man plans his course, but the Lord determines his steps. The verses Ole Jeb had repeated almost daily had lodged in his soul, a reminder God was in control. *Apparently You have other plans for me, Lord.*

His thoughts turned to the dark-haired infant. Abigail. His *daughter.*

Cole's chest ached as unexpected grief swept over him. He'd missed so much. Rachel's pregnancy. Abby's birth. What if there had been complications? What if—

His gloved fingers tightened on the reins. No. He wouldn't let his mind go there. The good Lord had seen fit to protect them both, and he could only be deeply grateful.

Looking back, he'd been a fool not to question whether or not there'd been consequences to his and Rachel's actions. But his sole focus had been on escaping with his heart and soul intact. Slowly but surely, his wife had begun to breach the fortress guarding his heart. She'd started to *matter.* He'd panicked. Left before it was too late. He'd learned early on that he didn't really have a way with people, was better off alone. And thanks to his pa's duplicity, most people kept their distance.

Apparently he was a dead ringer for Gerald Prescott. Which meant, of course, that when people looked at Cole, they were reminded of the man who'd duped them. A churchgoing man who'd pretended to be a godly, upright pillar of society when he was in fact a swindler and a cheat, skimming money from the church offerings for years. The fact that he skipped town, evading punishment, had rubbed salt in the wound.

When his childhood home came into view, weathered and neglected, memories of his dear ma swirled in his head, along with a rush of bitterness and anger. When Gerald's crimes had been revealed, gentle, mild-mannered Rosalie Prescott had been appalled and ashamed, so much so that she became a recluse. The supportive friends who'd come out to encourage her gradually stopped coming. Facing everyone was too painful, and she eventually died a lonely, broken woman. All due to his father's selfishness and greed.

Dismounting, he stalked to the door, brittle underbrush crunching beneath his boots. The door hinges were still attached, but inside the shadowed interior revealed an unpleasant scene. Broken glass and soot littered the floor, chinking was missing from between the wall logs and the sour odor of rotten meat hung in the still air. A far cry from Rachel's cozy, neat-as-a-pin cabin.

For a moment, he allowed himself to wonder what life might be like if he'd stayed. Would they have somehow found happiness? Instead of passing the night alone in this ramshackle ruin, would he be holding his wife, snuggled with her in a warm cocoon of quilts?

"You're dreamin', Prescott," he muttered as he lit a cracked kerosene lamp.

He wasn't the kind of man who deserved happy ever after, nor did he believe in such a thing. The best he could hope for was a friendship with Rachel, if she would allow it, and a solid father-daughter relationship with Abigail. He wouldn't dare hope for more.

Ensconced in her rocking chair before the fireplace, sewing basket at her feet, Rachel stitched wings onto an angel's costume while a contented Abby kicked and rolled on her pallet. The few bites of breakfast she'd managed to swallow roiled in her stomach. Thoughts of Cole tormented her.

The room was quiet save for Abby's soft babble and the occasional pop and shift of the logs in the fireplace. With each breath, she inhaled the crisp, hearty pine scent emanating from the evergreen garland decorating the mantel. Handmade ornaments were tucked into the greenery, splashes of bold color against the drab grays and browns of the stacked-stone fireplace. The sparse decorations were her halfhearted attempt to revive her holiday spirit.

She hadn't bothered with a tree. What was the point? It would only serve as a reminder of her and Cole's first and only Christmas, an awkward day to be sure, two reluctant acquaintances thrown together on what was supposed to have been the most special of days. Watching as he'd hauled in a tree and helped decorate it, she'd felt as if they were playing house.

She checked the mantel clock again. Where was he? Had he changed his mind about staying? The needle slipped and pierced her skin. With a frustrated sigh, she sucked on the wound and crossed to the water basin to wash the stain out of the white material. This was a disaster!

As she draped the damp fabric over the nearest straight-backed chair, she heard the thud of Cole's boots on the porch. Her lungs constricted as a sense of unreality settled over her. Her husband was here, and he knew about their daughter. What was he planning to do? How long was he planning to stay? One night? A week? Forever?

What's happening here, God? My world has been flipped upside down, and I can't find my footing.

Smoothing the folds of her full, floor-length skirt, she sucked in a fortifying breath and pulled the door open. Cole's hooded gaze met hers. "Good morning."

Rachel's skin flushed hot despite the low temperatures. Without the distraction of shock and fatigue, she was able to take in every inch of impressive male. His dusky brown cowboy hat sat low on his forehead, in the way men who didn't want to be noticed wore them. A fawn-hued canvas duster flowed in straight lines to his ankles, beneath which peeked a pair of brown leather riding boots that appeared to be new and of fine quality. Soft deerskin gloves protected his large hands from the elements.

"May I come in?" He interrupted her inspection. His

freshly shaven cheeks held a tinge of pink, his breath puffs of white smoke in the crisp air.

Face flaming, she jerked a nod, moving back to allow him to enter. She watched silently as he removed his gloves, then deftly unbuttoned the duster and slipped it off. His lanky frame had filled out. She couldn't help but notice his thick, ropy shoulder muscles stretching taut the cream material of his shirt or the way his walnut-colored vest hugged a firm, sturdy-looking chest. His obvious strength and power drew her, made her feel irrationally safe.

But she wasn't safe with him. She had to remember that.

When he'd set his hat and gloves aside, he turned to regard her with hands on his hips and questions in his eyes. "Are you not speaking to me today?"

She clasped her hands tightly at her waist. "Of course I am." She didn't have a choice, did she? "Can I get you a cup of coffee?"

His tension eased off. "Yes, thank you."

"Have a seat at the table." She crossed to the kitchen, expecting him to follow her. Reaching for the kettle, she glanced over her shoulder and caught her breath. He'd moved closer to where Abby lay playing on the floor, his intense, uncertain expression squeezing her heart. Rachel stilled. How would he be with their daughter?

"Can I hold her?" he asked quietly.

"Y-yes, of course."

Heart in her throat, she didn't move as he crouched beside the pallet and ran a fingertip along the curve of Abby's cheek. "Hey there, darlin' girl. Can Daddy hold you?"

Big blue eyes focused on his too-handsome-for-words face, Abby burst forth with a string of gibberish.

As he reached over to scoop her up, Rachel thought she saw his hands tremble. In one swift motion he was on his feet, cradling her against his chest as he smoothed her cap of dark hair. Father and daughter took stock of one another. Then, with a sigh, she rested her head against his shoulder and snuggled closer. His gaze shot to Rachel's.

The pained wonder in his eyes cut deep. Remorse dripped into her veins. She should've done *something* to try to find him. She could've asked around, searched for clues as to where he may have been headed. Or, as he'd suggested, hired someone to track him down. Only now did she understand that in keeping Abby's existence a secret, she'd aimed to hurt him. The same way he'd hurt her.

Whirling around, she fought to keep the tears from flowing over. She refused to lose control in front of him. Focused on pouring water into the kettle, she jerked when she heard his step directly behind her. Water splashed onto the work surface.

"There are some things I'd like to know."

His velvet voice wrapped around her like a warm quilt. His body heat radiated outward. For a split second, she forgot everything except the loneliness. The ache to be held. She very nearly leaned back against him. Thank goodness her sanity returned before she gave in to the impulse. Cole Prescott was not the man to offer her comfort or anything else.

Snatching a towel from the row of knobs above the dry sink, she wiped up the spill and set the kettle on to boil. "Like what?"

"How did you fare during the pregnancy?"

Startled, Rachel swung around. "What?"

He shifted his stance, uncomfortable but clearly

wanting answers. "I've heard pregnant women are sometimes very ill, and I was wondering if you had been."

"I experienced some mild nausea," she reluctantly admitted.

"Any fainting spells?"

"No."

His sun-browned hand spanned Abby's back as he cradled her close to his broad chest. Already she could sense his protectiveness, his paternal pride. She had to admit, her husband and daughter looked natural together.

His voice deepened. "Tell me about her birth."

She lowered her gaze to the floor. That was too personal a matter to discuss with a man she hadn't seen in nearly a year and a half. "Ask anything you want about Abby. She's your daughter and you deserve to hear about her. But you forfeited the right to know anything about me the minute you walked out that door, so I'd appreciate it if you didn't ask me anything more."

"I regret not being here for you," he said in a pained whisper. "If I could go back—"

"Well, you can't," she blurted, raw inside and out remembering how frightened she'd been that night her water broke. All alone, the pains coming faster and harder…

Despite everything, she'd called out for him. Longed for her husband's familiar presence, his strength and quiet assurance.

When she felt the warm pressure of his hand on hers, her lips parted and her gaze shot to his face. Cole rarely initiated physical contact. No doubt living with rejection had made him reluctant to show affection.

"Did you have someone here with you? At least give me that much."

Drowning in his hazel eyes brimming with concern, she slowly nodded. "My mother came to check on me, and she found me…."

"Thank the Lord."

Again, she was speechless. Cole hadn't attended church in all the years she'd known him. And not once had she seen him read the Scriptures or bow his head to pray. So what—

A sharp rap on the door shattered the silence.

He dropped his hand and stepped back. "Expecting anyone?"

"No."

She circled the table and walked to the door, relieved at the interruption. That exchange had been too intense for her peace of mind. Her relief died a rapid death when she pulled open the door and found her mother standing on her porch. She was not ready for this.

"Mother, what are you doing here?"

Lydia wrenched her hands together, her brow deeply furrowed beneath her black bonnet. A covered basket was looped over her left forearm. "I just came from Clawson's. I overheard Lucille and Mr. Moore talking about a stranger in town." Her brown-black eyes shimmered with worry. "A man they say bears an uncanny resemblance to that no-account husband of yours."

Rachel blocked the doorway, but she had no doubt Cole could hear every word spoken. She had to get rid of her mother without alerting her to his presence.

Lydia stepped forward and patted her arm. "I'm sure it's a coincidence, dear. I just thought you should be aware of the talk going round." The undercurrent of worry in her voice belied her words.

"Mother, I don't mean to be rude, but it's nearly time for Abby to eat and I—"

To her dismay, Cole appeared behind her. Reaching across her shoulder, he swung the door wide and edged into Lydia's line of sight.

"Your friends were right, Lydia," he said matter-of-factly. "I arrived in town yesterday."

"You." Her mouth hung open, her eyes narrowing to angry slits. "How dare you show your face around here! And you, daughter—" her attention swung to Rachel "—what possessed you to allow him into your home?"

Frustration set Rachel's teeth on edge. The war had begun.

Chapter Three

Beside him, Rachel stiffened. Her face had leached of all color save for two fiery patches on her cheeks, and her mouth was pinched with strain. It was a familiar sight, unfortunately. Didn't her parents see that putting her in the middle upset her? In expressing their hatred for him, they caused her no end of distress.

"As you can see, Cole is getting acquainted with Abby."

"That man doesn't deserve to be a father," she spat, jabbing a finger in his direction. "He's bad seed, Rachel, the son of a swindler and cheat of the vilest kind. How can you expose this innocent child to his influence?"

Cole ground his teeth together, ruthlessly tamping down the fury churning in his gut. Perhaps sensing his turmoil, Abby began to fuss.

Rachel gasped. "Mother, please. Don't make this any harder than it already is."

"If you won't choose to use common sense, your father will." Jutting out her chin, she glared at Cole. "I'm warning you. I'm going to fetch my husband. If you're still here when he arrives, you'll find yourself on the wrong end of a shotgun."

"No!" Rachel gasped.

For the second time that morning, Cole intentionally touched his wife. He settled a restraining hand on her shoulder. Jolting from the contact, she turned to stare at him, her wide blue eyes troubled. He was stunned to see an apology there, as well.

Breaking eye contact, he leveled a look at his mother-in-law. "This is my land. My home. I built it with my own hands. Make no mistake, I will defend it and my family if necessary. You and your husband are welcome here if and *only* if you plan to be civil and watch your manners. I won't subject Abigail to your hostility."

Lydia's chin dropped, obviously stunned that he'd dared speak against her. But he refused to be bullied. If he had any chance at all to stick around and see his daughter grow up, he had to set the boundaries now. He just hoped it wouldn't cause more problems for Rachel.

"Cole," Rachel began, but her mother cut her off.

"You're nothing but trouble, no better than your pa," she found her voice. "Just you wait until my husband hears about this! And the rest of the fine folks of Gatlinburg. They'll run you outta town." Looking pointedly at his hand on Rachel's shoulder, she raised an imperious eyebrow. To Rachel, she said, "Think real hard about what you're doing."

Then she stomped away, crossing the yard and disappearing on the forested path that connected the two properties. Rachel shivered. In the heat of their conversation, the cold had failed to register. He dropped his hand and, urging her inside, shut the door and lowered the latch.

She stopped in the middle of the room, shoulders slumped. She looked lost. Defeated. Brushing past her, he placed the baby on her pallet and gave her a toy. Then he went to stand before Rachel.

Dressed in a high-collared lilac blouse and royal purple flower-print skirt, she was a delicate bloom in the midst of a colorless winter. The floral scent clinging to her hair and skin unearthed forbidden memories. Memories best forgotten if he wanted to maintain his sanity.

"Talk to me." During those first months of marriage, he'd shied away from any deep conversations, fearful of both revealing his own emotions and caring about hers. But he was fighting for the right to raise his child, and he'd do anything to make that happen.

A spark of anger flared in her eyes. Flipping her long ponytail behind her back, she jammed her fists on her hips. "*Your* land, huh? You're awfully territorial for a man who abandoned his wife and home, aren't you?"

"And what would you prefer me to do?" he asked evenly. "Stand idly by like I did before?"

"No. I..." Her brows drew together. "Can't you see? I don't want this...this turmoil in my life. Like everybody else, my parents have their faults, but they want what's best for me and Abby. If it weren't for their support, I don't know how I would've made it through the past year and a half. I don't want to hurt them."

"And yet, they're hurting you by putting you in this position."

"They don't trust you, Cole. And neither do I."

"Considering my actions, that's only fair." He deserved her anger and mistrust. He'd certainly earned it. Still, he cringed at the words. "Look, the last thing I want is to cause more trouble for you. I came here to release you from our commitment, remember?"

She stilled, her expression unreadable, her eyes watchful.

"But that little girl over there changes everything," he went on. "She deserves to grow up knowing she's loved by both her parents. Somehow, we have to find a way to make this work. 'Cause I'm not going anywhere. I won't abandon my daughter."

Hours later, Cole's words beat a steady rhythm in her head, the finality and conviction with which he'd spoken a clear sign he meant to follow through. He wouldn't be swayed on this, she knew. Not after the childhood he'd endured. *Can you blame him for wanting to be a part of his daughter's life?* an unwelcome voice prodded her. *You should be thankful.*

Thankful? That was a tall order considering that at this very moment, the news of his homecoming was surely spreading like wildfire through the town. She shuddered.

"What are you thinking about?"

Rachel looked up from her sketch. Megan sat beside her on the pew with her own paper and pen. Together they were compiling a list of props they needed for the pageant. A tiny worry line appeared between her pale brows.

Rachel heaved a sigh. "Cole has returned."

Megan's gaze shot to Abby, who was practicing rolling from side to side on her pallet in the aisle. "Does he know about…?" Her big blue eyes filled with compassion.

"Yes."

"And?" The blond-haired beauty appeared to hold her breath.

"He vows he's home for good. For Abby's sake," she tacked on.

"He wasn't angry?" she asked, surprised.

"He was at first. He was under the impression that I had his address. He claims to have sent me a letter a couple of months after he left, but I never received it."

"I wonder what happened to it."

She shrugged. "It could've easily gotten lost."

"How do you feel about all this?"

"I'm not sure." At present, her emotions were an impossible tangle. "His being here will make things difficult. At least he's staying at his ma's old place across town. I don't believe I could handle having him around day and night."

"Do you—" She broke off and shook her head, her curls dancing about her face. "Oh, never mind. It's none of my business."

"Whatever it is, you can ask me. We're friends, remember?"

Growing up, Rachel had had lots of friends. But that was before the scandal, before her marriage to the town outcast. Megan was one of a handful of confidantes who'd remained loyal. She trusted her implicitly.

"In the beginning, I got the impression you were fond of him. I was wondering if those feelings ever changed…if you love him."

No. Of course she didn't. He'd made that impossible, maintaining cool distance between them, his steadfast reserve impossible to breach. Only near the end, in the quiet of night, had she experienced any sense of closeness with her husband. Cole had stunned her with his tenderness, the ease with which he made her feel like the most desirable woman on earth. When he left, she banished those memories. They were too painful.

"You don't have to answer," Megan rushed to say. "I can see it's a difficult subject."

"It's all right," she started, only to halt when the church door creaked open.

Both women twisted in the pew to glance back at the alcove. Heavy thuds on the floorboards sounded seconds before an imposing figure turned the corner. Cole's dark gaze found hers and held.

Her pulse jumped as she stood to her feet. "Cole." What was he doing here? In church, of all places?

His gaze slid reluctantly to her companion for a split second before returning to her. "I saw your horse outside—" he jerked a thumb over his shoulder "—and thought I'd stop in."

"Oh. Well. Megan and I were working on the plans for the Christmas Eve presentation." She motioned to the younger woman standing beside her. "Cole, you remember Megan O'Malley, don't you?"

His hat in his hands, he slowly advanced, his guard up. "Yes, of course. Pleasure seeing you again, Miss Megan. I trust you and your family are well."

The O'Malleys were one of a handful of families who hadn't lumped Cole in with his pa. Instead, they'd gone out of their way to be kind.

Megan's smile was genuine. "My family is doing exceptionally well, thank you. We've recently had two weddings. Juliana and Josh are both married now."

Sincere pleasure lit his eyes. "Is that right? I look forward to seeing them again."

"Juliana lives in Cades Cove with her new husband, but Josh and his wife are here. Kate is from New York, and she's the sweetest thing. Wouldn't you agree, Rachel?"

"Indeed, she is." Her thoughts were a jumble as she was still trying to reconcile his presence in this house of worship.

He nodded to their sketches visible on the pew. “How are the plans coming along?”

When Rachel didn’t answer right away, Megan tossed her a curious glance and answered, “Rachel has the costumes well in hand, however, we don’t have any props yet. We need a volunteer to build the larger set pieces.”

“What kind of props?”

“A stable and a manger, for starters.”

He addressed Rachel. “I can do it.”

“You?” Her brows shot to her hairline.

His shoulder kicked up. “I’ve had a lot of experience working with my hands. Building things.”

Not for the first time, she wondered what type of work he’d been doing while he was away. From the looks of his tanned skin and bulked-up frame, it must’ve involved manual labor. Probably outdoors. Not that she planned on asking.

Megan didn’t appear to have any reservations. “Thank you, Cole! We appreciate your willingness to help.” She handed the sketches to Rachel. “Would you mind going over the particulars with him and answering any questions he might have?”

That would mean spending time with him, something she wanted to keep to a minimum. But how could she refuse without seeming petty?

“Uh, sure. No problem.”

Slipping a timepiece from her skirt pocket, Megan frowned as she examined the face. “It’s later than I thought.” She snapped the lid shut and replacing it, began gathering her things. “Nicole’s working on yet another dress, and I promised to help her with the lace trim.” Moving into the aisle, she cooed a sugary farewell to the baby. Then she smiled up at Cole. "Thanks again. And it's really nice to have you back."

"I'm happy to do it," he murmured with his gaze lowered, clearly unaccustomed to such warmth.

"See you in the morning, Rachel," she called as she swept around the corner.

The door thudded closed and, in her wake, uncomfortable silence blanketed the spacious room. He cleared his throat. "I see there's a new café in town. Do you want to discuss the projects over coffee?"

He wanted to take her to Plum's? Smack in the middle of town? Where prying eyes would watch their every move? She could just imagine the reaction. *"No."*

His dark brows drew together at the alarm threading through her voice.

She rushed ahead. "I—I mean, no, thank you. I'm sure we'd get much more accomplished at the cabin. I can make coffee or tea or even hot cocoa, if you'd like."

"Whatever makes you happy."

He said it without a trace of sarcasm, but she sensed he knew the real reason she'd discarded his suggestion. Well, too bad. He wasn't the one who'd been cast aside, unwanted and pregnant, pitied by most and ridiculed by others. No. He'd gone off to the land of sunshine and freedom, wherever that was. He'd gotten a fresh start, while she'd been left to deal with the shattered pieces of her life.

Happy. What was that? Acceptance was a more reasonable goal. Now that he was back, she wondered if she could hold on to even that much.

"Give me a moment to gather Abby's things."

Cole strode forward, his reserve slipping as his focus shifted to his daughter. Rachel paused to watch as, setting his hat on the seat, he scooped her up and held her suspended in the air inches from his face. Abby giggled. His wide grin, the unabashed delight spreading across his face, sucked the air from her lungs. She stood transfixed. Here was a rare glimpse of the man behind the mask. The power and truth of the moment twisted something deep inside and she longed to be included, to share in his joy. To be the *source* of that joy.

But that was a schoolgirl dream. She was rooted firmly in reality. There'd be no happy endings for her.

Deliberately turning away, she picked up her cloak from where she'd draped it over the pew back and wrapped it around her shoulders. Keeping her gaze averted, she brushed past Cole and bent to fold the blankets into a neat bundle.

"Do you need a hand?"

The subdued quality of his voice indicated he had his guard firmly back in place. A depressing thought.

"I have everything," she retorted, angry at herself for wanting the impossible. She stood too quickly and black spots danced before her eyes. She swayed.

He was at her side in an instant, his hand gentle on her arm, his gloved fingers warm through her thin cotton blouse. "Are you all right?"

He smelled of leather and fresh air. In choosing not to look up, she was confronted with his wide, capable-looking chest, the firm expanse inviting her to rest her head and surrender her troubles. Jerking her arm from his grasp, she stepped back.

"I'm perfectly fine." Was that breathless voice truly hers?

"Rachel, do you not want my help with your play? Maybe I should've asked before I volunteered. I know this isn't easy for you."

She looked up then, into his beautiful hazel eyes,

searching for hidden meaning. Did he know how his touch affected her? Feeling heat climb into her cheeks, she fervently hoped not. Not only was it embarrassing, it was irrational. Not to mention irresponsible. This man was adept at wreaking havoc in her life.

She was tempted to answer truthfully, that she was not okay with this, but no one else was stepping forward to help out. Time was growing short. If they wanted to have a play, they needed those props.

"The important thing is that the children have what they need." She held out Abby's coat. "Do you mind holding her a minute longer while I put this on?"

"Sure." He held the baby securely in the crook of his arm, slightly away from his body.

Like most babies, Abby didn't relish being dressed. As Rachel attempted to slip the coat on her without getting too close to Cole, Abby squirmed and stiffened her arms, her small face creasing in protest. At last, Rachel managed all the buttons. Moving quickly, she tugged the dainty white cap down over her dark curls.

"There."

When she stepped back, Cole was staring at her with quiet approval. "You're good with her."

The unexpected praise warmed her inside and out. Every woman needed to hear that sometimes, that someone appreciated her hard work and thought she was doing a good job. To hear it from Cole made it that much more meaningful.

"Thank you," she murmured, gathering her belongings from the seat. "Shall we go?"

He motioned with his free hand. "After you."

Exiting the church, she prayed for fortitude. She was a lonely woman, and her husband's very presence drew her, his obvious strength and physical beauty a distraction from her goal. No matter what, she must always remember the grief he'd inflicted. She wasn't certain what their future held, but she knew this—she would not grant him the power to hurt her ever again.

Chapter Four

Sitting at Rachel's table, Cole drained the last of his coffee while balancing Abby on one knee, his left arm curled around her middle to keep her steady. Her chubby little hands, damp from sucking on them, opened and closed over his fingers. Lowering his face, he pressed a kiss to her curls and inhaled her sweet scent. His daughter was warm and wriggly and wonderful. Love like he'd never known expanded in his chest.

But along with the giddy feeling came a powerful urge to protect her from all of life's sorrows. He wanted to be here for his daughter, to kiss away her hurts and guide her to make better choices than his own. Somehow, he had to convince Rachel that his sticking around was for the best. Their daughter's well-being was priority.

Lifting his head, he caught his wife's wary gaze. She'd been reserved and aloof this past hour, almost businesslike in her instructions. He guessed it was because—like him—she was affected by their close proximity and it frightened her. He'd witnessed the flash of longing in her eyes when he'd touched her, a longing that mirrored his own. They were husband and wife, both of them lonely. She was wise to keep her distance. He prayed he would be wise, as well.

Cole didn't want to do anything to mess this up. One wrong move, and she'd bar him from their lives.

He despised himself for hurting her. He'd been selfish, thinking only about his own need to escape without considering how his leaving would affect her. He wouldn't do it again.

"I should get going."

Scooting back his chair, he rose and crossed to Abby's pallet. But when he lowered her, she arched her back and cried out in protest. He tossed a confused glance at Rachel. What now? He had zero experience with infants.

Rachel rose and placed their empty cups in the dry sink. "I'll take her. She's probably getting hungry."

When he'd delivered her into her arms, he stepped back, reluctant to leave. However, it was nearing supper time, and she hadn't offered an invitation to share the stew simmering on the cook stove. Cold beans, cornbread and mind-numbing solitude waited at his ma's cabin.

Beside the door, he shrugged into his duster. "I'll stop by the lumberyard first thing Monday morning for the supplies." His fingers made quick work of the buttons. "Will I see you in church tomorrow morning?"

Her brow furrowed. "Church?"

He paused in pulling on his gloves. "Yes. Are you going?"

"Y-yes. You, ah, attend services now?"

Plunging his fingers into the soft deerskin, he tugged the gloves up and over his wrists, then looped his thumbs in his waistband. "About two months ago, I got real sick. Since I don't have much patience with lying about, I continued to work until one night, I collapsed in the street. An old man by the name of Jebediah Olsen found me and took me in and nursed me back to health."

Rachel's blue eyes grew dark with needless worry, trembling fingers covering her mouth. That she cared about his suffering filled the empty spaces in his heart.

"During my recuperation, Ole Jeb read the Scriptures to me. Day and night, he read whether I wanted him to or not. I was irritated at first, but gradually the words began to sink in." Recalling Jeb's stubborn kindness, he couldn't help but smile. "I realized that without God's help, I'd never become the man I wanted to be. I'm a believer now. What you'd call a Christ follower."

Moisture flooded her eyes as a glimmer of a smile tilted up her lips. "I'm thrilled for you, Cole."

"I'm just glad God placed me in Jeb's path. I wouldn't be here if it weren't for him."

"I don't understand."

"I told him about you. He encouraged me to come and see you one last time. Although I knew it wouldn't make up for my behavior, I wanted to apologize in person. I intended to release you from any obligation to me. I didn't think it fair for you to be bound to me for a lifetime, not when this marriage wasn't what either of us wanted."

Rachel's lashes swept down, hiding her eyes. Her skin was pale, her lips colorless. What was she thinking?

"Can you understand why I can't follow through with it? Why we need to try again?"

"*I'm* not the one who stopped trying!" She bristled, her slender form quivering with suppressed fury. "I had every intention of honoring my commitment to you. Unlike you, I took my vows seriously. I've had no say whatsoever in this marriage, no choice. Well, that's changed. The past year and a half has shown me that Abby and I can make it just fine on our own. We don't need you."

He flinched. "You're wrong. Abigail needs a father."

"A father who is steadfast and trustworthy. A father who will never, ever abandon her. You aren't that man, Cole."

Closing his eyes against the accusation and disappointment in her expression, he fought to tamp down the roiling sickness in his gut. No stranger to rejection, he'd developed thick skin over the years. And while Rachel had every right to feel this way, it still stung to hear her voice the words.

The tension in the room made it difficult to breathe. When Abby started to cry, Cole settled his hat on his head and stepped to the door. Setting his jaw, he challenged her with his gaze.

"We'll finish this conversation later." He hesitated in the open doorway. "Just a warning. I won't give up easily."

The bitter wind buried its icy fingers beneath the collar of his duster, and he shivered. In his haste, he'd forgotten his neckerchief, and his skin prickled from the exposure. His ma's place was on the opposite side of town, about five miles from Rachel's. With nothing to distract him from his thoughts, the ride seemed interminably long.

What did you expect? A welcome-home party? You're lucky she didn't shoot you on sight.

He had to make her see that he meant business. He wasn't going anywhere, not when his daughter needed him. Rachel was reacting out of hurt, refusing to see the truth of the situation. Time was his ally. Luckily, he had plenty of that.

Moonlight illuminated the trail. High above the valley, it glistened on the snow-covered peaks of Mt. LeConte. The shadowed forest on either side of him stood silent, frozen.

On alert, his searching gaze swept his surroundings, unable to penetrate the gloom. He kept one hand on the reins and one on his hip, in close proximity to his weapon, the remainder of the way home. He breathed a sigh of relief when the old cabin's dark outline loomed before him.

Dismounting, he jerked at the clicking sound of a gun hammer.

"Turn around," a man barked the command, "and keep your hands in the air."

Cole did as he was told, his mind scrambling to formulate a plan. Whatever this man wanted, it couldn't be good.

Make that two men. On horseback. Both masked, hats pulled low to hide their eyes, guns trained on his chest. If they wanted money, they were out of luck. He kept the bulk of it in the bank.

"What can I do for you, gentlemen?" He drew out that last word, letting them know his true opinion of them.

"Cut the sarcasm," the larger man snarled, "and toss your weapons over here. Nice and slow."

Cole had a good ear for voices and this man's sounded vaguely familiar. Were they passing through? Or worse, locals?

Jaw locked in anger, he carefully removed his pistols and tossed them to the ground. *I could use some help here, Father.*

"What do you want? Money?" he snapped, his blood beginning to boil.

The larger man laughed, but it wasn't a pleasant sound. "We don't want your filthy money," he spat. "What we want, Prescott, is for you to hightail it outta here. You're not fit for the fine folks of Gatlinburg. You made a big mistake showing your face around here again."

This was not good. He'd expected resistance in the form of dirty looks, threats and maybe even a fistfight if someone forced him to it. But this…what were their intentions? To scare him? Or something more sinister?

"And if I don't want to leave?"

The man doing all the talking hesitated. "We can do this the easy way or the hard way. It's up to you. Either way, you *will* leave." He looked to his silent companion and jerked his head in Cole's direction. The other man got down off his horse and advanced on him, gun outstretched.

Cole's heart thudded wildly. What now? Rachel's lovely face swam before his eyes. He would never get a chance to prove he'd changed….

"Turn around."

"You don't wanna do this," he forced out, panic climbing up his throat and closing off his airway.

In response, the man seized his shoulder and spun him around. The next instant, blinding pain exploded in his skull and he fell facedown in the dirt.

He wasn't coming.

The piano music was starting, and Reverend Monroe was approaching the podium, motioning for everyone to stand and join in the singing of hymns. Rachel glanced over her shoulder once again at the doors. No sign of him.

Beside her, her mother intercepted the look and arched a disapproving eyebrow. Rachel faced forward again and sang the familiar words, her heart not in it. Why couldn't he have stayed away? Her life was so much simpler without him in it.

What bothered her was that ever since he'd announced his intentions of attending the service, she'd half hoped he wouldn't show. She felt guilty about that. He had the right to worship the same as everybody else. Yet now that he wasn't here, she experienced a sliver of worry. An irrational one, considering he wasn't someone she should count on to keep his word.

He might've slept late. Or maybe he decided he wasn't up to facing everyone just yet.

Even now, as everyone stood singing, she witnessed half a dozen curious glances. No doubt they were wondering if the rumors were true. Anticipating the convergence of *concerned* folks following the sermon, she considered slipping out during the closing prayer. Why couldn't everyone mind their own business?

The sermon passed in a blur. She didn't hear a word of it, her untamed thoughts swirling round and round in her head like snowflakes tossed by the wind. Every time she looked at her precious daughter, asleep in Lydia's lap, her conversation with Cole rose up to accuse her.

You're wrong. Abigail needs a father.

His determination hadn't affected her so much as the hint of pleading in his dark eyes, the desperation he fought to mask. He clearly adored Abby and longed to be a part of her life, longed to be a father to his child as his own father had not been. But was it wise?

What if she agreed to give him a second chance and then six months or a year or three years down the road he decided he wanted out? What then? Abby would be crushed. *And so would you,* an unwanted voice pointed out. *Just like last time, only worse.* There was no way she could spend that amount of time with him and not lose her heart. She wasn't willing to take that risk.

Oh, Father God, I'm so confused. I don't know what to do. Please give me wisdom. Guide me in the decisions I'm facing.

When everyone stood for the closing prayer, Rachel couldn't help herself. She escaped outside and went to wait at her parents' wagon. Shivering in the cold, she extracted her black leather gloves from her reticule and put them on, eyeing the canopy of white clouds hovering above.

"Rachel Prescott," her mother admonished as she drew near ten minutes later, Abby still asleep and tucked against her shoulder, "what on earth were you thinking? Sneaking off like that? People will assume you have something to hide."

Behind Lydia strode her father and younger brother, Stephen. While Lawrence looked disapproving, Stephen's expression was one of compassion. A thoughtful, mature twenty-year-old, he hadn't once spoken against Cole.

The church doors swung open and people began to trickle out.

"Can we please leave? I don't feel up to answering questions today."

Lawrence's lips curled. "If Prescott had stayed away, you wouldn't have to deal with any of this."

Taken aback by the venom in his voice, Rachel could only stare. This wasn't mere outrage over his son-in-law's treatment of his daughter, this was outright hatred. Unease slithered through her veins, and she wished she hadn't accepted their dinner invitation. No doubt the conversation would be unpleasant.

"Not here, Lawrence," Lydia admonished as Stephen tied Rachel's horse to the back of the wagon. As they rolled past the church, Rachel was acutely aware of the stares and whispers aimed her way. She lowered her gaze to her lap and wished her father would urge the team to go faster.

Dinner was indeed a disaster.

Her father's twenty-minute tirade chased away her appetite. She picked at her food, silent while he and her mother lamented the injustice of her life and argued what her next move should be. From under the table, Stephen nudged her foot. She glanced across the table and caught his sympathetic smile. His attempts to redirect the conversation had failed miserably.

Tuning them out, she exhausted all the possible reasons for Cole's absence.

She felt a finger on her sleeve. "Divorce him."

"Mother!" Rachel gaped at her, stunned at the suggestion. "I can't do that! What would everyone say?"

Besides the fact that divorce was frowned upon, it was so very…final. A divorce would sever forever all her ties to Cole. And yet, that's exactly why he came back to Gatlinburg. To rid himself of her.

Her father swiped a napkin across his mouth and smirked. "It won't come to that."

All eyes turned to him. Despite the gray hair and creases in his face, Lawrence Gooding was a vigorous, healthy man. Large-boned and well muscled, he could still do the work of two. Rachel loved and respected him, but she couldn't claim to know him all that well.

He wasn't one to talk about his feelings or invite others to do so. He tended to keep people at arm's length.

Much like her husband.

She stifled a sigh. She'd desired so much more for her own marriage.

"Why do you say that, Lawrence?"

Tossing his napkin on his scraped-clean plate, he leaned back with a huff of satisfaction. "I'm certain that once Prescott figures out how unwelcome he is around here, he'll leave on his own. Rachel will be rid of him for good."

She shook her head. "I'm not so sure he cares what people think. He's adamant about being a part of Abby's life."

His pale gaze hardened. "You're that girl's ma. Refuse him the right to see her."

"That's not exactly fair—"

His meaty fist struck the table with such force, the dishes rattled. Rachel jumped. Seated in her high chair, Abby's lower lip folded down in a whimper.

"You've always been too softhearted!" His voice rose. "That blackguard walked away from you and never once looked back. Tell me, was that fair?"

Her patience stretched thin, Rachel realized the conversation was futile. In his current mood, her father would not be reasoned with.

Rising, she began to clear off the table. "It's time for me to nurse Abby."

Lydia rose to help. Disgusted, Lawrence scraped back his chair and stomped outside, slamming the door behind him. Stephen scooped up the baby and handed her to Rachel.

"Go. Take care of her. I'll help Ma clean up."

She managed a tight smile. "Thank you."

By the time she'd finished nursing Abby, Rachel had made up her mind to go and see Cole. Just to make sure he was all right. She wouldn't know a moment's peace until then.

Not wanting her parents to know her destination, she rode over to Megan O'Malley's farm, where she lived with her widowed mother, Alice, and her sisters, Nicole, Jessica and Jane.

"I know it's short notice," she said when Megan came to the door, "but would you mind watching Abby for an hour? I have an errand to tend to."

Smiling, the blonde reached out to take the baby. "Of course not. I can show little Miss Abby the new kittens in the barn." Settling Abby on her hip, her smile turned impish. "Would this errand have anything to do with Cole?"

Rachel blushed. "He was supposed to be at church this morning. I'm just going to see if everything is all right."

Her friend turned thoughtful. "I see. Well, don't rush." She addressed Abby. "We're gonna have fun together, aren't we, princess?"

Grinning in response, Abby jammed her fist in her mouth. Rachel reached out and caressed her downy soft cheek. "I'll be back soon, sweetheart."

Thanking Megan again, she mounted her horse and headed in the direction of the Prescott homestead, conflicting emotions coursing through her. This was a fool's errand. Cole would probably enjoy a good laugh at her expense. But she pressed on until she approached the run-down cabin on the outskirts of town.

Tucked deep in the forest, the Prescott place felt isolated and abandoned, dead vines engulfing much of the dilapidated structure. Expectant silence hung in the motionless air as Rachel swung her leg free and dropped to the ground. A parade of towering tree trunks spread out in all directions, the hard forest floor scattered with decaying leaves and moss. She shivered beneath her green wool cloak.

Rachel was not fond of winter, of the deadness and desolation. Nevertheless, without it there'd be no spring, no glorious rebirth.

Tucking loose strands beneath her bonnet, she rapped sharply on the door, her pulse jumping when she heard a soft, "Just a minute." The curtain at the window flickered.

Cole pulled the door open and, leaning his weight against it, stared blankly at her.

"Rachel?"

His normally golden skin had a pasty tinge. Sweat darkened the hair at his temples. And his clothes, the same from yesterday, looked as if he'd slept in them.

"I was worried when you didn't show up to services." Annoyance made her tone sharper than normal. Had he been drinking? He hadn't touched a drop of alcohol in the time they were together, but who knew what bad habits he'd picked up in the time he'd been away?

Foolish, foolish, foolish. Worrying about this man was a waste of energy.

"Forget it." She turned to go. "I can see you simply changed your mind."

"Rachel, wait," he called out, "I'm sorry."

The instant he let go of his knuckle-tight grip on the door, he swayed forward, his mouth twisting in pain. She rushed forward to catch him. Only he was a good six inches taller than she, and made of solid muscle. "Cole, what's wrong?" She panted, gripping his shoulders and struggling to keep him upright.

He sagged sideways against the door frame, his right hand going to the back of his head. He winced. When he pulled his hand away, Rachel gasped in horror. Blood stained his fingers.

"What happened to you?" she cried, fingers twisting his shirt.

But he didn't answer. His lids drifted closed and his head lolled back.

Rachel screamed as he slipped from her grasp and collapsed, unconscious, on the floor.

Chapter Five

Pain ricocheted through his skull. Cole struggled to force his lids open as frantic hands clutched his chest. Rachel was moaning. Or wait. Was that him? Another low moan rumbled through his chest. Definitely him.

"Cole, talk to me."

He felt her cool hand on his cheek, her sweet cinnamon breath fanning across his mouth. He opened his eyes. Rachel hovered over him, her bonnet askew and dark tendrils skimming her pale cheeks. Her eyes were huge in her face, turbulent waves of blue. Fright marked her features.

Gratitude seeped into his soul. In that awful moment before his attacker struck, he'd feared he'd never see her again. He'd been drifting in and out of consciousness ever since. Sometime during the night, the cold had forced him up and inside the cabin.

"I'm all right," he tried to reassure her as he attempted to sit up, "just light-headed."

"You're not all right, you're bleeding!" Gripping his shoulders, her hands possessed both strength and gentleness as she assisted him into a sitting position.

The movement sparked a fresh wave of nauseating

pain radiating outward from the gash in his head. He stiffened, clamping his eyes closed as breath hissed between clenched teeth.

"I know you're hurting," she said on a ragged whisper. "But I need to take a look at that injury. You might require stitches."

He didn't want anyone anywhere near his head, but she was right. It must be tended to.

"Fine. Where do you want me?"

When she hesitated, he risked a glance at her. Even, pearly white teeth worried her full lower lip. "Do you think you'd be okay sitting in that chair? Or do you need to lie down on your stomach?"

"The chair."

"You won't pass out again?"

"I can't promise anything," he drawled softly, "but I'll do my best."

Curling her arm behind his back, she anchored her hand on his waist. "We'll take this nice and slow."

With her help, he managed to stand without toppling over. A few steps later, he sank with a grunt into the lone wooden chair in the room, the only one he'd been able to salvage. The rest he'd broken up to use as firewood. The worn square table before the fireplace was nicked and scratched, but it was sturdy and that was all that mattered.

When Rachel made to move behind him, he snagged her wrist. "Are you squeamish? I doubt I'd be able to move fast enough to catch you if you were to pass out again."

"Blood doesn't bother me."

Satisfied she wasn't bluffing, he let go.

Rachel was being honest. Blood didn't bother her. What did bother her—made her sick, really—was seeing Cole suffer. Weak and pale, his body was rigid as he attempted to remain conscious.

The wound was a jagged, two-inch gash. Beneath the dried blood matting his hair, she could see a plum-size knot. A small amount of fresh blood still leaked from it.

Removing her bonnet and cloak, she went to stand in front of him in order to gauge his expression. "Who did this?"

A muscle twitched in his jaw. Behind the haze of pain in his hazel eyes, anger bloomed. "I don't know."

"You didn't see your attacker?"

"There were two of them. And no, I didn't. Their faces were covered."

Cole had been ambushed. He could've been killed! Rachel swallowed back the threatening tears. Now wasn't the time to break down. She'd deal with her emotions later. Alone. He couldn't find out how this was affecting her.

Her fingers curled into fists. "Why?"

"To welcome me to town," he snorted.

"Cole," she warned.

"They want me gone." He stared at her without blinking. "Just like everybody else."

He meant *her.* She'd made her feelings clear, hadn't she?

Unable to meet his gaze, she moved into the kitchen and rifled through the practically bare cabinets for a pot in which to boil water. When she found one, she dipped water from the barrel into it and placed it on the cook stove. But the stove was cold. As was the room, she belatedly realized.

"You need stitches, but first I need to clean the wound." Gathering kindling from the stack near the fireplace, she tossed it in the stove and lit it. "Do you want to lie down while this heats?"

"No. I'll wait." He tracked her movements with his gaze. "Where's Abigail?"

"At the O'Malleys'. Megan watches her sometimes. She's good with her."

He nodded, then winced.

While waiting for the water to boil, she gathered what cloths she could find, noticing as she did the sorry state of the one-room cabin. What had it been like when he was growing up? They had never discussed his family or his past, but she'd often wondered about both. It couldn't have been easy being judged unworthy when he was innocent of all wrongdoing, condemned to a solitary life because of his unfortunate resemblance to a man everyone despised. The condescension she'd experienced because of their abrupt wedding and his subsequent departure was nothing compared to what he must've endured.

Cole, who'd sat resting with his eyes closed while she'd been moving about, now regarded her with his dark gaze. His color hadn't improved. And a fine sheen of sweat clung to his forehead. He should be lying down, but it was futile to argue with him. One thing she remembered about her husband—he had a stubborn streak the size of this valley.

"What are you thinking?" he murmured.

She stacked the cloths on the table. "I was wondering about your father."

His eyebrows jacked upward seconds before he cleared his face of all expression. "Oh?"

"Do you believe he's guilty of everything they accused him of?"

"I don't know. Probably." He sounded resigned. "If

he did skim money for years, we didn't see any signs of it. Ma and I were constantly struggling to make ends meet. Maybe he stashed it somewhere for when he decided to make a run for it."

"Do you think he's still alive?"

His mouth flattened. "I don't know, and I don't care."

"It's not fair," she exclaimed, her chest burning with injustice, "the way this town treated you. You were *innocent*."

"I suppose they figured like father, like son. The apple doesn't fall far from the tree…isn't that what they say?"

"No!" She shook her head. "You're not like that. I know for a fact you wouldn't deceive anyone or…or take advantage of people who placed their trust in you."

He studied her, no doubt surprised by her outburst. "Not everyone treated me like dirt. The O'Malleys and the Timmons families. Reverend and Mrs. Monroe." He swallowed hard. "You."

"Me?"

"You didn't think I'd forget, did you? The times at school when you'd try to draw me into your circle of friends, inviting me to join in the games. Back then, you didn't care what anyone else thought. You saw a lonely, hurting boy and extended the hand of friendship."

Her eyes smarted. "It didn't make a difference, though, did it?" she whispered, shamed by his words. Since when had others' opinions become so all-fired important?

He took hold of her hand, squeezing gently, his thumb grazing back and forth across her knuckles. His hazel eyes glowed with tenderness. "It did to me. More than you know."

Rachel felt herself drowning in those eyes. Only

inches separated them. How easy it would be to lean forward and match her mouth with his, to get lost in his embrace…

Sucking in a breath, she slipped her hand free and took a step back. "The, um, water is boiling. I'd better get that wound taken care of."

Schooling his features, he carefully re-erected his protective shield. A small part of her experienced a stab of disappointment, wished that he'd caught her back to him. *And just what would that solve?* Getting close to him had proven disastrous in the past. Nothing had changed. If anything, the stakes were higher. She had Abby to think of now.

Cole sat silent and unmoving as she cleaned and prepared the gash for stitching. She would've liked to disinfect it with alcohol, give him a drink to dull the pain, but he didn't have any. So she worked as quickly and efficiently as possible. Only afterward did her hands tremble. She'd seen him grimace, heard that first harsh breath and his subsequent efforts to control his breathing.

"All done," she murmured, laying aside the needle and scissors. "Come, I'll help you to the bed."

"I can manage," he retorted, shoving to his feet and moving stiffly to the narrow bed. The effort cost him. His lids drifted closed as soon as he was settled on his side, his back to the wall. She noticed he hadn't removed his boots or gun belt. Was that because he lacked the energy or because he thought his attackers might pay him another visit?

Cold fear knotted in her belly. *God, please keep him safe,* she pleaded silently.

"I'll clean up here and go pick up Abby. But I'll bring a plate of food by later."

"No," he said without opening his eyes. "Too dangerous for you to be out after dark."

"Dangerous?" Her brows drew together. "I don't have enemies."

"Rachel." He did look at her then, his gaze penetrating, his voice weak yet commanding. "What happens if those men decide to come back? If you were to see them…you don't wanna give them any reason to want to silence you. I won't put you in harm's way.

"Besides," he went on before she could protest, "I'm not the least bit hungry. There's jerky and tinned fruit if I get desperate. I'll stop in at the café for a hearty breakfast first thing tomorrow."

She hated leaving him like this, but what other choice did she have? Besides, he wasn't her responsibility anymore.

When the bloodied cloths had been rinsed and hung to dry, the dirty water dumped out back, she pulled on her bonnet and cloak. Cole was asleep, so she kept her step light against the floorboards. One creaked.

"Rachel?"

She turned back. "Yes?"

"Thanks. For everything."

She nodded, determined to reinstate the formal distance between them. "I would've done the same for anyone. Good night."

"Right. Of course." Was that dejection in his voice? "Good night. Give Abigail a kiss for me."

Her foolhardy heart begging to stay, she closed the door firmly behind her and rode out before she did something she'd regret.

Cole woke the next morning with a killer headache and ferocious growling in his belly. He hadn't eaten in at least twenty-four hours. He'd slept deep and hard, a fact that bothered him. Anyone could've entered the cabin, and he wouldn't have known a thing.

Thank You, Father, for Your protection.

He managed to change his clothes and make it into town. It was early enough that the café wasn't crowded, and the patrons who were there were people he didn't recognize, possibly just passing through. As he attacked his breakfast with gusto, cathead biscuits drowning in sausage gravy, fried potatoes and light-as-air eggs, he pondered his predicament. Who were those men? And how far were they willing to go to run him out of town?

Other unknowns troubled him. Were they working alone or were there more? It was certainly possible. The nature of his father's crimes had created deep-seated hatred. For years, Gerald Prescott had deceived everyone with his oh-so-holy, virtuous demeanor. That he'd stolen from the church, and in essence, *God,* made his deeds that much more reprehensible. Dirty. Evil. A wolf in sheep's clothing.

And what of Rachel and Abigail? Were they in danger because of their connection to him? His gut clenched, his fingers flexing on the delicate cup in his hands. Sipping the stout coffee, he stared unseeing out the plate-glass window overlooking Main Street. Surely no one would want to harm them. Still, he'd warn her to be on her guard. His wife had already suffered enough because of him. He wouldn't be able to live with himself if he caused her any more pain, even inadvertently.

He settled his bill with the waitress, then guided his horse down the street toward the opposite side of town where the lumberyard was situated. This time he did encounter folks he recognized. Mr. Moore, the owner of Clawson's Mercantile, out sweeping the boardwalk.

Claude Jenkins, bank proprietor. Lucille Gentry, an old schoolmate. Instead of avoiding eye contact, he boldly met their gazes and nodded friendly greetings. He was done with skulking in the shadows. He was innocent. And now, he understood, a beloved child of God.

Their stunned expressions were almost comical.

Billy Johnson, owner of the lumberyard, was clearly not happy to see him. The same age as Cole's father, he'd been one of Gerald's closest pals. Once the scandal broke, he must've been incredibly embarrassed for not having guessed Gerald's true nature.

"I heard you'd slunk back into town." He stalked around the counter and spat a stream of tobacco juice that nearly landed on Cole's boot. "I'd hoped it was just a rumor."

"No rumor." Cole stood his ground. "I need some lumber."

His eyes narrowed to slits. "I don't do business with slugs like you."

"I see." He held his temper in check, reminding himself this man's quarrel was with his father, not him. "Well," he shrugged casually, "I suppose I'll have to tell Rachel and Miss Megan there won't be a manger or stable or any other props for the Christmas pageant. The children will be mighty disappointed."

He turned to go.

"Wait," Billy growled.

Careful to keep his expression blank, he pivoted back.

"I'll sell you the lumber, but only because it's for the pageant." Displeasure radiating from his stout body, he stomped back behind the counter and snatched up a pen and piece of paper. "And don't think I'll do business with you for any other reason. This is a one-time-only deal."

Cole gave him the list of supplies, not surprised when Billy quoted him an amount twice the going rate. But he didn't complain. This was for Rachel. He wouldn't disappoint her.

Because of the sound of saws and machinery, he didn't hear the approach of the man behind him. Cole jerked around when he heard the man's greeting, his hand going for the gun at his waist. Then he recognized the face and the familiar, steady blue gaze of Josh O'Malley, the closest thing to a friend Cole ever had.

He hesitated, unsure of his reception. After all, he *had* done the unthinkable and deserted his family. Josh was a family man now. He wouldn't understand Cole's desperate drive for self-preservation.

"Cole Prescott." His mouth curved in a wide grin. He extended his hand in welcome.

They shook hands, Cole swallowing back surprise. "O'Malley. How ya been?"

"Good. It's been a busy year. My cousin Juliana was married back in August. And I got hitched last month." His expression brightened, practically glowing with happiness.

"Congratulations," Cole said, meaning it. If anyone deserved happiness, it was this man. Still, he couldn't stop the wave of jealousy splashing over him. If only he and Rachel could find some way…

"Her name's Kate. She's a photographer." He gestured outside. "We have a combined furniture store and studio at the end of Main. Stop in sometime when you get a chance. She's not working today, but you'll get to meet her at the church decorating party this weekend. You are coming, right?"

He shrugged. It was the first he'd heard of it. He wondered if Rachel would want him to go or not. Probably not.

Billy interrupted with a baleful glare. "I'll be right back to take your order, O'Malley."

When he'd disappeared through the door leading to the machine room, Josh's demeanor turned serious. "He's charging you double, you know."

"I figured. But I have to have the supplies."

"I can speak to him—"

"No. That would only make things worse." He had to fight his own battles. Or, in this instance, admit defeat.

Josh's gaze turned speculative. "How's the head?"

Cole stared at him. "How did you know?"

"I was at Megan's last night when Rachel came to pick up Abby. She's worried about you."

"I'm fine."

"Any idea who did it?"

"No. Although, the larger man's voice did seem familiar. I think it's someone I know."

Josh settled a hand on his shoulder. "Whatever you need, I'm here for you. My family, too."

Cole nodded past the lump in his throat. This show of support was as rare as snow in summer. It meant a lot coming from someone he admired. And suddenly he felt the urge to confess.

"I shouldn't have left her," he pushed out. "I didn't know...about Abigail. I hate that I wasn't here for her." Bitter regret swirled in his chest. He'd failed her. "I was a fool. She got too close, and that scared the daylights outta me. I had to escape. It's not an excuse, just an explanation."

Josh nodded in understanding. "We all make decisions we later regret. The important thing is you're here now."

Billy reappeared then, wanting Cole's money and Josh's order.

When he'd paid the man, he tipped his head in silent farewell.

"See you Saturday night." Josh gave him a parting wave.

Yeah. Saturday night. He didn't share Josh's confidence. The last thing Rachel wanted was to be seen with him. If she didn't mention it, neither would he.

Chapter Six

Standing on Rachel's front porch later that morning, Cole tugged his collar up as a stiff wind whistled past. She hadn't answered his repeated knocks. His impatient gaze swept the yard and the empty woods, snagging on a flash of color just inside the barn door.

Rachel, her deep green cloak swirling around her, emerged from the shadows leading her horse, Cocoa. Her cloak gaped open at the neck, and he caught the barest glimpse of Abigail's white cap. Where were they headed? Descending the steps, his long strides closed the distance between them.

Her eyes flared wide the moment she spotted him. She jerked to a stop, her penetrating gaze engaging in a full-on, head-to-toe inspection of his body. His stomach flip-flopped.

The wind whipped her loose tresses about her face. As he drew closer, he noticed the creamy whiteness of her skin, her enormous blue eyes and cherry-red lips the only spots of color. She looked like a Christmas package. All that was missing was a red ribbon.

When he reached her, it took all his willpower and then some not to pull her into his arms and kiss her senseless. She must've sensed the danger, for she retreated a step.

"Where are you headed?" His voice came out gritty, like sandpaper.

"I was going to check on you."

He hadn't expected that. Pleasure coursed through him. "Really?"

Nodding, her eyes tightened with worry. "How are you feeling?"

"Almost normal." In truth, his head throbbed in time with his heartbeat, but it was something he could live with. At least the dizziness was gone.

"It hurts, doesn't it?" It was more of a statement of fact than a query.

Lifting his hand, he fingered loose strands away from her cheek and, tucking them behind her ear, lingered against her slender neck. She watched him warily, her unfathomable eyes neither inviting him closer nor urging him away. If only he could whisk her to a far-off place, a place where the past no longer existed, the power it held over them erased. A place of love and acceptance, joy and laughter.

That knock on his head must've done more damage than he'd previously thought.

Rachel reached up and encircled his wrist, again not moving his hand but not encouraging further touch.

"I'm fine," he exhaled. But he wasn't fine. Not really.

Loneliness and need battled with caution. This was his wife. His child. His *family.* A lifetime of solitude had created a ferocious yearning in his soul for connection, for belonging, for affection. And Cole wasn't sure if he had the energy to subdue it anymore.

Look what happened the last time you unleashed it. You hurt Rachel. Left her pregnant and alone.

Wrenching his hand away, he spun around, his chest heaving as if he'd run a mile through the woods.

"Cole?"

He felt her feather-light touch on his arm, there and then gone again.

"I'm fine," he said again. Maybe if he said it enough, he'd believe it.

The wind pushed against him, nearly knocking his hat off his head. The cold cooled his fevered mind.

Turning back, he took Cocoa's reins from her. "I came to ask a favor."

She waited for him to explain, her features wreathed in concern.

"I need a place to work." He gestured to the supplies in the back of his newly purchased wagon. "Ma's barn, or what's left of it, is almost completely caved in. Would you mind if I used yours? I went inside the other day and noticed my tools are still there."

Her brow puckered, then smoothed. "Sure."

"I won't bother you, Rachel. You won't even know I'm here." He led Cocoa in a wide circle. "Go inside and get warm. I'll get this girl settled back in her stall."

"Cole—"

He glanced back, eyebrows raised.

"Let me know if you need anything."

He nearly choked. He needed a lot. Too much. That was the danger.

Unable to speak, he nodded and headed for the barn and the safety space from her allowed. Space and solitude. Always solitude.

Leaning over the crib, Rachel tucked the pink and white blanket around Abigail's small body, careful not to disturb her. The baby had nursed fitfully, in stops and starts, unusually dissatisfied. Perhaps she'd eaten too many mashed-up carrots beforehand. But she'd nodded off quickly enough. Rachel hoped she'd have a good, long nap and wake in a better mood.

Gazing down at her cherubic face, Rachel's heart swelled anew with gratitude. There would always be sorrow associated with the memories of her pregnancy, but nothing could detract from the miracle and wonder of this tiny life. Every day she fell deeper in love with her daughter.

Cole loved Abby, too. He wanted to be a part of her life, and wasn't that only right and fair? That a father and daughter should be together?

It was like beating a dead horse, she knew, but again her mind conjured up what-if scenarios. What if Cole had been here through the entire thing? How would he have taken the news of her pregnancy? Would he have been overly protective of her, pampering her at every turn, or would he have retreated into himself, ignoring her sick spells and burgeoning belly?

An image of her husband, his large hand splayed across her belly, his handsome face struck with wonder as he felt their child move within her, flashed through her mind. Her heart twisted with anguish for what could've been.

Irritated with herself, she pivoted and approached the fire, staring unseeing into the flames. The mantel clock chimed the hour. Two o'clock. He'd been out there working for five hours. Had he stopped to eat lunch? She'd half expected him to come knocking around noon, then she'd remembered his promise not to bother her.

Worry pricked at her.

He'd been so weak yesterday. And in pain. He should be resting, not doing hard physical work. What if he passed out again? The remembered fear and uncertainty propelled her into action.

With unsteady fingers, she quickly sliced off two pieces of sourdough bread and several hunks of cheese and, together with a slice of apple pie, wrapped them in a cloth. Taking him a snack was a better sounding excuse than checking to see if he was conscious or not. After checking to make sure Abby was resting comfortably, she swung her cape about her shoulders and, closing the door softly behind her, hurried to the barn.

Lanterns cast a soft, golden glow in the corner where he was working to measure and cut the pieces for the backdrop. His back was to her, his hat discarded, offering her a clear view of his injury. The knot beneath his wound was a deeper purplish-yellow than it had been yesterday, but the gash didn't appear to be infected. A good sign.

She cleared her throat. "I brought you a snack."

He laid aside his measuring ribbon and turned around, his gaze flicking to the bundle in her hands. "Thanks. What time is it?" Dusting his palms against his pants, he strode forward to take it from her.

"Two."

"Already? Time got away from me."

Was he pale or was it the lighting? "How are you feeling?"

He paused, his gaze reproving. "You really should stop asking me that. I'm all right. Don't worry about me."

Without giving her a chance to respond, he eased down to the floor and, leaning back against the barn wall, unwrapped her food offering. Rachel sat on a nearby hay bale, her hands clasped tightly in her lap. Not worry? Easier said than done. Someone in this town wanted him gone badly enough that they were willing to resort to violence. What happened when they realized their first warning didn't have the desired effect?

"Abby's taking a nap."

"How long does she normally sleep?" he asked between bites.

"About an hour and a half. Sometimes longer."

He finished off the sandwich and turned his attention to dessert.

"Cole, those men—"

He stopped midchew, his hazel eyes growing stormy.

"What if they come back?"

Swallowing, he spoke slowly, weighing his words. "There's a good chance they will. This time, however, I'll be prepared."

His words didn't reassure her. "You can't be on guard twenty-four hours a day. What if they come while you're sleeping?"

"I'll keep the door locked and sleep with my gun. If they try to bust in or break the window, I'll hear it."

"But—"

"Rachel. We'll have to trust the good Lord to watch over us and protect us. Remember, He's got everything under control. Nothing happens without His consent."

"Yes, but sometimes He allows bad things to happen."

"Yeah, I know," he said, his tone softened, threaded with patience, "but He gives us the grace and strength to see us through the tough times." A glimmer of a smile hovered about his mouth. "That's wisdom passed on from Ole Jeb. You see, he and I had a similar conversation."

At the reference to his absence, burning curiosity temporarily shoved her fear aside.

"Where did you go?"

She wouldn't ask *why* he left. She already knew the answer to that one. Cole had found life with her unbearable. That he was willing to give it another try proved how much he loved his daughter.

His almost-smile vanished. He looked as if the topic made him uncomfortable. Dread flared in her middle. Had he done something he was ashamed of? Something unlawful?

A more depressing thought occurred to her. A year and a half was a long time for a married man to be on his own. Had Cole sought the company of a woman during his absence? Or perhaps more than one?

"I won't ask what you're thinking," he stated darkly. "From the look on your face, I doubt I'd like it."

Rachel attempted to school her features. He'd always been able to read her too well. Unfair, considering his thoughts were an unrelenting mystery to her.

Setting the remainders of his food aside, he drew his legs up and balanced his muscled forearms on his knees. He'd rolled up the sleeves of his green-and-blue-checked shirt and she could see the light dusting of hair against golden skin.

"There was an advertisement at Clawson's. Vanderbilt Shipping was looking for able-bodied men to build ships. So I headed down to South Carolina. To Port Royal. Hard labor and long hours, but the pay made up for it."

That explained his tan, his hardened, muscular body and financial security. There was no hint, however, about his non-work-related activities.

"Where did you live?"

"I shared a company cabin with a man named Lionel Jergins. It was kind of like a camp. There were roughly one hundred cabins, along with two bath houses and a large dining hall where we could eat cheap. There was a small general store, too."

He didn't seem to mind her questions, so she asked another. Not the one she really wanted to ask, but close. "What did you do during your off time?"

"There wasn't much of that, but once a week I went into town with the others. We played games. Chess. Nothing too exciting. The company warned us not to get into trouble. If we did, we'd be let go with no explanation." He turned thoughtful. "A couple of men didn't heed the warning. They got drunk. Engaged in fistfights. They were gone the next day."

It all sounded very…innocent. But it wasn't the answer she sought. *Why does it matter if there were other women? Your marriage ended the day he walked out. A divorce decree would be redundant at this point.*

"I should go and check on Abby." Irritated with herself, she rose to her feet and shook the bits of hay out of her skirt. He was at her side immediately, the heat of his body drawing her.

"Something's bothering you. What is it?"

"Nothing."

When she turned to go, he placed a restraining hand on her arm. The sizzling skin-on-skin contact, the imprint of his strong fingers on her inner wrist, hauled her down memory lane so fast it made her head spin. Cole's touch, as rare as a solar eclipse, resurrected forbidden feelings. Yearning. Affection. Love.

Love? No. Never that. Surely she was smart enough to know that loving Cole could only lead to heartache! He'd been alone too long, had learned to rely on no one else but himself. For the span of a few short weeks, she'd allowed herself to hope, to believe she was penetrating his wall of self-protection….

"Don't shut me out," he urged, his warm breath stirring her hair.

"That's unfair, coming from you," she accused, glaring up at him.

"What's that supposed to mean?"

Angry now, she wrenched her arm free. "You're the one who refuses to let me in. If I dare to get close, you retreat back into your shell. I never had a chance, did I?" To her horror, a tear escaped to slip down her cheek.

The remembered anguish and humiliation of their final month together pulsed through her body, flooding her lungs and threatening to smother her. Nothing in her life had prepared her for the emotional extremes she'd experienced with him. Like an out-of-control sled on snow-slicked hills, her hope had skyrocketed with each precious night in his arms—only to plummet with bone-jarring intensity when, time and again, he reverted to his cold, distant self with dawn's arrival. Almost as if he was two different men.

Cole reached for her, but she flinched.

"Don't."

Fleeing the barn, she thought she heard him whisper "forgive me" but that was no doubt a trick of the wind.

Cole stood rooted to the floor, unable to breathe, unable to move or even think. Rachel's pain held him in a viselike grip. He'd done *that* to her?

The headache that had been building all afternoon exploded to full strength. *Oh, Lord, I didn't realize. I didn't intend—*

He rubbed a shaky hand down his face. He should've known. She wasn't like him. His wife was compassionate, tenderhearted, sweet as maple syrup. Of course his behavior had confused her. If he, an expert at keeping people at arm's length, had been affected by their intimacy, then certainly she had been. *Idiot!* That's what he was.

He began to pace, his boots scattering the straw. Cocoa watched him with solemn eyes from her stall.

She'd hidden her true feelings from him. Until now. The expression on her face… He cringed, remembering. Her grief provoked an answering grief in him. *Her* pain caused *him* pain. And that could only mean one thing—Rachel mattered. Time and distance hadn't accomplished his purpose. As far as his heart was concerned, it was as if he'd never left. What he felt for her was not love, he was certain, but it was dangerously close.

Leave now, while you still can.

He ground to a halt. The temptation to run was strong, seductive. If he left now, never to return, how long would it take to forget her? To forget the feel of her silky soft skin against his? The impossible blue of her eyes? The texture of her hair? The airy floral scent that was hers alone? How long until the dreams stopped?

Running didn't do any good last time.

True. His wife had lodged herself in his heart and refused to leave. No matter where he went, she'd still be there. And he truly didn't *want* to leave. Not all his memories of this place were unhappy. He loved these mountains, the endless forests and streams, valleys and peaks. The abundant wildlife. The breathless beauty each season displayed.

There were people who mattered in his life. The O'Malleys. The Timmonses. The Monroes.

Rachel. Abigail.

If he concentrated really hard and was very careful, just maybe he'd be able to pull it off. Exist around her without sliding in too deep. It was perfectly natural to care about the mother of his child, right? Love didn't have to be the end result.

Caring and loving weren't the same thing at all. So why did he still feel like running?

Chapter Seven

At the decorating party that night, Rachel was preparing to eat when she sensed a change in the room's atmosphere. The quiet hum of conversations all around her faltered, stammering into acute silence. Everyone stopped what they were doing, even those who'd been dishing food onto their plates, and stared at the newcomers. Trepidation slithered down her spine. She didn't have to turn around to know who it was.

Standing just inside the alcove were Josh and Kate and, slightly behind the pair, her husband. Like an outlaw, Cole was dressed in head-to-toe black, silver-handled Colts shimmering on his hips underneath his floor-length black duster. His dark, hooded gaze dared anyone to approach him. The only thing missing was his signature scowl.

Not the best way to win over a crowd already inclined to distrust him.

Was he attempting to send a silent message to his attackers? His wary stance screamed *hands off.* Rachel quickly scanned the familiar faces. Could it be someone in this very room? She shuddered.

Megan stepped closer to her side in a show of silent support.

When her gaze returned to Cole, he was looking directly at her. Uncertainty flickered in his hazel depths. The mask slipped for a split second, revealing a vulnerability that shook her to the core. Of course. He had every right to be cautious. Experience had taught him to expect the worst.

Suddenly the gossip and speculation no longer mattered. Cole needed her.

Hugging Abby closer, she approached the trio, the tap of her boots on the wooden planks echoing in the hushed room. Cole's handsome face registered stunned surprise. Josh and Kate exchanged pleased smiles.

"Good evening, Rachel." Dark-haired, petite Kate reached out and smoothed Abby's curls. "What a doll! I declare, every time I see her, she's grown another inch."

"She has a good appetite," she murmured with a strained smile, aware their conversation could be heard by everyone in attendance. Nerves quivering, her lungs were working overtime and she felt light-headed. She hated being watched.

The second Abby spotted Cole, she squirmed and strained toward him. This past week he'd spent his days in the barn and his evenings with them. Feeding him supper was the least she could do, she'd told herself, considering he'd bought the supplies and was providing free labor. He'd quickly won the little girl over.

As Rachel transferred her to his arms, he murmured a quiet thank-you for her ears alone. Gratitude colored his husky voice. The baby splayed her chubby hand over his mouth, and he grinned down at her. Abby grinned her toothless smile in response. Rachel's mouth went dry. There was something irresistible about a strong man with a baby in his arms. Seeing Cole with their daughter never failed to stir her emotions.

The sound of papers rustling and the beginning strains of *Silent Night* flowed from the piano. Reverend Monroe urged everyone to go about their business before joining their group near the door. Whispered conversations sprang up again.

His smile encompassed them all, but he addressed Cole. “It’s good to see you here. I’d heard you were back in town and was wondering when I’d get a chance to welcome you.”

Absently rubbing Abby’s back, Cole shook his outstretched hand and nodded solemnly. “Thanks, Reverend.”

The older man curled an arm around Cole’s shoulders, his kind gaze touching on Rachel’s. “What do you say we go and fill our plates before it’s all gone? I’m determined to get a piece of the O’Malley twins’ apple crumb cake this time. I missed out at the last gathering.”

“I’m sure Jessica and Jane would make one especially for you and Carol, if you asked,” Kate interjected.

His eyes lit up. “Thanks for the suggestion.”

Then he steered Cole toward the table. Rachel followed, her gaze trained on their backs. Josh and Kate walked behind her. Megan intercepted the men and took Abby so that Cole would have his hands free.

The sheriff of Gatlinburg, Shane Timmons, appeared at her side, his somber expression troublesome. In his mid-thirties, he was a tough-as-nails, no-nonsense lawman. Married to his job. Had he come to advise her and Cole to leave?

“Evenin’, Rachel.”

“Sheriff.”

“That knot on Cole’s noggin. Was that an accident?”

"No, I'm afraid not."

His lips pursed, displeased. "Who did it?"

"He doesn't know. They concealed their faces."

His jaw hardened. "Tell Cole I'd like to speak with him before he leaves. If trouble's brewing, I need to know about it."

At her acquiescing nod, he left her side to assume post on the side of the room, his sharp gaze scanning and rescanning the crowd. At least he was a fair man. He didn't hold a grudge against Cole like so many others. Like her father.

Since that first confrontation, her parents hadn't come near the cabin. Usually, her mother came by once or twice a week. And Rachel and Abby spent every Saturday morning and Sunday afternoon at their place. She'd stayed home this morning, however, partly because of Cole's presence and partly because she'd had pies to bake for tonight. And, coward that she was, she hadn't wanted to face a lecture.

Rachel missed her conversations with her mother, missed Stephen's good-natured gibes and comforting hugs. She couldn't avoid the fact that Cole's reappearance had driven a wedge between her and her family. It hurt, but she couldn't blame him. Lawrence and Lydia hadn't ever attempted to build a relationship with their son-in-law. She had to wonder if, by not sticking up for him from the beginning, she'd made things worse.

She moved through the line, not paying attention to what she put on her plate, and followed the men to a pew. The reverend did all the talking. As she picked at her food, Rachel felt Cole's gaze on her.

It wasn't until about an hour later that she found herself alone with him. Seated on the last pew, they threaded red and gold ribbons through the evergreen garlands.

"You're awfully quiet," he murmured, his eyes on his task. "How are you holding up?"

She shrugged. "So far, so good."

"I hadn't planned on coming tonight," he said in apology. "I know you wanted to avoid a scene. But then Josh and his wife showed up and insisted I accompany them. They gave me no choice."

Determined to keep the peace, the two O'Malley families had formed a human buffer around the two of them. Even now, Megan and Nicole sat nearby playing with Abby, while Sam, Mary and Alice placed candles in the windows behind them.

Rachel couldn't help but smile, thankful for such good friends. "They are a force of nature, to be sure." At her touch on his knee, he lowered his hands to his lap and gazed at her. "I'm glad you came."

One dark brow quirked up. "I find that hard to believe."

"It's true. I've been thinking…maybe the best way to stop the gossip is to let them see us together like we are now, talking and acting normally. They'll soon realize there's nothing to talk about. Their curiosity will be assuaged."

"Perhaps you're right." Still, his shoulders were set in an uncomfortable line.

"Cole, you never gave anyone the chance to get to know you. All they remember is the surly loner with a permanent scowl on his face. Once they've had a chance to talk with you, to see you interact with Abby, they'll realize you're a normal man. Not a threat."

"I'm not sure they'll ever look at me and not see my father."

The defeat in his flat tone saddened her. "So you're not even going to try? Look, maybe if you get more involved in the community, those men will abandon their plan to run you out of town."

He covered her hand with his own, the heavy weight and warmth of it soothing. Cole's touch felt right and good.

"Hey—" he dipped his head to catch her gaze "—let me worry about that, all right? A week has passed and nothing more has happened. Maybe they decided to back off."

Rachel couldn't help but think they wouldn't give up so easily. And she was fairly certain he didn't think so, either.

"Cole—"

A commotion to their left brought both their heads up.

"What's the meaning of this?"

Her father's booming voice halted all conversation, and for the second time that night, everyone froze, their attention swinging back and forth between her and Cole and her parents.

So much for acting normal.

Beside him, Rachel went rigid. The tension radiating from her body ensnared him, spiking his pulse, his own muscles bracing for the coming confrontation. He removed his hand from hers and, setting the garland aside, stood to his feet, foolishly wishing he could spare her this humiliation.

Lawrence advanced, eyes blazing and nostrils flared, meaty hands fisted. Lydia and Stephen hung back. Out of the corner of his eye, Cole noticed Sam O'Malley move in close, ready to defend. Somewhere Josh and his brother Nathan were no doubt making their way toward them. At least he had help.

His father-in-law loomed at the end of the pew a few feet away, his disgusted gaze passing over Rachel to latch on to Cole. “You have some nerve, Prescott, insinuating yourself into this gathering as if you’ve done nothing wrong. What makes you think anything’s changed? No one wants you around. You’re not welcome here.” He glanced around, addressing the crowd. “Why are you all standing idly by while this filthy animal works his wiles on my daughter?”

Rachel gasped. Her head jerked up. “Father, please—” her face twisted in embarrassment “—don’t do this.”

Uneasy murmurs skirted the room.

“Have you forgotten who he is and what he’s done? The man is a coward, Rachel. Like his pa, he took what he wanted and walked away without a thought! It was *easy* for him to walk away from you!”

Rachel’s wide eyes shot to Cole, tears shimmering in the blue depths. Her face crumpled.

White-hot fury burned in his belly.

“This is not the place to discuss my sins,” he growled, barely reining in his temper. “Think of your daughter and granddaughter.”

“He’s right, Lawrence,” Sam O’Malley inserted, “family business should be discussed in private.”

“He’s not part of *my* family,” he shouted, his face flushing. Something wild entered his eyes. “Get out!” He lunged forward. “Leave before I drag you out by your—”

“That’s enough.” Sheriff Timmons’s voice cracked like a whip. He clamped his hand on the older man’s shoulder and hauled him backward. "If you don't calm down, you'll be the one leaving this party."

"Come on, Pa," Stephen urged. "Let's go outside for a bit. Get some fresh air."

"I'm not sticking around to watch this." He shook a finger at Rachel. "This ain't over, missy."

As the sheriff escorted him outside, conversations sprung up once again. Cole dropped to his seat beside Rachel, longing to comfort her but guessing she wouldn't welcome his touch right about now. He was the reason for her unhappiness.

"I'm sorry." Useless words, but he felt the need to say them.

Her head was bent so that he could see only the curve of her cheek. In her lap, her fingers were clenched tight, knuckles white. "I'm going outside for a few minutes," she uttered softly, "please don't follow me."

"Rachel, please—"

"Can you ask Megan to bring Abby out in a bit? I don't feel like decorating anymore tonight."

"Sure."

"Thank you."

Torn, Cole watched her leave. He felt like punching something. Outrage thrummed through his veins. How could a father do that to his child? Was the man blind? Had he not seen how much his outburst had hurt her?

Sam, whose presence he'd quite forgotten, squeezed his shoulder. "Give it some time, son. Lawrence will cool off eventually." His kind face was wreathed in sympathy.

"I'm not convinced."

"He needs time to adjust. Once he realizes you're not going anywhere, he'll have no choice but to accept your presence in Rachel and Abby's lives."

"You sound pretty sure of yourself. How do you know I won't skip town again?"

Behind the glasses, Sam's blue eyes were wise. "I can see it in your eyes. The way you look at those two, it's plain to see nothing in this world could tear you away." When Cole just stared at him, he laughed and patted his back. "If you need anything, anything at all, let me know."

Cole finally found his voice. "I appreciate that, sir."

Watching him walk away, he prayed he'd be half as good a father as Sam. The thought brought him up short. For the first time, a crack splintered his rock-solid determination to be a father to Abby. What if things didn't improve? What if the townspeople never accepted him? What kind of life could Abigail have? He'd die before he subjected her to the same kind of behavior he'd endured. The sneers and stares. The blatant snubs. Always on the outside looking in, wishing for acceptance while pretending he didn't care. He wanted far better for his sweet little girl.

Troubled, he went to fetch her from Megan. He'd take her to Rachel himself.

When he emerged from the church, she and her mother were having a heated exchange at the bottom of the stairs.

"You're tearing this family apart!" The strident accusation carried on the wind.

Hearing his footsteps, Lydia glanced up, her mouth thinning in displeasure. Sniffing as if his presence tainted the air, she spun and hurried into the darkness toward their wagon.

Cole descended the steps until he reached her, the two of them not speaking as Lawrence led his team down the lane. When they'd gone, he turned to her.

"Let me take you and Abigail home in the wagon."

"All right."

He'd been prepared to argue the point, so he hesitated at her quick acceptance. He recovered quickly, though, balancing the baby on one shoulder and taking Rachel's arm with his free hand. Once they were settled, blankets tucked around their laps, he tied Cocoa to the back and then climbed up to take the reins.

They were about a mile outside of town when he finally broke the silence. "I'm sorry you had to endure that back there. Had I known your father would react that way, I wouldn't have come."

"Please don't apologize." Though moonlight bathed her face in a pale glow, her eyes were dark, shadowed. "I'm the one who's sorry. I should have put a stop to this from the beginning. If I had, perhaps things wouldn't have deteriorated to this point."

Cole gaped. *She* was apologizing to him? "Your parents made up their minds about me long before our marriage. I doubt anything you could've said or done would've made much of a difference."

"You're my husband. They should respect that."

A husband she didn't want, he reminded himself, one she'd been forced to accept.

"I should've stood up for you, and I regret now that I didn't."

"You're their only daughter. Naturally they want what's best for you. Let's face it," he huffed grimly, "I've caused nothing but heartache for you since the night of that ill-fated party."

Averting her eyes, she tightened her hold on Abigail. "If it weren't for you," she whispered, "I wouldn't have Abby. And I wouldn't trade her for the world."

Cole's throat grew thick, his own feelings mirroring hers. Abigail was worth it all.

He desperately wanted to make her grand promises. That he'd be everything she needed him to be, that they'd be happy and their future would be bright. But he couldn't. Too many unknowns stared him in the face.

At the cabin, she didn't invite him inside, murmuring a quick goodbye before slipping inside and shutting the door in his face. He stood there, shivering not from the crisp night air but from longing and need. This was *his* home. His and Rachel's. The one he'd built with his own two hands.

He should be in there with his wife, not alone out here, and certainly not in that flimsy excuse of a cabin his ma had let fall to ruin. Defeated, the loneliness weighing heavy in his chest, he climbed back up on the seat and signaled for his team to head out.

Chapter Eight

Sunday morning, Rachel and Abby arrived at the church later than usual, both exhausted and a tad cranky. Abby had slept fitfully, eager to nurse yet fussing when she attempted to do so. Rachel put it down to an upset tummy.

"May Abby and I sit with you?"

She paused at the end of the pew, her focus pinned on Cole, alone on the back row.

Surprised pleasure flashed across his freshly shaven face as he rose effortlessly to his feet and moving aside, gestured for her sit. When she was settled, her dove-gray skirts smoothed and the baby situated on her lap, Rachel dared to turn and look at him.

He was in black again, except this morning his vest was paisley silk in rich burgundy, an elegant addition that lent him a civilized air. Her gaze surveying his close-cropped brown hair, she decided she preferred this clean-cut version of him, as opposed to the longer locks and scruffy beard he used to wear. His chiseled bone structure and strong jawline were on display, his masculine beauty no longer hidden. She inhaled his spicy aftershave. Her fingers itched to caress his smooth skin....

His hazel eyes darkened and lowered to her lips, then slowly, reluctantly, lifted back to hers. Heat flooded her cheeks, and she wrenched her gaze to the empty podium. Services wouldn't start for another ten minutes, and here she was mooning at her husband. The attraction was still there between them, an invisible, magnetic pull. Risky. Tempting.

This weakness was exactly why she'd rudely left him standing on the front porch last night, all but slamming the door in his face.

Hurting and vulnerable, she'd battled the desire to invite him inside the entire ride home. She'd been so lonely, needing comfort, but at what price? Already, her heart was softening toward him, her mind conveniently forgetting the anguish he'd inflicted. *But he seems sincere in his apologies,* the hopeful part of her pointed out. *Determined to be a part of your lives.*

No, the more realistic side insisted, *a part of* Abby's *life. Not yours. He never said he wanted you back. He came here to divorce you, remember? The only reason he's staying is for his daughter.*

Right.

"Rachel?" He leaned in close, his breath brushing her ear and charging off a riot of goose bumps along her shoulders. "Are you sure you want to sit with me? Don't get me wrong, I want you beside me. It's just that, well, I don't want another repeat of last night, and I'm sure you don't, either."

"I'm sure," she said softly. "They will have to learn to accept my decision." She hoped the consequences wouldn't be too severe or long lasting.

With a swift intake of breath, he angled his face so

that their gazes met, his burning bright and intense. "What decision? Are you saying you're ready to give me another chance?"

She froze. He looked eager and...happy. "N-no. I haven't...that is, I was referring to my decision to present a united front to the community. And to cease tolerating my parents' hostile behavior. You're right, it isn't healthy for Abby to be around that."

The flame of hope sputtered out, leaving his green-gold eyes flat and cold. "I see."

She hated hurting him, but how could she trust him? Or herself? "Cole—"

Abby wriggled in her lap and began to fuss.

"It's okay, Rachel. I simply misunderstood." Avoiding her gaze, he lifted the baby into his arms and held her against his chest, patting her back and gently bouncing her. The movement silenced her. Her fist made its way to her mouth, and she contented herself with gnawing on it.

Cole frowned. "She doesn't seem like herself today."

"She didn't get much sleep last night."

"Which means you didn't, either."

There was movement directly behind them. And then her father and mother passed them without a word, making their way up the aisle to their regular seat near the front. Stephen followed, aiming a wave and a smile their direction before going to join Lawrence and Lydia. The hushed conversations stalled as everyone waited to see if there would be another incident. But the reverend approached the podium then and, signaling his wife to start the music, led the crowd in a hymn.

Her emotions were a mess, a curious mix of sorrow and anger and longing concerning Cole and dread in regard to her parents. She found it nigh to impossible to heed the sermon, but she did catch the words about not judging others and not having a critical attitude. A coincidence? She didn't think so. She only hoped his message would have a positive effect.

By the time he concluded the services, her stomach was queasy and palms clammy. Her heart beat an uneven rhythm against her ribs. Would her father cause another scene?

Cole, perhaps thinking the same thing, quickly ushered her outside into the weak sunshine and escorted her to Cocoa's side. When she looked back at the church and saw her father strong-arming his way through the crowd streaming down the steps, she gasped in dismay. She would not escape his wrath as she'd thought.

"Do you want me to stay?" Cole asked in a strained voice.

Of course she did. But neither did she want the two men to come to blows. "No. I think it would be best if you didn't."

He gestured to a sleeping Abby. "She's pretty comfortable. I'll wait by the wagon until he's finished." Before turning away, he cast her a warning glance. "If things get out of hand, I will step in."

Rachel watched him go, praying it wouldn't come to that. *Please, Lord.*

Her father drew closer, his expression thunderous, more angry than she'd ever seen him. Her mother's drawn face appeared more worried than angry.

"I can see you've decided to disregard my warnings."

"Cole is my husband and Abby's father. He deserves some sort of respect, which you've never given him. Why can't you just try to get to know him?"

"Treat him with respect?" he spat. "That vermin? You're not thinking clearly, daughter!"

Rachel choked back her indignation. Arguing wouldn't solve a thing. "I'm doing what I think is best. I'm not a little girl anymore. Both of you will have to accept that our marriage is our business."

His manner immediately turned frosty. "If you insist on accepting him back into your life, then don't bother coming around anymore. You are no longer welcome in my home."

Her stomach dropped. Lydia gasped and jerked his arm. "Lawrence, don't! Think of what you're doing!"

"Surely you don't mean—" she began, but he was already turning away, stalking in the direction of his wagon.

"Ma, please." Her parents had been there for her in her darkest hours, and while they didn't always see eye to eye, she loved them. That her father found it so easy to banish her from their lives stung. She swiped at the moisture on her cheeks. "Can't you talk to him?"

Her mother seemed to age before her eyes, sorrow deepening the lines and creases. "You know your father. Once he sets his mind to something, he won't sway. The only thing that will change his mind is if you turn Cole away." She seized her arm, pleading. "Make him leave town, Rachel. Then life can go back to the way it was."

What if she didn't want it to go back?

"I can't."

"You mean, you won't." Disbelief thinned her lips. "When he hurts you again, you know where to find us."

Rachel watched her mother leave, wanting to call her back yet knowing it would gain nothing. She'd made her decision. She didn't sense Cole's presence beside her until his fingers lightly grazed her arm.

"Are you okay?" The compassion lacing his quiet

question brought all her emotions rushing to the forefront. Blinking fast, she nodded.

"That was a dumb question." He shook his head in disgust. "Of course you're not okay. Let me take you home."

Allowing him to guide her, she trained her gaze on the brown grass beneath her boots. People were watching the drama unfold, she knew. Wouldn't they think it hilarious if she lost it right here and now? When he abruptly stopped, she opened her mouth to question him but was cut off.

"Afternoon, Prescott. Rachel."

Jimmy Scruggs and his wife, Bea, stood awkwardly regarding them. In their mid-fifties, the couple owned land next to Cole's parents'. She and Cole had gone to school with their two girls, who'd both married and moved away.

Cole stiffly inclined his head. "Mr. and Mrs. Scruggs, I'm afraid now isn't the best time to talk. Another day, perhaps?"

When he made to move around them, Jimmy moved to block his retreat. Cole tensed. Fear shot through Rachel.

"Wait! I'm not here to cause trouble." He held up his hand. "I, uh, just wanted to apologize. What the preacher said today, well, it made sense. I shouldn't have judged you. You aren't responsible for your pa's actions, and we were wrong to ostracize you and your ma. I know it won't undo the past, but we'd like to ask your forgiveness."

Rachel's jaw dropped. Cole had gone stock-still, his brow furrowed in disbelief. He cleared his throat. "I, uh, don't know what to say. I wasn't expecting…of course, apology accepted."

"I'm certain we're not the only ones who feel this way," Bea interjected, her gaze moving over Abby and Rachel. "It will take time for folks to admit it, but we're glad you're home. Families should stay together."

Beneath her fingers, Cole's biceps bunched. "Thank you."

"If there's anything you need, just let us know. You have our support."

She and Cole watched silently as they walked away. "Did that really just happen?" he said at last.

"I'm having a hard time digesting it, too."

"This is a good thing, right?" He looked like a lost little boy then.

"A very good thing." She smiled gently. "You just need time to absorb it."

"You're right." He caressed Abby's head and frowned.

"What is it?"

Pressing his palm against her tiny cheek, his mouth turned down. "She feels warmer than usual."

"Let me feel." She replaced his hand with her own. Abby's skin was dry and hot, her cheeks pink. Unease sifted through her. "She may have a fever. Let's get her home."

Eyes dark with worry, he reluctantly relinquished her so he could guide the team. Rachel held her close and prayed this was nothing serious.

Seated on the stone hearth that evening, Cole's gaze tracked Rachel as she circled the room with an unhappy baby in her arms. His wife's expression worried him. She was trying so hard to be upbeat, to mask her concern, but her eyes told a different story. He may not have much experience with infants, but he did know they were extremely vulnerable at this age.

Abigail's whimpers made his chest seize up, made it difficult to breathe. He hated feeling helpless. His sweet little girl was hurting, and he was powerless to do anything about it.

Pushing to his feet, he intercepted her. "Why don't you rest for a little while? Let me take her."

Her brows pulled together. "I'm fine."

With his fingertip, he traced the delicate shadows beneath her eyes. "You need to keep up your strength, sweet pea. At least go eat dinner. You're still eating for two, remember."

Her lashes swept down as her face flushed bright. He was her husband, yes, but his time away had erased all sense of familiarity between them. Would she ever be comfortable around him again?

"You've been on your feet most of the day," he went on. "It won't hurt to take a break."

"You've been walking her almost as much as I," she pointed out, even as she passed Abigail to him.

"I'm glad I'm here to help."

"Me, too," she whispered. She opened her mouth then shut it.

"What?"

"Will you stay tonight? This is the first time she's been sick, and I'd rather not be alone."

Cole searched her features. This was strictly for Abigail's sake, he knew, but he couldn't help but be pleased. The fact that she needed him didn't frighten him as it once had. He wanted to be here for her, to support and comfort her. Did this mean she was beginning to trust him?

"I'll be here for as long as you want me."

"For Abby."

Now was not the time to argue the point. Abigail demanded his attention. Pressing his mouth to her ear, he murmured soothing, nonsensical words. While he walked, Rachel ate and, instead of resting as he'd suggested, pulled out her sewing basket and the costumes she was still working on. An hour later, his legs demanded a rest, but the moment he eased down into the rocking chair, Abby set up a wail.

In the glow of the firelight, he glimpsed a swollen red spot on her lower gum. Peering closer, he gently rubbed the spot and she immediately bit down on his finger. Hard.

"Ouch."

Rachel put aside her material. "What is it?"

"I think she's cutting a tooth."

Coming to stand beside his chair, she bent down to get a closer look. "You're right. That would explain her fussiness the last few days, especially when nursing."

"Could it be the cause of her fever?"

"Maybe. So far, she hasn't had any other symptoms."

Smiling at Abby, who was going to town on his finger, he said, "Don't worry, little one, as soon as that tooth breaks through, you're gonna feel a lot better."

Rachel yawned for the second time in five minutes. Glancing past her to the mantel clock, he rose. "It's after midnight. I'm gonna see if I can get her to sleep. No more sewing. Have a seat and rest your eyes."

Looking slightly less worried, she nodded, shoulders drooping with fatigue. Abigail was exhausted, too. Within minutes, her eyes drifted shut, her head heavy against his shoulder. Just to make sure she was truly asleep, he walked and prayed some more, asking God to give her relief and a good night's rest. When he'd successfully tucked her in her crib without waking her, he gazed down at the tiny being who'd so completely and effortlessly captured his heart. Pride and wonder and gratitude swelled in his chest. *Thank you, Father, for putting Ole Jeb in my path. For changing me and leading me home. And giving me another chance with my family.*

With quiet steps, he ducked under the quilt partition separating the bedroom from the kitchen and living area and approached the dwindling fire. Exhaustion pulled at him. The knot on his head was still tender, softly aching. He turned to speak to Rachel, but she was fast asleep, her head tucked to the side and her hands limp in her lap.

A rush of tenderness swamped him. Her sable hair curved softly about her face and streamed past her shoulders, gleaming like a rich pelt in the golden light. Relaxed in sleep, worry smoothed from her forehead, she appeared much younger than her twenty-four years. Carefree and unacquainted with heartache. So lovely he could hardly stand it.

He took one step forward. *What are you doing, Prescott?* What *was* he doing?

Standing stock-still, he allowed his gaze to touch her, snagging on the glint of gold around her neck where her lemon-yellow shirtwaist gaped open. He hadn't noticed her wearing any type of jewelry, so this discovery intrigued him. Moving closer, he squinted at the simple necklace. Shock ripped through him when he saw her wedding ring dangling there, the gold band he'd bought on a whim the morning of their wedding.

What did this mean? Why would she wear it about her neck, hidden next to her heart, if it wasn't special to her?

Heart pounding, Cole acted on impulse and, going on his knees before her, leaned in close and touched his lips to hers.

Rachel was having the most delicious dream.

She was in Cole's arms, his mouth a whisper against hers, his fingers gently cradling her face.

Joy exploded deep inside. How long had she yearned for her husband's embrace, to be held by him once again? With a soft moan, her arms encircled his neck and she pressed him closer, kissing him back with all the pent-up longing she'd kept locked inside.

Cole. My Cole. I've missed this. Missed you.

"I've missed you, too, sweet pea," he breathed before capturing her lips again.

His voice, his touch seemed so real. But it was just a dream. A dream she never wanted to wake from. Sorrow stole her joy, weighing heavy on her heart.

Slowly, she became aware of the tears streaming down her cheeks. And Cole's enveloping heat. Her lids fluttered open. He'd pulled back slightly, his eyes dark and probing yet curiously gentle as he reached up to wipe away the moisture.

Oh, my.

"Why are you crying?" he implored huskily as his brows drew together. "Have I upset you? Was I wrong to kiss you?"

"It wasn't a dream," she said wonderingly, her arms still around his neck. Her lips tingled.

His arms tightened around her. "No."

She must've drifted off to sleep while waiting for him. And he'd kissed her. Warmth spread through her.

"You haven't answered my question." His thumb brushed away more wetness. "What has you so sad?"

"Because I wanted it to be real," she whispered the truth.

His eyes flared, his lips parted. His mouth descended on hers, and she let herself forget for a moment why this was a bad idea. But reality couldn't be ignored forever. Somehow, she dredged up the strength to pull away.

"We can't."

His chest flexed beneath her palms. "Why?"

Needing space to clear her head, she exerted pressure and he responded, standing to his feet and staring down at her with a lost expression that tore at her resolve. Rising on trembling legs, she moved past him to stand in front of the fire.

He followed but didn't touch her. "Tell me what you're thinking."

"You've changed, you know." She faced him. "Before, you didn't ask me how I was feeling or what was on my mind. You hardly talked to me, except to ask what was for supper or comment on the weather. Whenever I tried to steer the conversation to more serious matters, you either made up an excuse and left the room or you turned cold, glaring at me, daring me to cross the barrier. You confused me, Cole. Those last weeks, I'd hoped..." She closed her eyes, willing herself not to cry. "Why did you leave?"

There. She'd asked the one question she vowed not to.

Then she felt his finger beneath her chin, urging her to look at him. His handsome features were twisted with remorse. "I left because of you."

Wincing, she called herself a fool. Hadn't she known this would be his answer?

"You weren't happy with me."

"No." His brows descended. "That's not it. I—"

A sharp rap on the door broke them apart.

"Who could that be?" A visitor at this time of night could only mean bad news.

"Stay here." Stiffening, Cole crossed to the door and, grabbing his pistol, edged the curtain aside with the barrel. His lips compressed into a thin line. "It's Timmons."

Opening the door, he nodded to the sheriff. "What can we do for you, Sheriff?"

The blond-haired man looked grim. "Cole, I need you to come with me."

"What's happened?"

Her heart in her throat, Rachel moved to stand beside Cole.

"I'm afraid I have bad news. Your ma's cabin has burned to the ground. We were too late to save it."

Chapter Nine

Oblivious to the rush of cold air, Cole stared at the lawman. Dread gnawed at him. The men who wanted him gone had sent another message. Where would it end?

"I'd like for you to come with me and take a look around."

"It was them, wasn't it?" Gripping his arm, Rachel gazed anxiously up at him. "Cole, what if you'd been there? If you'd been asleep when it started…."

Covering her hand with his own, he said carefully, "But I wasn't. God saw fit to arrange for me to be here, safe with you and Abigail."

Her eyes shimmered with unshed tears. All he wanted was to take her in his arms and soothe away her distress, but he couldn't. Not yet.

"I need to go and check things out. Maybe find what started the fire. I'll be back as soon as I can. Will you be all right on your own?"

"Yes, of course." She looked as miserable as he felt.

Not caring that the sheriff stood watching, Cole bent and placed a quick kiss on her cold lips. "Don't worry, okay?" he murmured. "Everything will be fine."

She didn't speak, just stood there looking troubled, her arms hugging her middle, as he slipped on his duster and buckled on his gun belt, tying it around his thigh. Picking up a lamp, he left her standing in the doorway and strode to the barn to ready his horse. By the time he rejoined Timmons in the yard, the cabin door was closed.

The ride across town was completed in silence. While this new threat demanded his attention, the interruption couldn't have come at a worse time. He hated leaving their conversation unfinished. Hated that she'd mistaken his meaning. Of course she hadn't made him unhappy. In fact, just being near her had filled him with disconcerting delight, and that's the reason he ran. Cole hadn't known how to be happy, how to love someone and be loved in return.

He still didn't. But Rachel made him want to try. Made opening up his heart worth the risk.

When they rode into the yard, the sight of his childhood home reduced to a pile of charred wood kicked him in the gut. Nothing would be salvaged. His belongings, including the Bible Ole Jeb had given him, burned to a crisp. And then there were the photographs of his parents on their wedding day and the three of them shortly after his birth. He didn't particularly want to remember his father, but it hurt that he wouldn't have a likeness of his ma to show Abigail someday. Some things couldn't be replaced.

Still, he thanked God for preserving his life. Otherwise, Sheriff Timmons might've had to deliver radically different news to Rachel tonight.

Watching as three men, lanterns held high, searched the area for clues, Cole attempted to smother the fury smoldering in his chest, the flames of outrage licking his skin. *Father God, it would be so easy for me to hate my enemies. Help me to seek justice and not retribution.*

Timmons looked over at him. "Any idea who would want you gone bad enough to do something like this?"

"Could be anybody. It's no secret how people around here feel about me."

"Your father-in-law has certainly made his feelings clear. Think he could be involved?"

He wanted to deny the possibility, but in truth he'd wondered that himself. Lawrence's large build matched that of the man who'd done all the talking the night of his attack.

"Sheriff?" The man closest to them, who Cole now recognized as his neighbor Jimmy Scruggs, waved them over. "I think I found something."

Both men dismounted and, lanterns swinging, strode over to where the older man stood waiting.

"Mr. Scruggs—" Cole nodded a greeting "—I appreciate your help."

"Scruggs was the one who first noticed the fire," Timmons inserted. "Said he was out checking his traps when he heard laughter and later, the sound of horses riding hard and fast toward town."

"I didn't think anything of it at first. After about ten minutes, I smelled smoke." He gestured with his hands. "I came over to investigate, and that's when I saw the fire. I hollered for ya, but when I didn't get a response and I didn't see your horse, I figured you weren't here. I went and fetched my hired hand to help me put out the fire. We did what we could, but it was too late."

Cole's gaze swept the smoldering ruins, the acrid smell of scorched wood burning his nostrils. In the glow of the lanterns, steam curled toward the night sky where they'd tossed pails of creek water in an effort to put out the flames. Scruggs appeared to be telling the truth. And in light of his apology and offer of friendship yesterday, he couldn't imagine him setting the fire. Still, he had to be on guard, to consider all the angles.

"What did you find?" Timmons thumbed his hat up.

"A half-smoked cigar."

All three men crouched down to get a closer look. The sheriff reached out and picked up the discarded band, letting it dangle between his thumb and index finger. Cole recognized it immediately as the Prince of Wales brand out of Florida. He blanked his face even as his stomach churned with the revelation. His father-in-law smoked those. Vowed they were the best around.

"You smoke?" Timmons eyed him and frowned, perhaps sensing his turmoil.

"No," he croaked. Rising, he paced away from them and glared into the night.

Timmons followed closely behind. "There something you want to tell me?"

"Nope." How was he supposed to break this news to Rachel? Inflict further pain?

"Ya know," the other man drawled, braced his hands on his hips, "like you, I've lived here my whole life. In a town this size, you get to know people real well, their likes and dislikes. Their preferences. Take Scruggs, for instance. I know he prefers Pears soap. Mr. Moore eats his eggs sunny-side up and his steak still mooing. Sam O'Malley only wears Hyer boots. That brand of cigar, well, I know of only one man who smokes them. If it's the same man you're thinking of, then we have a case for arrest."

Cole remained silent, brooding. He would not be the one responsible for fingering Rachel's father as the perpetrator behind these attacks. Perhaps he should confront Lawrence in private. If he made it clear he wasn't leaving, Lawrence might give up the scare tactics.

"I get that you're trying to protect Rachel, but she's a big girl. She can handle the truth. How do you think she'd feel if things escalated and you got hurt or killed?"

"God has seen fit to protect me up until this point."

"He also expects us to use common sense," he retorted. "The evidence is right here—"

"You can't be certain Lawrence is the only one around who smokes that particular brand. What if it's someone else and I wrongly accuse Rachel's father? I'd have absolutely no chance of staying, then."

"You're grasping at straws."

"I'm erring on the side of caution." He turned back, heart-weary and feeling decades older than his twenty-four years. "I'm gonna look around for more clues."

"I am going to question him, Prescott. For yours and Rachel's sakes, I won't mention your suspicions, just mine. Let's hope that'll scare some sense into him."

Cole understood that, as the sheriff of Gatlinburg, Shane Timmons would not shirk his duty. "I just ask that you keep it under wraps. Rachel's dealing with enough right now."

"Agreed."

Joining the other men, they scouted the area for another hour. Scruggs's hired hand discovered an empty tin smelling of kerosene near the pile. No doubt the perpetrators had used it to start the fire. By the time Timmons ordered everyone to go home, Cole was numb with cold and exhaustion.

The entire ride home, he thought of facing Rachel and her onslaught of questions. Mostly he wondered how on earth he was going to keep the truth from showing in his face.

* * *

"Cole, wake up."

Bent over his sprawled form in the hay, Rachel jiggled his shoulder, exasperation replacing the anxiety that had seized her the moment she woke and discovered the pallet she'd readied for him had not been slept on. Irritation at herself for falling asleep fueled her ire. How had she slept the entire night through while he was in danger?

"Hmm?" His lids fluttered open, narrowed against the sunlight streaming through the open doors.

Still fully clothed with his boots on, streaks of soot clung to his forehead and cheeks. His hair was disheveled and peppered with bits of hay and he reeked of wood smoke.

"What time is it?" He sat up and, running a hand through his hair, looked her up and down. Heat climbing in her cheeks, she tugged the sides of her housecoat tighter. In her haste, she hadn't taken the time to dress or even tend her hair, which hung in wild disarray about her shoulders. What a sight she must be, standing here in her night clothes and unlaced boots.

"Why didn't you wake me the instant you got home?" Rising to put space between them, she countered with a question of her own. "I was worried."

Stroking his stubbly jaw, he stood and brushed the hay from his rumpled clothes. "I'm a mess. It was too late to clean up, and I wasn't gonna bring this filth inside, so I crashed here."

She shivered at the air penetrating her thin layers. "Weren't you cold?"

"I made do." He shrugged, his unwavering gaze stirring memories of last night, warmth spreading through her limbs as she remembered the feelings he'd aroused in her.

"How's Abigail?"

She forced the memories aside. "Still sleeping. In fact, she didn't wake all night. Her skin feels a touch warm but not anything like yesterday."

"Good."

"Tell me what happened."

His jaw hardened. The guard slipped into place, and she wondered why.

"I lost both the cabin and barn. Jimmy Scruggs and his hand tried to douse the flames, but it was too far gone."

"Oh, Cole." She wanted to hug him but, shy and uncertain, settled for touching his hand. "I'm so sorry."

He'd lost his childhood home and all ties to his past. All because of ignorance and close-minded wickedness.

Anger warred with stark fear. Cole could've easily been at home asleep when the fire was set. He could've lost his life last night. The knowledge turned her bones to jelly and the blood in her veins to sludge, her heart contracting painfully in her hollow chest.

She couldn't lose him. His exact role in their lives was uncertain, their future far from figured out, but she had to have him in her life. She cared about him too much to let him go. *Care is such a weak word to describe how you feel about him, don't you think? Just go ahead and admit it. You* love *him.*

"Hey," he said softly, brushing his knuckles down her cheek, "you've gone white as a sheet. You don't have to be scared. It's over. Everything's fine, now."

"It's not over," she choked out, her body trembling with fear. "Those men, whoever they are, won't stop until they get what they want. What if they come here next time? What if—"

He curved his hand around her cheek, steel-like resolve set in his features. "I'll leave town before I let them hurt you or Abigail. Perhaps...perhaps I shouldn't have come back. I never dreamed I'd bring trouble such as this to your door."

Covering his hand with her own to hold him there, she begged him with her eyes. "Don't say that! You deserved to know about Abby. You're good for her, and she adores you. I was wrong. You are exactly the father she needs. Please don't leave again."

My heart couldn't take it.

His hazel eyes shot with gold glowed with a fierce light. "Rachel," he breathed, "can you ever forgive me for leaving? You misunderstood earlier. I didn't leave because you made me unhappy. I left because you started to get to me. Your sweet spirit, generous heart, contagious smile. I thought I was safe." He shook his head in wonder. "All those years, I'd managed to keep everyone at a distance. Why should it be any different with you? But it was. From the very beginning, I felt the pull you had on me. I fought it. Believe me, I fought it. And when I realized I was losing, I panicked. And like a coward, I ran."

Rachel couldn't speak. Knowing this, it all made perfect sense. His night-and-day mood swings. His almost desperate tenderness, the intensity of those final nights countered with his frozen distance come daylight. She *had* made him miserable, but in an entirely different manner than she'd imagined.

Doubts and misgivings eclipsed her joy. If he got scared once, what would stop him from pulling away a second time? A lifetime of rejection and solitude had forged him into a man who feared intimacy, who kept his heart locked away, safe from further hurt. How could he shake ingrained habits?

"I forgive you."

His brow furrowed. "But?"

Dropping her hand, she pulled away from his touch. "That doesn't mean I want to try again. I want you in Abby's life. As for you and me…I'm not sure that's wise."

"What can I do to earn your trust?" His pained expression chipped at her resolve.

"I don't know." She ran a frustrated hand through her tangled waves. "I can't discuss this right now. I have to check on Abby."

He didn't respond, didn't try to stop her. At the door, she turned back. "If you'd like a bath, bring the tub inside and I'll heat some water."

"Thanks."

"Sure."

With his forlorn expression seared into her brain, Rachel hurried to the cabin, wondering if a happy ending was even possible.

Fresh from the bath and smelling like springtime, his hunger sated by a breakfast fit for a king, Cole should've felt a sight better than he did. But there was no getting around the fact he was in trouble with a capital *T.* He was, for all intents and purposes, homeless, with not much more than the clothes on his back to call his own. And he had his father-in-law to thank for it.

Striding down the boardwalk, he noticed not everyone looked away upon meeting his gaze. One or two even waved. The development should've improved his mood. It didn't.

His thoughts were consumed with Rachel and all that had transpired between them the past twenty-four hours. He did not regret kissing her, not in the least. However, that one act had forced his hand, and he didn't like the outcome.

She felt something for him, but apparently it wasn't strong enough to overcome her misgivings. She didn't trust him not to hurt her again. And if he were completely honest, he couldn't be certain he wouldn't. A depressing thought.

Scowling, he entered Clawson's and pulled the slip of paper from his coat pocket. The bell above the door announced his arrival, and almost immediately Emmett Moore approached him, his manner somewhat wary.

"Mornin', Mr. Prescott. What can I do for you?"

"Mr. Moore." He nodded, held up the slip. "I have a long list of items, I'm afraid."

Stroking his gray beard, the proprietor squinted at the list and frowned. "All that won't come cheap. For that amount of supplies, I won't accept trade or give you store credit. Cash only."

The cash wasn't a problem, but Cole had to wonder if it was the quantity that prompted the decision or his reputation, the fact that he was the son of Gerald Prescott, thief-at-large.

"Not a problem." He handed him the list. "You tally the total, and I'll run across to the bank and collect the cash."

The man paled, stumbled back. "Now see here, don't think you'll get away with robbing the bank—"

"Emmett Moore," a feminine voice scolded from behind the counter, "have you taken leave of your senses?"

Cole stared open-mouthed, stunned speechless by the man's assumption, as a plump blonde clicked her way down the aisle, brown eyes snapping with censure. When she reached them, she elbowed Emmett and turned in apology to Cole.

"Hello, we haven't met before. I'm Ruthanne, Emmett's wife."

"Uh, pleasure to meet you, ma'am. Cole Prescott."

"Oh, I know who you are." She waved a hand. "You'll have to excuse my husband, Mr. Prescott. Ever since the robbery back in the summer, he's as nervous as a turkey the night before Thanksgiving. He's suspicious of everyone these days. Please, don't take offense."

"Robbery?"

Her flushed face creased in consternation. "You haven't heard? A gang of outlaws ambushed Emmett, tied him up in the back and stole all our money. Even worse, they kidnapped poor Juliana O'Malley! Oh, it's Juliana Harrison, now. One of the outlaws wasn't really an outlaw, you see, and he saved her life. The good news is we got all our money back. Unfortunately, Emmett is still coping with what happened."

The man managed to appear sheepish and indignant at the same time. "You would, too, if you'd been trussed up and left to die!"

"I discovered you within an hour of the deed," she soothed.

"That savage could've put a bullet through my head."

"But he didn't, did he?"

A harrumph was all the answer he gave.

"Let's get started on that list, shall we?"

Cole watched, nonplussed, as the dynamo of a woman ordered her husband about. He still hadn't moved when the bell above the door jingled five minutes later and in walked the banker's wife, Merilee Jenkins, a covered dish in her hands.

"Mr. Prescott, I heard about the fire," she intoned, her face morose. "My husband and I are truly sorry for the loss of your things. I made this spice cake for you. And I have a basket of fresh rolls and some of my blackberry preserves out in the wagon."

He blinked, accepted the cake she thrust at him with a sense of unreality. This woman had made it a habit of crossing to the opposite side of street to avoid him. What had changed?

"Um, thank you."

She arched a brow. "Personally, I think it's a sign."

Uh-oh. Here it comes. The warning to leave town.

"Oh?"

"Yes," she said matter-of-factly. "A husband and wife should be living under one roof. You should be with Rachel, not clear across town. Look at this as an opportunity."

This day was getting stranger by the minute. "You may be right."

Her smile was one of self-satisfaction. "I usually am."

Rachel listened to him relate the morning's events with rapt attention. He omitted the last part of Mrs. Jenkins's conversation, and so was startled when she announced, "It's a sign."

"It is?"

Waving a hand toward the baked goods he'd placed on the table, her smile was tinged with optimism. "A sign that people are starting to change their minds about you. First the Scruggs. Now Claude and Merilee. You'll see, more and more people will follow their lead. They'll realize that it wasn't right to punish you for your father's sins."

Cole mulled over her assertion, glancing at Abigail playing on her pallet. Her fever was gone, and while her appetite hadn't fully returned, she wasn't as fussy as she had been yesterday. Rachel's sewing basket and a pile of unfinished costumes waited for her near the stone fireplace.

"Think about it," she continued, "Jerry Scruggs could've let your cabin burn to the ground without lifting a finger. If he didn't care, he wouldn't have tried to save it. He wouldn't have even bothered to alert the sheriff."

"True." He gazed at her, achingly lovely even in her simple, everyday dress of robin-egg blue, her hair pulled back with a matching ribbon. He tried not to want her, to remember she didn't trust him and that she refused to give their marriage another chance.

What did she expect from him? To rebuild his ma's cabin and come for daily visits? That would be akin to torture.

"I just wish…" Fiddling with the basket handle, she shook her head, her expression clouding.

"You're thinking of your parents." He composed his features to blandness, wary of revealing too much. He couldn't let the truth slip. It would devastate her.

"I wish they weren't choosing to be close-minded." Her gaze strayed to the baby. "I can't imagine they'll find it easy to shun their only grandchild for very long."

And what of their daughter? Resentment unfurled in his chest at their utter disregard for his wife's feelings. Guilt was there, too. His return had triggered this mess.

Both of them looked up in surprise when a team entered the yard. Cole's gut tightened. More bad news?

But it was the reverend and his wife, bearing more covered dishes and baskets of baked goods.

"We came to express our deepest regrets on your loss of property," Reverend Monroe explained as he passed by Cole carrying a load of food to feed an army. Carol Monroe, with her ever-present smile, followed behind. Cole took the dishes from her, and Rachel was there to help her off with her coat.

She offered them coffee and dessert, indicating Mrs. Jenkins's contribution already on the table. They quickly agreed, cheeks pink from the ride through town, the mild-mannered gentleman seeming pleased others were reaching out to help, as well.

Despite the regrettable reason that had prompted their visit, it was a pleasant one. The reverend and his wife hadn't once treated Cole as if he were responsible for Gerald's crimes. Instead they went out of their way to speak with him and invite him to services, their kindness and concern sincere. The only awkward moment was when the reverend, having seen Cole's wagon full of supplies, offered to help him carry everything inside the cabin. He and Rachel exchanged a quick glance before he smoothly declined the offer. He couldn't outright admit his intentions of sleeping in the barn. If the other couple had noticed anything amiss, they hadn't let on.

As soon as they departed, Cole slipped on his duster. "I'll be outside for a while getting my stuff situated in the barn. Need anything before I go?"

"Cole, I—" She hugged Abby close to her hip. "I've been thinking. Why don't you stay in here? A pallet beside the fireplace might not be as comfortable as a bed, but it beats the barn floor. At least you'd be warm and dry. And with the quilt strung up, we'll both have privacy."

He didn't want privacy from her, but he kept that

thought to himself. “Not to mention it smells a sight better in here.”

Her smile transformed her face. “With all that food, it smells like a bakery.”

Patting his stomach, he grinned back. “That suits me just fine.”

His soul lighter than it had been in days, he brought the crates inside and began to unpack. Hanging his clothes beside hers in the wardrobe felt right and natural, setting his shaving supplies on the washstand like staking his claim. Funny, he didn't feel like running anymore.

This was where he belonged. Was there any chance Rachel would come to the same conclusion?

Chapter Ten

They fell into a routine of sorts. During the day, Rachel cooked, cleaned and took care of Abigail while he sawed, hammered and painted props, in addition to caring for the animals and keeping the firewood stocked. In the evenings after supper, Cole entertained the baby while Rachel put the finishing touches on costumes. He cherished those special hours, just the three of them in their cozy cabin made cheerful with flickering firelight and crackling wood, the cleansing scent of pine garlands and swirls of bold ribbons and lace. Simply being with his wife and daughter filled him with unspeakable joy.

A steady stream of visitors dropped by each day to offer their regrets, bringing cakes, pies, cookies, bread, rolls, casseroles and even flowers. That meant stashing his pallet under the bed and taking down the quilt divider every morning. Neither he nor Rachel wanted people speculating about the state of their marriage. His gaze landed on the poinsettia gracing the center of the table, a gift from Alice O'Malley and the girls. Even Rachel had been surprised by the outpouring of concern. It seemed the tide was turning in his favor, a fact he couldn't quite wrap his head around. He couldn't overcome his hesitancy, curious why he was suddenly deemed acceptable.

Was it because of the reverend's message condemning the act of judging others? Pity because of the fire? Or because they cared about Rachel and wanted to smooth things over for her sake?

There was no clear answer. Rachel advised him not to study on it too much, to simply accept their kindness and be grateful.

Before services Sunday morning, he was escorting his two ladies to their seats when Elizabeth Jenkins intercepted them in the aisle.

"Oh, Rachel, I'm afraid I have bad news."

Conversation stalled around them. Rachel's fingers clutched his suit sleeve.

A quiet, thoughtful woman the same age as he, Elizabeth had married Lee Jenkins, the banker's only son, shortly after her eighteenth birthday. As far as he knew, the couple was still childless, a state that deeply saddened them both. He hadn't known she and Rachel were close and wondered what she had to tell her. And what was so pressing it couldn't wait until services were over?

"What is it, Liz?"

The pretty, brown-haired lady looked distraught, and she wasn't dressed for church. "It's Lee. He was moving things around in the barn last night and hurt his back. Doc Owens advised him to stay in bed the rest of the week. I'm so sorry, but he won't be able to participate in the performance."

Rachel rested a hand on Liz's, clamped tight with tension. "Please, don't worry about the performance. We'll figure something out. I'm sorry about Lee. I'll be praying for a speedy recovery."

"But who will play Joseph?"

"We'll find someone, I'm sure of it."

Elizabeth's gaze fastened on him, and he knew exactly what she was about to suggest.

"What about you, Cole? Would you be willing to fill in for Lee?"

Uh-uh. No way. He was the black sheep of Gatlinburg, or didn't she remember that? There was absolutely no way he could stand up in front of this town and portray Jesus's earthly father.

"I'm sorry, I can't."

"You're the same size as Lee," Rachel pointed out, her enthusiasm unmistakable. "I doubt I'd have to alter his costume."

"Rachel—" he pitched his voice low "—you aren't thinking this through. I want to help you, truly I do, but I'm the last person who should get involved."

"Nonsense." Sam O'Malley, who'd entered the church behind them, slapped a hand on his shoulder. "Why shouldn't you? I personally think you'd make a wonderful Joseph."

"I second that." Ruthanne Moore nodded sagely. Beside her, Emmett frowned but didn't offer his opinion. No doubt he wasn't expected to have one.

Rachel squeezed his arm. "There are only a couple of lines. I could go over them with you every day until the performance."

Christmas Eve was this coming Saturday. That didn't give him much time to prepare. Oh, what did it matter, anyway? He wasn't agreeing to this.

Elizabeth spoke up. "And if you agree, I can go home and tell Lee the good news. He'd rest easier if he didn't have to worry about this."

"I—"

"Please?" Rachel's luminous blue eyes begged him to reconsider. "For me?"

He couldn't be angry with her for putting him on the spot. This was the first thing she'd asked of him since his return. A small thing, really. How could he disappoint her?

"All right. I'll do it." He sighed, wondering what ramifications his involvement might have. Lawrence would not react well to this news.

"Thank you."

The smile she rewarded him with erased his apprehension, warmed him with satisfaction. Her happiness was worth any price he had to pay.

"Do you have a minute?"

Cole stood in the open doorway, his breath puffs of wispy smoke, snow clinging to his boots and lower pant legs. Sometime during the night, clouds had moved in and dumped about six inches of the white powder on the ground. Their first snow of the season.

Rachel placed the last dried dish in the cupboard and looped the towel over a hook. "Sure. What do you need?"

"I have a surprise. Bundle up and come outside. Bring Abigail."

Boyish excitement lit up his face. What was he up to?

"What—"

He wagged a finger. "No questions."

With a parting grin, he pulled the door shut behind him. She stared at the closed door, hands on hips, and shook her head in wonder. Then she looked at Abby, still seated in her high chair. "Your daddy is up to something."

Abby merely grinned and banged her toy against the table.

Laughing, Rachel swept the little girl up and hugged her close, kissing her soundly on the cheek. Quickly, curiosity brimming, she dressed Abby in her coat, hat and mittens. When she'd fastened her own cape and bonnet, she opened the door and, stepping out onto the snow-dusted porch, immediately noticed the sleigh.

Cole's head whipped up, and beneath the brim of his black hat, his brows raised in question. "Would you two ladies care for a sleigh ride?"

When she began to make her way toward him, he crunched across the snow and extended his arm. "Oh, Cole, this is wonderful." She smiled up at him. "It hasn't been used since..."

He glanced at her, serious again, remembering as she was their one and only outing in this sleigh. Nearly two years ago to the date, Christmas Day. Their wedding day.

It had felt suddenly as if they were strangers. Uncomfortable in each other's presence, the conversation stilted as they struggled to accept their new reality. Much had changed since then.

He paused, suddenly uncertain. "I thought you might like to go and find a tree, but if you'd rather not..."

"I'd love to."

He looked as if he wanted to say more, but decided against it. Helping her onto the seat, he settled Abby in her lap and placed hot bricks near her feet. Then he climbed in next to her and tucked a large quilt about their legs, enveloping them in a warm cocoon. With a gentle smile that melted her heart, his gloved hands closed over the reins and he signaled for the team to head out.

Above them, buttery sunlight streamed down from a brilliant blue sky, a kiss of warmth in the otherwise crisp air. As they entered the winter-wonderland forest, the harness bells tinkled merrily and the rudders glided smoothly over the hard-packed snow. A flawless white world enveloped them, white-laced tree branches appearing as intricate icicle webs. A cold, mysterious beauty.

Tucked against Cole's side, Rachel was content to simply absorb her surroundings. Surely it wouldn't hurt to forget—for one brief afternoon—past hurts and present troubles. More than anything, she wanted to abandon her cares and revel in the moment, to enjoy this outing with her husband and daughter. To pretend they were a real family, that he was with her because he loved her so desperately that he'd never dream of abandoning her again.

Cole met her gaze then, his hazel eyes unguarded for once and full of emotion she couldn't identify. His slow smile was like the sunrise, transforming his solemn face. Happy looked good on him. She decided she liked it very much.

The afternoon, filled with good-natured teasing and laughter as they bickered over which tree to choose, sped by, and all too soon they were approaching the cabin.

"You pop the corn while I get this monster situated inside, then I'll help you string it."

With Abby in her arms, she hesitated before accepting his outstretched hand. "I don't have any."

"Yes, you do." His teeth flashed in a grin. "I bought some when I was getting my supplies last week."

So he'd planned this in advance, had he? She arched a brow. "If I do, you have to promise not to eat it all.

That *monster,* as you call it, is gonna need a lot of popcorn to decorate those branches."

He'd pretended to grumble about the one she'd liked best, complaining it was a giant and far too large for their home. But she'd seen the teasing sparkle in his eyes, the suppressed laughter about his generous mouth. He was obviously as good at playing the pretending game as she.

"I guess I can leave some for the tree."

Without warning, he circled her waist with both hands and swung her and Abby down, then lowered a kiss on both their cheeks. Abby, tired and cold, rested her head on Rachel's shoulder. Rachel blushed, foolishly wishing for a different type of kiss, one like they'd shared the night of the fire.

Oops. She wasn't supposed to think of that disaster. Their fairy-tale afternoon wasn't over yet. They still had to decorate the tree and share a treat of steamy hot cocoa and gingerbread cookies.

While Abby slept in her crib, they strung popcorn and made paper snowflakes. The gorgeous pine stood tall and full in the corner, the fresh scent filling the space with anticipation of Christmas. Only five more days until the presentation. Six until Christmas, their second anniversary.

Having Cole here day and night was wearing on her resistance. His constant presence made it difficult for her to remember the reasons she shouldn't open her heart to him again. He *fit* here. That was the problem. He'd waltzed back into their lives as if the last sixteen months hadn't happened, and she'd let him.

What did that make her? Lonely? Desperate? A fool?

Joining her at the sink, he glanced down and grinned.

"What's so funny?"

"You have a chocolate mustache." He laughed softly, lightly wiping the moisture from her mouth with a cloth. "There. Perfection restored."

Their gazes locked. The humor in his eyes faded, replaced with admiration and longing. His touch and nearness ignited a flurry of butterflies in her midsection. Her limbs grew heavy, her fingers tingly, her being in tune with his.

With uncharacteristic boldness, she touched her palm to his cheek and glided her thumb across his skin, warm and still smooth from his morning shave. He blew out a breath. Covered her hand with his own and held it there. His expression slowly changed, his longing banked and replaced with questions. Questions she wasn't ready to face. Surely their afternoon of pretend wasn't over yet.

Quickly, before he could end it, she pulled his face down to hers. He didn't resist as she'd feared. They clung to each other, adrift in uncharted waters, the future a dark unknown.

"Rachel," he breathed, pulling away but keeping a firm grip on her shoulders, "I need to know what you want from me." His expression was torn between need and uncertainty.

"What do you mean?" But of course she already knew.

"How long am I welcome here?"

"I can't answer that." Biting her lip, she lowered her gaze to his chest. Her heart slowed with dread. The last thing she wanted was to hurt Cole, but how could she trust him after what he did?

Dropping his hands, he stepped back. "Do you expect me to rebuild Ma's place and live apart from you and Abby? To be a part-time family, sitting together in church and sharing meals on occasion? I have to be honest—" he ran a frustrated hand through his hair "—I don't know that I'll be able to live like that for very long."

The picture he painted was a dismal one. A kind of half-life that would only serve to frustrate the two of them and confuse Abby. What was the answer then? Her head and heart were divided. Trust him or not?

And what of his expectations? His feelings? He'd admitted she mattered to him, but not once had he mentioned love. Could she bear to live with him, to love him day in and day out if he didn't love her in return? Wouldn't that be a half-life, too?

"I need more time." Head bent, arms hugging her middle, she stared at the floorboards.

"I understand." With a heavy sigh, he crossed to the door and slipped on his coat and hat. "I'll be out in the barn for a while."

Rachel blinked back the sudden tears. If only he *did* love her, maybe then she'd have the courage to try again.

Feeling ridiculous in the shepherd's getup, Cole gripped the curved staff tighter, oblivious to the rough wood biting into his palm. His gaze didn't waver from Rachel's face. If he glanced down at the sleeping infant in the woman playing Mary's arms, he'd be reminded of Abigail's birth and all he'd missed. He'd wonder how she'd looked at that age, if she'd been peaceful like this one or fussy and demanding. If he looked beyond where Rachel stood directing the dress rehearsal to the back of the church, he'd encounter curious parents watching his every move, perhaps waiting for him to mess up. He should never have agreed to this.

But he'd wanted to make his wife happy. This play, the spur-of-the-moment sleigh ride and tree trimming had been for her. Unlike before, he was making an effort to please her, to lower the walls he'd erected years ago. It didn't come easy. Changing lifelong patterns. But to know her, to truly know her heart and mind, was a prize worth attaining.

Rachel glanced his direction then and offered him a quick smile of encouragement. He cocked a brow in response. *Please let this be over soon.*

The children were in the middle of *Angels We Have Heard on High* when the doors burst open and Lawrence strode in, looking entirely too pleased with himself.

Cole's chest constricted. This night had just taken a turn for the worse.

When Shane Timmons entered the room several paces behind the large man, his granite face colder than usual, Cole knew he was in trouble.

"Stop this!" Lawrence bellowed as he marched down the aisle.

Rachel jumped, her startled gaze bouncing between her father and Cole as the piano music ground to a halt and the children grew quiet. Fear leeched the color from her cheeks.

Pointing his finger in accusation, Lawrence managed to look outraged. "There he is, Sheriff! Arrest the thief!"

Gasps and murmurings filled the silence as the bystanders pressed closer. If he hadn't been the center of attention before, he certainly was now. Seething with anger, Cole removed his head covering and moved to stand in the aisle.

"What's this about, Sheriff?" He held Lawrence's calculating gaze.

With an air of grim reluctance, he angled himself

between the two men. "One of Mr. Gooding's horses is missing. He claims to have evidence you stole it."

"It's not just a claim, Sheriff. I have the evidence right here." He patted his coat pocket, then turned to address the crowd. "Cole Prescott has fooled you all. He's a crook, just like his conniving, thieving pa before him. He stole my horse, and I can prove it."

Cole's mind raced. He was innocent. What kind of evidence could the man possibly have?

"I was about to retire last night, smoking a cigar on my front porch, when I heard what I thought was a rider approaching. When I didn't see anyone, I went out to the barn to take a look around and discovered my best horse missing. Today, I found this in the hay next to the empty stall." He pulled out a gold pocket watch and let it dangle high in the air by its chain. "The initials on the inside lid are C.E.P."

Cole closed his eyes as reality crashed into him. He'd underestimated his enemy. Lawrence would go to any length to get rid of him, including framing him for a crime he didn't commit. How had he gotten hold of the watch? Unless…he'd searched Cole's ma's cabin before he set fire to it.

"Let me see that," Timmons ordered.

When Cole reopened his eyes, he met the sheriff's probing stare. He couldn't bear to look at Rachel, couldn't bear to witness her hurt and accusation. No way would she believe him over her father.

"Is this yours, Prescott?"

"It is."

More gasps.

Lawrence's smirk reeked of triumph. Cole curled his hands into fists, the itch to wipe that smirk off his face hard to suppress.

"Did you do what Gooding is accusing you of? Did you steal his horse?"

"No, I did not."

"Check his place," Lawrence challenged, folding his arms across his barrel chest. "If my horse is there, and I've no doubt it is, then you'll see I'm telling the truth."

"I don't care what evidence you have—" Rachel surged to his side and faced the two men with trembling conviction "—my husband is not a thief!"

Stunned, Cole's jaw went slack and he stared at her. She believed him?

Her father's face turned beet-red. "Are you calling me a liar?"

She flinched, but held her ground. "Cole couldn't have stolen your horse. He was with me last night."

"He must've slipped out while you were asleep."

"No, I would've heard him."

"Listen here—"

Timmons held up a hand. "There's an easy way to settle this. We'll take a ride out to the Prescott place. If the horse isn't there, we'll do some more digging. The watch alone isn't enough to convince me of his guilt. He's your son-in-law and has spent time there in the past. It could've been buried in the hay for some time."

"And if my horse is there?" Lawrence pressed.

The sheriff's mouth thinned. "Then I'll have no choice but to arrest Prescott."

Chapter Eleven

Rachel blinked to clear her vision, certain her mind was playing tricks on her. Blackie, her father's favorite horse, was here. In her barn. This didn't make any sense.

Cole's face was a frozen mask, his eyes flat, emotionless.

Shane looked equally grim. "I'm gonna have to take you in until we get this sorted out."

"There's nothing to sort out." Her father sounded almost gleeful. "This proves I was right all along."

No! Something was terribly wrong here. Cole wouldn't have done this.

Rachel tried to capture his gaze, but he appeared lost in thought. Why wasn't he fighting this? Proclaiming his innocence?

Shane ignored her father, obviously displeased with the turn of events. "I assume I can trust you to come with me of your own accord?"

Cole seemed to rouse himself. "Of course."

"Let's get this over with then," the lawman muttered before pivoting on his heel and stalking toward the door.

Over his shoulder, he called, "Gooding, I'll need you to come with us and fill out a written statement."

"It'd be my pleasure."

Panic bubbled up.

When Cole made to move past her, she sidestepped to block his path, her palms flat against his chest halting his progress. "Wait! Cole, talk to me," she pleaded, tears flowing freely now. "You can't go to jail for a crime you didn't commit! Why aren't you fighting back?"

The expression on his face, when he at last met her gaze, froze the blood in her veins. This was not the man who'd surprised her with a sleigh ride a few short hours ago, stringing popcorn and trimming the tree and…and kissing her as if she was his entire world. This was not the man she'd fallen in love with. This man was cold. Unreachable. His guard as impenetrable as ever. "Do me a favor. Don't come to the jail."

She gasped. "Please don't shut me out! Not now. Not when we need each other more than ever."

His hands settled heavily on her shoulders. Not to pull her closer or give comfort, but to move her out of his way. "Please just do as I ask."

Then he was striding out the door and into the night, vaulting into the saddle and riding out with her father and the sheriff. On his way to jail.

The metal bars of his cell mocked him. *You really believed you could turn things around? Start fresh? The no-account son of the most hated man this side of the Tennessee River? It would have been better for Rachel and Abigail if you never came back.*

Weary beyond words, he sank onto the narrow cot and tugged his hat down to cover his eyes. In his current mood, he didn't wanna see or talk to anyone. Anyone being Shane Timmons.

For the past hour, the astute lawman had sat at his desk without speaking, flipping through papers and occasionally eyeing Cole as if expecting him to say something.

The rustling paper stilled and the chair scraped back. When footsteps didn't immediately follow, Cole tipped up his hat and found the lawman leaned back in his chair, arms crossed as he regarded him with uplifted brow.

"You do realize what the punishment for horse thieving is, right?"

Death by hanging. He couldn't bring himself to say it aloud. Sweat rolled down his spine.

"Of course," Shane went on, "Gooding has agreed to drop the charges if you swear to leave town and never come back."

Should he be relieved by the knowledge? A life apart from his wife and daughter would be no life at all. Still, what choice did he have?

The lawman's gaze turned intense, scrutinizing. "I don't understand why you're doing this. One word from you as to the owner of that cigar butt and you can go home to your wife and child. We both know he's framing you, trying to run you out of town. With your testimony, Gooding would be in that cell instead of you."

Exactly. "I can't do that to Rachel."

"What do you think this is doing to her?"

Cole hung his head, unable to get the image of her stricken face out of his mind. *This is for the best,* he reassured himself. If not Lawrence, someone else would want him gone. What kind of life could Abigail have with him for a father? Folks had long memories. They would never let her forget who her father and grandfather were and would treat her with the same derision as they had him.

Yanking his hat down to signal he was finished with the conversation, he stretched out on his back and attempted to ignore the yawning ache in his chest. This time, leaving here would surely kill him.

With trembling hands, Rachel pushed through the sheriff's office door later that night, her gaze shooting past Shane, seated at his desk on the left, to the jail compartments lining the back wall. Only one was occupied. Stretched out on the cot, his hat covering his face, Cole appeared to be asleep.

"You have a visitor, Prescott."

Settling his hat on his head, Shane stood and locked gazes with her. "I'll be right outside if you need me."

She nodded, thankful for the small kindness, and slowly approached the iron bars. The bleak, sparse space compounded her despair. He should be home with her and Abby, not here. Not alone at Christmas. Imprisoned for a crime he didn't commit.

"Cole?"

He bolted upright, his hat sliding to the floor as he pierced her with his dark gaze. "You shouldn't be here."

"I couldn't stay away," she pushed out on a shaky breath.

"Who's taking care of Abigail?"

"Megan's at home with her." Gripping the bars, she pressed her face close. "Cole, I know my father orchestrated this whole thing with Blackie. Tell me the truth—is he the one who attacked you? Did he set fire to the cabin?"

Pushing to his feet, he covered her hands with his

own. She sighed at his warm touch, aching to be in his arms and draw comfort from his strength. The cold, metal barrier prevented that.

His expression gentled. “Everything’s going to be all right, you’ll see.”

“How can you say that?” she demanded, his lack of emotion stirring hers. “Nothing will be all right! Not with you locked up like this. Abby needs you. *I* need you…” Her voice broke. Tears shimmered near the surface.

“Please don’t cry, sweet pea,” he murmured, reaching through the bars to wipe away the escaped moisture.

“Who’s going to play Joseph? Who’s going to rock Abby to sleep? Who will take me on s-sleigh rides?” She sniffed. Pulling her hands free, she buried her face in her hands.

Not so long ago, she’d convinced herself a life without Cole was for the best. What she wanted. Now, she couldn’t imagine living without him.

“Rachel,” he groaned, torment lacing his voice, “go home. This isn’t helping.”

Lifting her head, she did nothing to hide her true feelings. “I’ve come to a decision.”

Wariness edged his mouth. “What’s that?”

“I want to share my life with you. For us to live together as a real family, as true husband and wife.”

A muffled moan rumbled deep in his chest. He squeezed his eyes shut. “That’s out of the question now.”

“There has to be some way to prove your innocence.” *And my father’s guilt.* She shied away from the notion.

“Listen to me, your father has agreed to drop the charges if I leave town.” Sorrow flickered in his hazel depths. “I think it would be for the best. My presence has caused you nothing but trouble. You and Abigail will be better off without me."

"He can't do this," she protested, indignation burning in her chest. Her father had no right! She would not allow him to interfere in her life this way. If Cole decided to leave, and she desperately hoped he wouldn't, it would have to be of his own accord, not because he was forced. Pivoting on her heel, she marched toward the door.

"Rachel! Where are you going?"

"To make this right."

Sick with nerves, her body flushing hot and cold, Rachel guided Cocoa through the darkness. *Please, God, give me courage to face my father. Comfort my husband and free him from this horrible situation.*

Entering the clearing, she saw light spilling from the open barn doors and headed that direction. She dismounted and, taking Cocoa's reins, led her inside. Her knees threatened to give out. Her father was an intimidating man, particularly when angry. But she had right on her side. She would not back down.

"Father? Are you in here?" Her gaze swept the stalls on either side, the scents of hay and horse and kerosene filling her nostrils.

In the shadowy corner, a tall figure unbent and stepped into the light. "Rachel, what are you doing here this time of night?"

"Stephen!"

At the sight of her brother, her fright and worry spilled forth and, rushing into his arms, she wept against his chest. He smoothed her hair.

"What's wrong, sis?"

"Oh, Stephen, it's a nightmare!" She eased back to

peer up at his concerned face. "Father has done something terrible." She told him everything that had happened, including the attack. "Cole was with me last night. I know he didn't do it."

His face clouded over, his words measured. "You think Father was behind it all? That he attacked Cole and set fire to the cabin in order to run him out of town?"

The admission was a difficult one. "I do."

His mouth compressed to a thin line. "How's Cole taking it?"

Rachel stepped back, surprised he didn't argue or defend their father. Did that mean he shared her conviction?

"It's like he's given up. I don't understand why he isn't defending himself."

"Consider his position. If he does, he's ultimately accusing Father of concocting this whole thing with Blackie. He wouldn't want to hurt you that way."

It made sense. He'd consistently protected her feelings, enduring her parents' verbal attacks without complaint. The love and respect she had for him expanded, eclipsing all doubts.

"Oh, wouldn't he?" Her mother appeared in the doorway, her brown-black eyes gleaming fiercely in the lamp's glow. "That man has inflicted hurt after hurt, and yet you still refuse to see his true nature."

Fisting her hands, she responded evenly, "No, Mother, *you* refuse to see his true nature. Cole is a good man. He left because he got scared. He was beginning to care about me, and for someone who'd spent much of his life alone, that couldn't have been easy to deal with. To make himself vulnerable, to expose his heart when he'd had nothing but hatred and derision aimed at him his entire life. You and Father didn't help matters. And I—" she pressed her palm over her heart "—was more worried about other people's opinions than my own husband's. I didn't stand up for him like I should've, but that's changed. I've changed. I love him, and I don't care what anyone else thinks. His opinion is all that matters."

Lydia's shoulders slumped with regret. "I did my best to protect you and Abby. When I destroyed his letter, I thought for sure we'd never have to deal with him again. But like a bad penny, he keeps turning up."

Rachel froze. "You did what?"

Beside her, Stephen muttered under his breath.

"I destroyed his letter." She lifted her chin in defiance. "Burned it, actually. I was in the post office a month or so after he left, and when Mr. Giles mentioned you had received one from him, I offered to deliver it to you. Of course, I had no intention of doing so. I was aware of your tender feelings for him, and I wasn't about to risk you doing something foolish, like asking him to return."

Reeling both from her mother's admission and utter lack of remorse, Rachel struggled to speak. He'd written, just as he'd said. Only, it hadn't gotten lost. Betrayal left a bitter taste in her mouth.

How was it possible she'd lived her entire life blind to her parents' true natures?

Fingers clutching the folds of her cloak, she stammered, "How could you do that to me? To Abby? H-he might've come back. In fact, if he'd known about the pregnancy, I've no doubt he would have." Her head jerked back. "Oh. Right. That's what you feared, wasn't it? That he wasn't the heartless villain you and Father made him out to be. That he would, in fact, do his duty to his wife and daughter."

"Don't make me out to be in the wrong here. I did what I did to protect you and my granddaughter."

"No, you did it to control me. You love and support me as long as I do what you want. I do love you, Mother, but I refuse to live that way."

Dazed and distraught, she snagged Stephen's coat sleeve. "If you see Father, will you tell him I was here?"

His face was a mask of concern. "Where are you going?"

"Back to the jail." Exhaustion pulled at her, but what was that compared to what Cole was enduring? "I want to talk with Shane and see if there is anything I can do to help get Cole released."

Placing both hands on her shoulders, he peered down at her with concern. "Rachel, it's late. There's nothing more you can do tonight. You need your rest. I'll ride over to the cabin with you, make sure you get home safe, then come by after breakfast and accompany you into town. I'd like to see Cole, myself."

"But—"

"He needs rest, too. Leave it until morning, all right?"

Knowing he was right, she nodded reluctantly, dreaded the long night ahead. How would she be able to get a moment's sleep with him locked in that horrible jail? Tomorrow was Christmas Eve. What if she couldn't get him released?

The presentation couldn't go on without Joseph. Even if there was someone else willing to play the part, she was in no position to direct. Her emotions were raw. On edge. The sight of rosy-cheeked children wearing the costumes she'd made and Cole's beautifully painted backdrops would cause a meltdown.

Lord, we need Your help.

Without it, she feared this Christmas would go down as the worst in her lifetime.

Christmas Eve morning, Cole watched, dumbfounded, as a parade of folks passed through the jail—some to bring food, some to offer a word of encouragement and some to pray with him. Exhausted, eyes bleary from a troubled night, he found it difficult to speak past the emotion clogging his throat.

These people, many who'd shunned him in the past, believed in his innocence. Believed *him,* Cole Prescott, over Lawrence Gooding. *Father God, it appears You've turned their hearts, allowed them to see the truth. I'm grateful, truly I am, but I can't help worrying what this will do to Rachel.* He knew from experience what it was like to have a father who thought himself above the law. Shameful. Humiliating.

He'd wanted to spare her the misery. Rachel's well-being and happiness had come to mean more to him than anything else. Plain and simple, he loved her. Lying in a jail cell gave a man plenty of time to think, to examine his life and heart. Only now did he realize he'd loved her from the start, perhaps even before that fateful night at Clawson's. Growing up, he'd admired her from afar, nursed a boyish crush, all the while knowing she was out of reach. Safe. When he'd suddenly found himself tied to her, sharing a living space with her, he had no chance at all of being safe.

Lost in thought, oblivious to the conversations on the other side of the bars, he didn't at first look up at the sound of newcomers. The sudden hush caught his attention.

When he raised his head and looked into Rachel's cherished face, his heart jumped in recognition. Without conscious decision, he stood and approached the bars, soaking in the sight of her. He couldn't bear to be apart from her for a single day. How could he possibly walk away from her for good? Seeing her current anguish, he entertained serious doubts about his ability to do it.

"Cole," her whisper came out as a plea. Her fingers were ice cold on his.

He managed a half smile. "Sweet pea."

Her hood slipped back, her shiny hair was arranged in a simple braid that hung down her back. Pale shadows beneath her eyes did nothing to detract from her beauty. He'd give anything to be able to hold her close…

Timmons lifted a hand. "I want everyone out except for Rachel and Stephen."

As folks streamed silently out the door, Cole studied his brother-in-law, who appeared a touch nervous, and transferred his gaze to Rachel. "What's he got in that flour sack?"

Worry lines marred her forehead. "I don't know. I asked him about it, but he refused to say."

Hands on his hips, Timmons leveled a narrowed gaze at the young man. "What ya got there?"

Determination tinged with regret marking his youthful features, Stephen set it on the desk. "A pair of pants Pa gave me the day after Cole's cabin burned down. He told me to get rid of them, but I didn't. I wasn't sure at first why he wanted them destroyed, but then I heard about the fire and…" He shrugged, obviously torn.

Rachel's hands fell away as she turned to watch the exchange. She held herself straight and still as a statue, braced for the worst. Cole was tense, as well. He was witnessing the disintegration of a family. A difficult thing to watch.

Extracting the article of clothing, the sheriff held them up to his face and sniffed. "They smell like kerosene."

"Yes."

He stared at Stephen. "You believe these are your father's pants and that he was wearing them the night of the fire?"

He snuck a glance at Rachel and Cole before nodding. A shudder tore through Rachel, and Cole reached through the bars and rubbed her arm.

Taking out his key ring, Timmons unlocked the top right drawer of his desk and pulled out a small pouch, tossing it to Stephen. "This was found in the rubble. Recognize the brand?"

His jaw firmed the moment he caught sight of the cigar butt. "It's the Prince of Wales brand my pa smokes."

Rachel raised a quivering hand to cover her mouth. It was one thing to suspect one's parent of misconduct, quite another to have those suspicions confirmed.

Satisfied, the lawman strode to unlock Cole's cell. "Looks like you're once again a free man, Prescott." He arched a sardonic, it's-about-time brow.

The door swung open, and he rushed forward, eager to have his wife in his arms. But she stopped him with an upheld palm, her moist gaze searching, intent on getting answers.

"You knew, didn't you?"

Aching to hold her, impatient with the delay and hoping against hope she wouldn't hold it against him, he nodded.

"You didn't say anything because you were trying to protect me." Two fat, silver tears snaked down her pale cheeks.

Cradling her face in his palms, he gently thumbed them away. "I would give my life to protect you."

Curling her fingers around his wrists, she gazed up at him as if he were a knight of old, a valiant hero come to rescue her. His chest swelled with fierce satisfaction and purpose. As long as there remained breath in his body, he would give everything he had to protect her and love her all of his days.

"Cole, promise me that from now on, you will be upfront with me. I can handle anything but losing you."

He suddenly became aware of their audience, and, seizing her hand, tugged her toward the door. "I am not having this conversation in a jail," he growled, desperate to bare his heart to her alone. To know, once and for all, if she'd have him or no. And he would not discuss it with his brother-in-law and the town sheriff looking on.

"Where are we going?" Rachel asked breathlessly as her husband, determined and seemingly unaware of folks' open-mouthed stares and exclamations, hurried her along Main Street.

"Somewhere away from prying eyes." His gaze swept both sides before alighting on the church in the distance. A satisfied smile curving his mouth, he squeezed her hand. "Perfect."

The brisk breeze brushing her cheeks did not cool her inner fire, the soaring euphoria incited by the promise in Cole's eyes. This was like a dream. Her husband was a free man, his good name restored. Later she would deal with the grief her father's betrayal had caused her. For now, it was enough that Cole was here with her.

Rushing her up the steps and inside the dim building, he shoved the door closed and, taking both her hands, pulled her farther inside, his hazel eyes shining brighter than the rainbow cascade glittering through the stained-glass windows. The hushed space bedecked with ribbons and garlands, holly berries and candles smelled of hearty pine and fresh hay. Cole's backdrops transformed the stage into a starry night in Bethlehem, the ancient village dwellings painted with impressive detail. Tonight, cherished hymns of exultation would fill this place, the treasured recounting of Jesus's birth once again brought to life.

"Rachel."

Standing very near, Cole continued to hold her hands in his. Calm and assurance radiated from his tall form, his eyes clear and warm as his gaze caressed her. His ever-present guard nowhere in sight. The unbridled emotion in his eyes took her breath away, weakened her knees.

"Two years ago we stood in this church and pledged our lives to each other. Not because it was our choice, but because it was expected. I didn't realize until recently what a gift God gave me that day. I wish I'd never left you." His voice roughened, the joy dimmed in his eyes.

"Cole—" She edged closer, wanting to assure him of her forgiveness.

"If I could rewrite the past, I would have been here for you and Abigail. I wouldn't have spent a minute away from your side," he insisted.

"I know." She couldn't dwell on his absence, not when he was standing here before her, vibrant and alive and whole…because he *wanted* to be. She could only be grateful beyond words he'd come home. If he hadn't… Her mind refused to go there. Too excruciating.

"I'm not scared anymore," he murmured, releasing her hands to set his on the curve of her waist, his fingers flexing against her. He eased her to him. "I love you, Rachel. I want to spend the remainder of my days proving just how much."

Looping her arms about his neck, she leaned into him and lifted her face to his. "I'd like nothing better."

His gaze flared, darkened, as he slowly lowered his mouth to hers. The soft yet insistent pressure of his lips, his all-encompassing heat as his hold on her tightened, the restrained strength of his embrace, fused together in one glorious sensation of homecoming. In Cole's arms was where she belonged. Always. Here, she was safe. Cherished. Loved.

He was hers, and she was his. One before God.

When he lifted his head long moments later, she said aloud the words she'd said in her heart almost from the very beginning. "I love you, Cole. You are everything my heart wants."

His brilliant smile nearly blinded her. "Marry me," he blurted.

"What are you talking about?" she laughed.

Startling her, he slid his finger beneath the collar of her blouse, snagged the necklace she wore hidden from view and held up her wedding ring. "Marry me a second time. Right here in this church. But this time, do it because you want me as your husband. Because you love me."

His voice deepened over the word *love,* his eyes intense with need. This was important to him.

"How did you know about the ring?"

"I spotted it the night Abby got sick. You were asleep in the rocking chair."

Ah. The night he'd kissed her awake. She trembled with the memories of that and his recent kiss. "You gave it to me moments before we exchanged vows. I couldn't bear to part with it, even if just to store it in my jewelry box. I wanted it with me, close but hidden. A reminder of you."

"Will you allow me to place it on your finger once more?"

When she moved to unclasp the necklace, he stayed her movements. "Not now. Tomorrow. At our wedding. This time, I want the whole town to witness our union."

She smiled then, delighted at the notion, her heart bursting at the seams. "I'd gladly marry you anytime, anywhere."

And then Rachel kissed him without reservation, deliriously happy that she no longer had to conceal her love. Tomorrow, on Christmas Day, two years to the day after their first wedding, she would walk down this aisle an eager bride. Cole would be waiting for her, ready and willing to renew his pledge to her. A family again, the three of them together on life's journey.

Epilogue

One year later

Cole sank carefully down on the edge of the bed beside his wife, unable to speak for the emotions expanding his chest—awe and pride and stark, cold fear. His anxious gaze swept her face, her damp forehead and rosy cheeks, her trembling yet smiling mouth, searching for the slightest sign of distress.

"I'm perfectly fine, darling." She lifted luminous blue eyes to his, her lips curving up in a smile so tender and sweet it made him want to weep. After what she'd just endured, why wasn't *she* crying?

Holding himself perfectly still, not daring to touch her, he cleared his throat. "Are you sure?"

"I would know if something was wrong."

"As would I," Dr. Owens spoke over his shoulder as he placed the last of his instruments in his black leather bag. Snapping the clasp and turning, his smile was wry. "I warned you, did I not, that most husbands choose to wait out the delivery in another room? Childbirth is the most natural thing in the world, but it can be quite a shock for a man who doesn't know what to expect."

Shock? He'd nearly passed out at least a handful of times. Thankfully, he'd managed to stay upright and focus his energy on Rachel, holding her hand, mopping her brow and murmuring who knows what in her ear.

"Your wife and son are both healthy. Just see to it that she gets plenty of rest. If you have any concerns, I'll come back out and check on them. Congratulations to you both."

The doctor bid them farewell and let himself out.

"You look a little pale. Are you all right?" Rachel asked softly, her brow furrowing. "Do you regret staying for the birth?"

"No, not at all. I wouldn't have missed it for the world." He managed a tremulous smile, his nerves calming a bit. Carefully, he smoothed her dark hair back from her forehead. "Remember the day you told me we were expecting?"

She nodded. "You promised you'd be here for me and this baby every step of the way."

"After all I missed with Abigail, I was determined not to miss anything this go-around."

Laying her palm against his cheek, she got that look in her eyes that made him feel ten feet tall, the one that made him feel invincible and vulnerable all at once. And loved. Always loved.

"You are the best husband and father. Have I told you lately how much I love you?"

Turning his face, he pressed a kiss on her palm. "I don't believe you have," he teased.

"I love you, my husband, more than the moon and stars, more than—"

Overcome, Cole pressed a light, sure kiss on her lips, murmuring, "I love you, sweet pea." Turning his attention to his newborn son, swaddled in blankets and resting peacefully against her chest, he brushed a reverent kiss on his downy head. "And I love you, little one."

"He's beautiful, isn't he?"

"Just like his ma," he agreed, in awe of this tiny life they'd created together.

His life was so full. He was ever aware he didn't deserve to be this happy. Whenever he thought about how close he'd come to throwing it all away, he choked up, grateful beyond words to the good Lord above for leading him back here. Sorting things out for his benefit. Blessing him with the family he'd always dreamed of.

Rachel rested her head against the pillows, a soft sigh escaping her lips as her lids drifted closed. A surge of concern swept through him. She must be exhausted. With careful movements, Cole lifted baby Daniel and tucked him in the crook of his arm, a warm weight against his chest.

"Just wait until your big sister gets a good look at you," he murmured, his gaze taking in the light covering of pale brown hair, the perfectly shaped nose and mouth. While Abigail was one hundred percent Rachel, their son had features from both parents.

Abigail was no doubt too busy to miss them. The O'Malley girls all adored her, the twins especially, who allowed her to help out in the kitchen despite her tendency to make a mess. Lydia had offered to watch her, but neither he nor Rachel had felt completely comfortable with the idea.

The relationship with his in-laws was not ideal, but it was progressing, more so with Lydia than with Lawrence. Thanks to Cole's recommendation, Lawrence's sentence had been reduced from six months to three. His partner in Cole's attack, lumberyard owner Billy Johnson, had gotten off with a warning. After Lawrence's release, he'd come home a somewhat humbler man. He kept his distance and his silence and that was all right with Cole. As long as he did nothing to hurt Rachel and the kids, he had no problem with the man, had forgiven him with God's help. It was easier with Lydia.

With her husband in prison and Stephen striking out on his own, the loneliness had gotten to her. She'd missed Rachel and Abigail. It hadn't taken her long to apologize for burning the letter and for all the hateful things she'd said to them both. Rebuilding trust took time, but they were working on it. Rachel was happy, and that was all that mattered.

"I wonder how the play is going?" Rachel had opened her eyes again, a tiny worry line between her brows.

"It won't be as good as last year's," he predicted with mock seriousness, "not without you directing."

"Megan will do a fine job, and you know it." She smiled, the line disappearing. "But I daresay Lee won't make as good a Joseph as you did."

"True," he teased, "but there's always next year."

"And the year after that." Her face glowed with peace and contentment, her eyes shining with promise.

"And the year after that..." He leaned over and kissed her, knowing they were no longer speaking of the play, but of their future together.

* * * * *

If you enjoyed these stories from Linda Ford and Karen Kirst, be sure to check out the other books this month from Love Inspired Historical!

Dear Reader,

Thank you for reading Smoky Mountain Christmas. When my editor told me she was looking for someone to write a Christmas novella to be paired with Linda Ford, I jumped at the chance. I'm really glad I did. Cole and Rachel's story was a joy to write. This was my first Christmas-themed story, and it worked out that I was writing it during the holiday season. The music, decorations and endless supply of cookies helped get me in the spirit. This time of year, we're reminded how important family and friends are in our lives. Please take the time to let them know how much you love them.

I love to hear from readers. You can email me at karenkirst@live.com. Or catch me on Facebook. For more information about my Smoky Mountain Matches series, visit my website, www.karenkirst.com.

Have a blessed day!

Karen Kirst

Questions For Discussion

1. Rachel is concerned with how other people view her and despises being the subject of gossip. How do others' opinions affect you? What does the Bible say about this?

2. Have you ever been treated unfairly because of someone else's actions? How did you handle the situation?

3. Not everyone in Gatlinburg treats Cole unfairly. Rachel, the O'Malleys and others are kind to him. Have you ever befriended someone in a similar position?

4. How difficult is it to stand up for what you know is right, especially when it's unpopular?

5. In the beginning, Rachel did nothing to attempt to mend the relationship between her parents and her new husband. What do you think she should've done differently?

6. When townspeople begin to show their support, Cole wonders what caused the change—the reverend's message on judging others, pity because of the fire or their affection for Rachel. What do you think was behind their change of heart?

7. Cole keeps silent about his suspicions in order to protect Rachel. What do you think of this decision?